The 5 star book b...

...enge, a
...f the
...father's
...draw...se
...dare I say, beautifully
...d but kick ass ending.'

Sharon **Bairden, Chapter i...** 'Alan Jones is a hidden Scottish talent and deserves to be discovered.'

Lorraine Rugman, Thebookreviewcafe 'Bloq at times is a very disturbing read, it's also dark and full of suspense, well plotted with characters who were so realistic I shed a tear for them, because I totally bought into their story.'

Shell Baker, Chelles Book Reviews 'This is a must read for all crime fans which I cannot recommend enough…Giving it 5 massive stars.'

Neats Wilson, The Haphazardous Hippo. 'For me, Alan Jones has an incredible way of drawing you into his books right from the outset; he then throws you around for a bit and then spits you out at the end and I love every minute of it.'

Caroline Barker, Areadersreviewblog 'It is delicately and beautifully written in the places it needs to be. A truly outstanding read.'

Dee-Cee Taylor, It's all about the books 'This is a gritty crime novel that had me gripped from page one. In Bloq we are taken on a rollercoaster ride and there are so many twists throughout the book I was left speechless and breathless.'

Rebecca, Becca's Books 'It was thrilling, sharp, and full of danger. And as for the ending? Wow. Absolutely spot-on. I really don't think the author could have ended this novel in a more powerful way.

Clare Ogden, TheAddictionofbooks 'There is so much depth to this excellent novel, so much I haven't mentioned and so much you simply need to discover for yourself....but be careful, once you are hooked.....there is no turning back.

Betty, Bookishregards 'Bloq is a mind-blowing crime novel that hooks you right from the start; a superbly written thrill ride that builds to an electrifying climax. Its fast pace keeps you on the edge of your seat, anxious to know more, and unwilling to put it down.

Helen Claire, Baatty About Books 'I found the chapters racing by and everything was on hold until I had finished this well thought out, well executed book that has the perfect blend of emotions, tension and drama and it is a book that I urge lovers of the genre to read.

Caroline, Lazysundaybookreviews 'Gritty, gripping and compelling, I can't recommend this book enough. It is by far one of the best books I have ever read and I'll be making Alan Jones my 'go to' author in future.

Sandra, Beauty Balm Blogspot 'Fast paced and un-put-downable. I sort of wished the ending was different but it was one of hope. Loved this book. Highly recommended.

Bloq

Alan Jones

First Print edition

Copyright © Alan Jones 2016

Published by

This book is a work of fiction and, except in the case of
historical fact, any resemblance to actual persons, living or
dead, is purely coincidental.

Remembering Nancy Stephen

CONTENTS

ACKNOWLEDGEMENTS

I would like to thank Shell Baker for being the first draft reader to read Bloq, for getting back to me so quickly and with such a positive reaction; also for pointing out that Stephen Gately was never a member of Take That, therefore sparing my blushes.

I'm indebted to both of my London proof-readers who checked Bloq for its accuracy and realism in the depiction of the London streets where the story unfolds. I was relieved when both Nick Short and Rowena Hoseason told me that I had, in the main, achieved it, but both pointed to a number of areas where I could improve my portrayal of the London they lived in. Rowena also extended her advice to other areas and made many suggestions which improved the authenticity of the story.

Thanks to all my other proof-readers for finding my silly errors and for their very positive feedback. In no particular order, they were Michael, Lauren, Liz, Peggy-Ann, Teresa Murphy, Carol Mason and Elaine.

A special thanks has to be given to Fergus Hay for suggesting suitable locations down under, to Martin Stanley for letting me run the initial London locations past him to see if they sounded likely candidates, and to Thomas Kiernan for his information on the technicalities of running a bar. I'd also like to thank 'Hendo Beast' for inadvertently supplying the homeless alcoholic's utterances.

Thanks also to Julie Lewthwaite, who has now edited three books for me; she told me each book was getting easier to edit but she's maybe just getting used to my writing foibles. As always, she's quick and as well as finding more mistakes than I'd like, she has good ideas about tweaking the structure and phrasing to improve the readability. My books always feel better when I get them back from her.

My cover team expanded this year, and included Pedro in a creative role and big Dave Frankland behind the lens. Cat as usual berated my meagre attempts at artwork and came up with the final cover which is a bit of a departure from the first two books.

Thanks to all the book bloggers who have supported my writing. There are too many to list, but they know who they are. Without bloggers, there would be no way for self-published authors to have any chance of competing with established writers.

And once again, thanks to my wife, children and all my extended family and friends for their general support and encouragement.

There is a glossary of computer technology terms used in the book at the end, and also at *www.alanjonesbooks.co.uk*

PROLOGUE

As a funeral, it was nothing much. Only four people were present; one of them was dead and none of the others gave a fuck. And there were one or two omissions from the service. Flowers. Music. Mourners. A priest. And, oh – a coffin.

The body was badly wrapped in a polythene sheet, the kind used as a damp-proof membrane by builders, laid under concrete floors. From the size of the feet sticking out one end and the sad straggle of matted blonde hair at the other, you would probably have guessed it was a young woman.

"Grab fucking end each, dickheads." Built like a tank and with a shaved skull, his words, in heavily accented and broken English, carried a low but effective menace that made his two companions, of lesser bulk but almost as intimidating, jump to comply.

The hole was no more than a foot deep, but it had been scraped out of the only level piece of ground in the immediate vicinity. All around the solitary flat patch, mountains of rubble, of various grades, crowded the small burial party and hid them from the houses to the north and west, and from the river to the south. A sludge barge sounded its horn as it made its way slowly downriver.

"Hurry it up, for fuck's sake. We've not got lot time; it will be soon dark."

Neither of the two subordinates, both born-and-bred Fulham hard men, would have dared to mock the Albanian's diction.

"Don't you think we should tie the ends up?" the taller of the two reluctant gravediggers asked, struggling to grip the polythene, slippy and damp in the drizzle of the grey evening.

"No, put fucking thing in fucking hole and get the fuck out of here, before get seen by some cunt."

Grunting and stumbling, they managed to get the plastic-wrapped corpse into the shallow depression, but the feet wouldn't quite fit, protruding above the level of the surrounding packed earth.

"You couple useless lazy cunts." He picked up the spade and made as if he was going to take a swing at his two assistants, who cowered from his advance. Instead, he used the spade to loosen a little of the gravelly soil around the feet in an attempt to lower them, but the ground had been heavily compacted by the lorries and heavy plant that had run over it for years and it was hard going. He began to appreciate why his two companions had dug the minimum depth they could get away with and he regretted not having used a small excavator, even though it would have been difficult to get it into this corner of the yard.

His efforts had allowed the legs to sink further into the hole, but he could see that the toes were still going to protrude when it was filled in. He lifted the spade above his head and swung it hard down on to the corpse's left ankle, shattering it with a sickening thud. A piece of flesh flew off and hit him on the side of the face and he irritably wiped his cheek with the back of his hand and spat a mouthful of saliva on to the ground, in case any of it had gone in his mouth.

He swung the spade again, at the other ankle; this time it took a couple of blows before it was severed enough to allow the foot to lie flat and to the side like the first one.

He stuck the spade into the ground a couple of times to clean it then threw it towards his helpers, who had to move sharply to avoid it.

"Always end up do it fucking self," he swore at them. "Fill fucker in and get fuck out this shithole."

He watched as the pair filled the hole, one shovelling and the other using the sides of his feet to level off the thin layer of soil on top of the body. Finally, they stamped around on the surface to compact it down, kicking some of the looser stuff on top to hide the footmarks.

"That looks OK, boss, doesn't it?"

"No thanks to you two phidi, but is going OK. It not matter anyway after tomorrow; no cunt will find," he replied. It felt good to curse in his native tongue, even if his audience didn't get it.

-o-

The wires grumbled as the grab line bucket lifted a tonne and a half of material from the pit where it had been tipped by the last of a steady line of trucks that had filed into the yard since first light. The crane operator swung the massive boom around and released its load on top of the nearest pile, causing a minor avalanche down the back of the mound. A rivulet of rubble trickled down on to the unmarked grave below and each subsequent release of the bucket caused the small space to shrink, until it had disappeared entirely. By lunchtime there was no sign that there had ever been a flat bit of ground there at all and when the edge of the mound reached the perimeter, the

9

shallow grave that had been hastily excavated was buried under seven feet of rubble and dust.

CHAPTER 1   BILL

Bill Ingram tried to ring his daughter's mobile just before he left the house at six o'clock, to see if her train was running on time, but her voicemail message told him that her number was unavailable. *She must be in a tunnel, or something,* he thought. He headed for the station, always a stickler for leaving himself plenty time to spare for everything he did, especially when meeting Carol. Everything was ready, so there was no point hanging around at home.

She'd sent him a text around the beginning of December informing him that she'd be travelling up from London on Christmas Eve, and giving him the time her train was due in.

He parked in the multi-storey in Mitchell Street and strolled the short distance to Central Station. It had a real Christmas buzz about it, with families being reunited, last-minute shoppers laden with bags rushing for trains, and revellers heading home after boozy office Christmas parties. Even the obligatory policemen looked quite cheery; as if they expected the seasonal goodwill to moderate the drunken carnage they'd normally have to deal with on a Friday night.

He was nearly half an hour early and on checking the arrivals board he saw that Carol's train was due in ten minutes late, so he decided to nip into Costa Coffee to treat himself to a latte and a muffin. He watched the flow of passengers to and from the trains as he waited for the late arrival of the 14.23 from Euston.

He was back at the arrivals board five minutes before the train glided in, marvelling, as he always did, at the effortless elegance of such a mechanical leviathan coming to rest so gracefully.

He scanned the platform as all the doors simultaneously opened, spilling their human cargo; a river of faces flooded towards him.

At first he watched only with interest, observing the usual rich tapestry of humankind, knowing that he wouldn't miss her, or she him, but as the mass of people dwindled, a prickling anxiety crept up on him, and when the last few stragglers walked down the platform without her appearing, he turned around to see if she'd somehow passed him by.

As the concourse emptied of its recent influx, the number of passengers milling around thinned out to a few solitary souls. If she'd been there, he would have spotted her within seconds. He checked both exits and hurried back to the platform.

He tried her mobile again but she didn't answer. He realised that he had her landline number on his mobile and he stood in the centre of the almost deserted station and tried it. Her voice answered but it had the hollow echo that identified it as the recording on her answering machine. He waited until the long tone had sounded and left a message telling her to contact him as soon as she got in.

He asked one of the Network Rail employees, standing talking to the train's driver, if he could check the train to see if his daughter had fallen asleep on it. He felt stupid even asking, but when the man told him to go ahead, he hurried up the platform, peering through each window as he did for any sign of her.

The guard had just stepped down from the rear of the train when Bill reached the last carriage, and he asked him if he'd lost something.

"My daughter," said Bill, "she was supposed to be on this train. I wondered if she'd fallen asleep."

The guard looked at him sceptically.

"There's definitely no one remaining, sir. I've just walked the length of the train, clearing up litter and checking for stuff folk have left. I think I would have noticed a girl."

"Yes, sorry. I just thought ..."

The guard wasn't unsympathetic. "She could have caught a later train, sir. There's another two due in from London tonight."

"She would have phoned me to let me know, she's very good that way."

"These phones aren't always all they're cracked up to be. Maybe her battery's gone."

"I suppose that's possible. Listen, thanks, I'll just wait for the next one. Do you know when it's due in?"

"One gets in at 21.38, the other at 23.54." He looked at Bill again and felt sorry for him. He had a couple of daughters himself and he knew what it was like to worry about them. "Come with me. I'll ask my manager if you can sit in our office until then."

He guided Bill to a doorway at the side of the concourse and climbed the stairs inside, motioning for Bill to follow. After talking briefly to a smartly dressed older woman, he directed Bill to sit in one of the chairs in what looked like a staffroom, with a low table in the centre and a hot beverage vending machine in the corner.

The woman, who introduced herself as Sheila but whose badge told him she was *Mrs S. Crainey, Operations Manager, Virgin Trains*, looked after him once the guard had signed off and headed homewards with a last "good luck" aimed at Bill on his way out.

She fetched them both a cup of tea and sat down opposite him.

"How old is your daughter, Bill?"

"She's twenty-five." Bill thought it must have sounded premature to be so worried about an adult who had effectively missed a train.

"What does she do for a living?"

"She's a trainee journalist with *The Times*. She has a degree in journalism." Bill couldn't keep the pride out of his voice.

"That's fantastic. One of my boys wanted to be a sports writer, but he didn't get the grades. Kids, eh."

Bill wasn't really in the mood for polite conversation, but it wasn't in his nature to be impolite. "What does he do now?"

"He works in a bank. It's a good job, but it's not what he wanted. The money's good, though."

"Carol was always good at school and through university. She finished as one of the top students in her year. That's why she got a job at *The Times*."

"You and your wife must be very proud of her. Do you have any other children?"

Bill's face clouded over. "My wife died earlier this year. We had no children other than Carol. It's been a bad year for us."

The rail manageress apologised. "I'm so sorry, I didn't realise."

"No, you weren't to know. It's probably why I'm so worried about Carol."

He looked at the woman sitting across from him. Concern was written all over her face, but he could see that she didn't know what to say. "She died of breast cancer in August," Bill said, to spare the woman from any awkwardness. "She was diagnosed in April and, despite treatment, she didn't even get a small respite from it. They did a mastectomy and gave her chemotherapy, but it was too far gone. I think she hid it for a while. Maybe if she'd gone to the doctor earlier …" His voice tailed off.

"That's awful. It's a horrible thing, cancer. It must have been hard on your daughter, too."

"It hit Carol hard, but she was great. She came up from London every weekend from when her mother told her about the cancer, taking her to clinics, visiting her in hospital during her treatment and in the hospice towards the end."

"She sounds like a marvellous daughter. She must be a comfort to you."

"She is. She stayed with me for a week after the funeral, sorting all Alison's things out and helping me with the paperwork, and all the formalities that come with a death."

Sheila Crainey could see that Bill was happy to talk, and she was a good listener. It was part of her role to deal patiently with her customers' problems and although it wouldn't have appeared in her job description, she considered it her duty to do what she could to look after Bill's wellbeing.

There may have been a degree of him off-loading some of his cares on to a stranger because Bill, who normally kept himself to himself, felt comfortable talking to the friendly and sympathetic woman who had time to spare for him.

After descending to the platform with Bill to meet the next train, still with no sign of Carol, she sent him back upstairs while she sorted out a few minor issues resulting from the latest arrival, then followed him back up to sit with him until the last train arrived.

Bill told her how he'd made a special effort with the Christmas tree because he knew that was what his wife, Alison, would have wanted, but he'd booked a nice local restaurant for Christmas dinner, figuring that the two of them sitting at the family table without Alison might be a little too morbid.

Sensing that Bill had unburdened himself enough, she told him a little about her own family, and it seemed to help the time pass for Bill, listening to the stories of the exploits of her three boys. He even managed an odd smile, reflecting that they'd had a much easier time bringing up Carol than Mrs Crainey had dragging up her tribe.

When it was time to meet the last train, she went down to the platform with him again and waited until it had emptied. Her heart went out to him when it became obvious that his daughter hadn't been on it. Her shift finished, she reluctantly advised him to go home and try to contact Carol again in the morning.

-o-

He looked around and spotted the two policemen he'd noticed earlier, encouraging a young woman, somewhat inebriated, to make her way out of the exit and catch a cab home.

He hesitated and, after the drunken girl clacked noisily and unsteadily down the slope towards the taxi rank in her three inch heels, he approached the two officers.

"Excuse me, I wonder if you could help me."

They both looked very young. He spoke to the one who looked the marginally older of the two. "My daughter was supposed to be on a train from London tonight and she hasn't appeared. She's not answering her mobile or the phone in her flat."

"What age is your daughter, sir?"

"She's twenty-five. Why?"

"Well, sir, if she was under sixteen, we would be a little more concerned and the procedure we'd follow would be totally different."

"Oh, I suppose that's fair enough; if she was a child I could understand that it would be more critical, but should I report her missing? I'm very worried about her."

"What's your name, sir?"

"Bill Ingram."

"Well, Bill, we don't normally take a formal report of a missing person until they've been gone for twenty-four hours, but that depends on circumstances. If there could be a reasonable explanation why the person hasn't turned up,

17

we generally allow that amount of time and most people do get in touch by then. If I were you, I would go home and wait for her to contact you."

Bill was disappointed that they couldn't help, but could see that they had a point. He was too polite and reserved to insist but he knew, deep down, that there was something far wrong. She would never have left him like this, not knowing where she was or what had happened to her.

He took one last look round then made for his car. Fumbling in his pocket, he couldn't find his car park ticket; his mind was in turmoil and he could feel the panic taking over. He retraced his footsteps in case he'd dropped the ticket in the station, but he couldn't see it, and anyway, a man in an electric sweeping buggy with a yellow flashing light and a loud beeper had already cleaned half of the concourse. Fortunately the policemen had gone, or they might have thought he was losing the plot.

He returned to the car park and read that he'd have to pay for the full twenty-four hours if he couldn't find his ticket; in the light of Carol not showing up it shouldn't have mattered, but it did. He emptied all his pockets, standing under the harsh blue-white light of the car park entrance.

He found the ticket in between the folded sheets of paper he kept in his jacket pocket to write lists of his daily tasks on. Without them, he would be lost. It wasn't an age thing; he'd always done it and he kept separate pages for home, work and shopping.

Driving out of the multi-storey, he took the wrong one-way street and had to circle around to get back on to the road home. In his mind all sorts of scenarios kept popping up, some perfectly reasonable, where at any minute the phone would ring and she would be all apologetic and full of explanations; others dark imaginings, where she'd been in an accident, a victim of a terrorist bombing, or was lying ill in her flat, unable to get to the phone. The darker ones repeatedly came to mind, ousting the less frightening possibilities.

There was no message on his answering machine when he got home, and only one missed call. He recognised the number as that of his cousin, Robert, and made a mental note to phone him in the morning.

He sat at the dining room table, looking at his phone, willing it to ring, for about fifteen minutes then, wondering if anything big had happened in London which she might have got caught up in, he switched on his laptop and waited for the icon that told him the Internet was connected to appear.

He liked the BBC news site and it was one of his bookmarks, so it loaded quickly. It was what they called a slow news day. The top story was the big freeze and the second was the level of consumer spending in the run up to Christmas, followed by an item about a New York man who'd been released from prison despite shooting dead one of a mob who'd attacked his home.

He couldn't see any London stories that could have impacted on Carol's travel plans, and if the ice and snow had been the problem, the trains wouldn't have been running so well and on time.

He looked up his usual rail information website to find out what he already suspected – there were no trains running on Christmas Day, almost everywhere, so even if she wanted to come up, she wouldn't be able to. It also stifled the germ of an idea that had crept into his mind – that he should jump on the next train and head down to London to see what had happened to her – and as that option was taken away from him, he steeled himself for what he knew he had to do. The thought of a three hundred and fifty mile overnight drive in darkness through ice and snow made him feel sick. He wondered if an ill-conceived rush down the M6 was the worst thing he could do for her, but he knew if he didn't, the night would be even longer.

And if he left now, he would be easily there first thing in the morning, even with a couple of stops for coffee or a short sleep.

Once he had made the decision, Bill moved quickly and efficiently. He packed a change of clothing, a sleeping bag and the basic toiletries, along with a flask of hot soup, a couple of slices of hastily buttered bread, and a second flask, filled with strong black coffee.

He was always extremely thorough in everything he did; he'd filled the car up with fuel that afternoon in preparation for the festive period and he always carried a spare container of diesel in the boot, but anyway, he was pretty sure that there would be a service station open somewhere on the motorway should he get low on fuel. There was no reason to hurry, so he could travel at a steady sixty and one tankful might just take him all the way.

Passing through the front door with his bags and provisions, he took a last look at the telephone, willing it to ring. Seeing the answering machine, he realised that he should leave a message for Carol on it, in case she phoned the house. Alison had purchased the thing before she had a mobile phone, when she'd been the chairperson for two local charities and had become exasperated at missing calls. It was old, but it still worked. Bill found it useful for screening out calls he didn't want to answer and now he was glad he'd hung on to it. After depositing his luggage in the car, he returned to the house and changed the outgoing message, taking a few attempts before he got it right: "It's Bill here. If it's Carol calling, leave a message saying where you are and how I can contact you. If it's anyone else, please phone my mobile if it's important."

He didn't leave his cell phone number; anyone who he wanted to contact him would have it already. He picked up the little card that was under the machine showing him how to connect to it remotely and, seeing the old spiral-bound notepad that functioned as a family address book, he pocketed it as well.

Finally, he switched off the Christmas tree lights that he'd left on to make the place festive for Carol and double locked the front door. Sitting in the car, putting on his seatbelt, he suddenly realised that he hadn't left a light on. *Shit.*

Even in his haste to get going, he wasn't the sort of person who could just ignore it. Alison and he always left a light on when they were going to be out in the hours of darkness, with a plug-in timer to convince potential burglars that the house remained inhabited.

He went back in and switched it on, checking the time on the little mechanical wheel, then locked up again. Reversing out of the drive, he felt slightly more comfortable seeing the glow of the light behind the curtains of the living room. He steered the car out of the quiet suburban cul-de-sac, heading for the motorway and his long trip south.

-o-

During the first part of his journey Bill constantly ran over in his mind how he was going to tackle his search for Carol. He drove for about an hour then stopped, not because he needed coffee or felt compelled to empty his

21

bladder – although both were welcome – but to make notes of his thoughts and plans so that he wouldn't forget any of it.

As he drove across the border into England, he thought back to happier times, trying to dispel the dark cloud of fear that had enveloped him.

He had a happy childhood, with parents who cared deeply for him but didn't stifle him, and his teenage years were fun-filled and, in a gentle way, adventurous. Four years followed at university, where he learned how to be an engineer, experimented with drink and girls, and watched from the sidelines as some of his friends dabbled in the softer end of the drug scene.

He met and married the love of his life in his gap year, while working his way around Europe, and secured a good job with one of Scotland's largest engineering groups just in time for the couple to move into their first house in a secluded but dull suburb of Glasgow a few weeks before Alison gave birth to their daughter, Carol, seven months after the nuptials. They managed to obtain a mortgage, helped by a loan from Bill's parents and the money Bill had somehow managed, even as a student, to save.

As Bill climbed steadily up the management tree in the company and moved home a couple of times to reflect his growing income and aspirations, Carol glided smoothly through her childhood, youth and further education, culminating in her gaining a degree in business journalism from Stirling University.

Her parents were disappointed when she moved to London, but realised that it was the best chance for her to further her career. They still saw her regularly; she came home to see her friends and family every two months or so and they would spend a weekend with her in London in between these visits. Her job as a junior reporter with the business section of *The Times* was just the opportunity she'd headed south for. The nearer Bill got to London, the harder it became to keep the anxiety from overpowering his memories.

-o-

Three short breaks and seven hours later, Bill found a parking space vacated by an early morning worker in Leybourne Street, fifty yards along from Carol's flat in Camden Town. He was cursing himself for forgetting, in his panic and worry, to lift the spare set of flat keys that lived in one of the kitchen drawers at home.

It wasn't a major disaster. He knew that Mrs Hamble, the neighbour in the flat below Carol's, had a spare set. He and Alison met her often on their visits down to London; she was a pleasant older lady who was very good to Carol, as their daughter was to her. But although the worry was eating into his bones, he still couldn't bring himself to ring her doorbell at six o'clock on Christmas morning, so he sat there for a while, putting the scribbled notes he'd made into some semblance of order, refining a plan in his mind for the day ahead. He could see that the curtains in Carol's flat were closed, but there was no answer when he'd rung her doorbell. He hadn't expected anything different; he'd rang both her house phone and her mobile every time he'd stopped during his journey and again when he'd first arrived. He could faintly hear the phone ringing from the direction of the flat and wondered why it didn't wake up Mrs Hamble below.

He sat in the car, turning over and over in his mind that, if he looked back, he should have known that something hadn't been right. The more he thought about it, the more it seemed that his previously charmed and untroubled life had started to fall apart on the 13th of January, 2010, the day of his forty-seventh birthday.

The first indication that Bill's almost utopic existence had been nearing its end was when, for the first time ever, Carol missed his birthday. A few friends and relations were coming round that Wednesday evening and Bill was supposed to pick his daughter up from Glasgow's Central Station late the previous night, but he received a phone call in mid-afternoon saying that something had come up in London that she couldn't get out of and, although she felt really bad at missing his birthday, she wasn't able to make it up for the few days with them that she'd intended.

Bill and Alison were disappointed, but not upset, and thought nothing of it. They supposed that it might have been something to do with work or with one of her friends – she was the type of girl who would go out of her way if someone needed help or support. *Besides, she was home at Christmas for a few days.*

She managed to come up the weekend following Bill's birthday, but didn't elaborate on her reasons for postponing her visit and her parents weren't the kind to pry. Despite Carol being their only child, they hadn't smothered her. Bill liked to think they'd given her the same space and freedom that his own parents had given him but, over the next six months, the period between her trips up north stretched a little. On a couple of occasions, when they'd suggested an extra visit down to see her, she'd had other things on that would have made it silly for them to make the journey.

That all changed with Alison's breast cancer diagnosis in mid-April. She'd noticed a small lump a few days before Bill's birthday, but a natural reticence to tell him or see the doctor about it, and the familiar slow progress through the grind of the National Health Service's diagnostic machine meant that it was exactly five months after Bill's birthday that she was admitted to hospital for a breast removal.

During Alison's illness, Carol wasn't her usual self, but Bill knew the effect his wife's slow and inevitable deterioration was having on him, and he could only assume that Carol felt the same; struggling to cope with the knowledge that each time she visited, more flesh had melted from her mum's shrinking frame and her eyes disappeared a little further into her head, leaving her more skeletal with each passing week.

Bill's father had died a few years before and his mother was in a home, with advanced dementia, so at Alison's funeral, he and Carol felt very much alone, despite the presence of a number of friends and acquaintances, and Alison's parents, who lived in Aberdeen. Carol's maternal grandparents had never been a big part of their lives; Bill had always thought that they'd never forgiven him for their only daughter's unplanned early pregnancy and short engagement.

Bill knew that Carol had waited until she was quite sure he was coping before heading back down south. She phoned him twice a week and travelled the West Coast Main Line to and from Glasgow on a fortnightly basis until late October, when the phone calls suddenly became less frequent and there was only one trip to Glasgow in the two months leading up to Christmas. During her visit Bill noticed that Carol was a bit pale and subdued, but didn't say anything. He'd thought to himself that she would eventually speak to him if something was bothering her. And anyway, she'd told him she had plans to come home for Christmas. She didn't know, but he'd booked them a week in the Lanzarote sunshine over the New Year. He felt

25

that they both deserved a break after the horrendous year it had been for them.

But she hadn't turned up.

By eight o'clock, his nerves were frayed and his patience had given out. He rang the old lady's doorbell, despite having vowed not to do so until he saw signs that she was up.

Nothing happened for a while, so he rang it again. This time, after a few minutes, he heard sounds from behind the door and eventually the letter box popped open.

"Who is it?" said a slightly croaky voice, as a pair of tired looking eyes peered at him through the slit in the door.

"Mrs Hamble, it's Mr Ingram, Carol's father. I was hoping you still had the spare keys for her flat."

"Wait a minute." There was a pause, then a rattle of chains and the sound of two locks being undone. Finally, the door swung open. The old lady had on a rather elegant purple dressing gown and green slippers. Her silver hair was unbrushed and loose, in contrast to the usual tight bun he was used to seeing; he apologised for waking her up so rudely.

"Don't fret about it. I normally get up between eight and nine. I probably wouldn't have heard the door if I hadn't already been awake." She motioned for him to come in. "Now, what's up with Carol?"

She fumbled for the keys as Bill explained what had happened and told her about his worries. She gave him the keys and gamely followed him upstairs to Carol's flat, one of two at that level.

He unlocked the door and stepped inside, his heart thumping in his chest, dreading the worst. He quickly checked the living room and kitchen, subconsciously leaving her bedroom until last, but despite his uneasiness as to what he might find, when he pushed open the door he saw her bed was empty and unslept in. He stood for a few seconds, gasping with relief that she wasn't lying in bed, severely ill or worse. Those few seconds of respite died as the full impact of her absence hit home.

"She probably stayed the night with friends, Mr Ingram. I'm sure she'll be back."

"She would never have done that without phoning; even if her mobile was broken, she would have found a phone somewhere. No, something's far wrong. I'm going to contact the police."

He wanted her to leave, needing to be on his own to gather his thoughts, irritated by her platitudes, but knowing that she meant well.

"Mrs Hamble, thanks for your help. I'll hang on to these keys, if that's all right." He paused, willing her to go, but she stood resolutely, as if her being there was a comfort to him. Bill tried again. "I'm going to go to the nearest police station. Do you know where it is?"

"There's one in Kentish Town. It's not far from here, but it may not be open today. You'll probably have to go to one of the larger ones, or just phone them. Would you like me to stay here until you get back, in case she phones, or comes home?"

He bit back his exasperation, not wanting to offend her, even in his worried state. "No, Mrs Hamble, that won't be necessary. You go down and get some breakfast. I need to do a few things, then go and report Carol as missing." He took her arm and guided her gently towards the door. He watched her as she carefully went down the stairs, looking back at him with concern a couple of times.

He closed the door and sat on the edge of Carol's bed for a minute. He then got up and started to look round the flat, searching for any clues to her whereabouts.

Carol had always been an organised and tidy person, and at first glance the flat seemed to look the way it should do, but on closer inspection there was something not quite right. A fine layer of dust covered every surface, and when he checked the fridge, he found no foodstuffs that he would have described as perishable, like milk, eggs or butter; there was only some cheese in a sealed packet which, although it looked all right, was long past its sell-by date. It was almost as if she hadn't lived in the flat for a while. When he checked the bin, it was half-full of empty spirit bottles, mainly vodka, which he found strange as there were no signs that any sort of party had taken place.

Looking out the window, he realised he hadn't displayed Carol's resident's permit in his car. He picked it out of the drawer in the chest in the hall, where she kept it handy for their visits. She'd sold her car nearly a year before – an Oyster card was much cheaper and she found it just as easy to get about on public transport – but the permit had a couple of weeks still to run.

He retrieved his bags from the car, placed the permit on the dashboard and returned to the flat. He noticed that the light on the answering machine was blinking and pressed the play button anxiously, hoping it was Carol, but disappointment flooded over him when he recognised his own voice on the message he'd left the night before.

Despite his anxiety, when Bill sat down on the chair his eyelids started to droop. He didn't fight it and before long he drifted off to an uneasy sleep, exhausted after his overnight journey.

CHAPTER 2   CAROL

7th November 2009

"Where are we going tonight, then?" Carol held the phone to her ear with her shoulder, wrapping the last remaining length of hair around the hot curling tongs, checking out the result in the mirror opposite the bed as she did so. *Hmmm, not bad.* She laughed to herself.

"Alice says she's found a fucking awesome club over the river in Walworth. Bloq, she said it was called. She was there last week with girls she knew from school; said there were a few celebs in but it's not right up itself and the drink's not extortionate." Heather was always up for trying somewhere new and liked to drag Carol along with her.

"What celebs were in? Not that I give a toss, anyway."

"You know him in Skins; the one that plays Cook?"

"Yes. Is he as wild in real life as he is on the telly?"

"Alice didn't say, but she also mentioned a couple of tennis players, the girl from one of the morning shows who was on Strictly and, inevitably I suppose, some football players and their WAGs. But not Thierry Henry, unfortunately."

"He lives in Spain now. I saw it in a magazine."

"OK, smart arse. But he is gorgeous. Anyway, are you coming?"

"I don't know. It sounds a bit upmarket for me. I'm not sure I want to make an arse of myself staring at second rate glitterati who are probably completely up their own arses, pardon my French."

"Oh, shut up. Don't be a tight Scottish mare. You always whine when we talk about going somewhere different then you end up having a ball."

"Yes, I know, but we'll probably go there, spend all our wages on one night and have nothing left until payday."

Heather laughed. "It won't be that bad. I, for one, intend to find some rich, good-looking bugger to buy me drinks all evening, so that won't be a problem."

"You'd settle for not-so-good-looking if he had enough money."

"Carol Ingram, you *are* a bitch. But you could be right. It's not all about looks; it's what's inside that counts."

"Aye, inside their wallet, more like."

"Right, that's it. I've booked a taxi for nine thirty. If you're lucky, I'll pick you up on the way. Not that you deserve it."

Carol grinned for a while after she'd put the phone down and carried on with her make-up. She'd been lucky falling in with Heather, who she worked with, and Alice, Heather's crazy friend from school. She'd fitted in so well with them and their wider social circle, making the transition from Scotland to London much easier than she'd expected.

-o-

31

"That's the guy who owns this place." Alice nodded towards the bar. Although the music was loud, they could make each other out without shouting too loudly.

"Which one?" Carol could see several men at the bar, all striking poses and mostly, as far as she was concerned, failing to pull them off.

"The one with the goatee. Aleksander, he's called. Spelled with a 'K', so defo foreign. Quite tasty, if you like that sort of thing."

Carol grimaced. "He's not my type. Too full of himself and I hate beards."

"Mostly, I agree, but some men suit them. What about Hugh Jackman, Ben Affleck and, of course, Sean Connery?"

It was Heather's turn to pull a face. "For fuck's sake, he's old enough to be your grandfather. That's disgusting."

Carol disagreed with her. "To be fair, I don't think that would put me off. I'm with Alice on that one. And the others are pretty hot, too, but on normal guys, gross."

Carol looked around. "Anyway, how do you know there's a 'K' in his name? And where are all those footballers and soap stars you promised?"

"I didn't say they were in every night, did I?" Alice shrugged. "And his name's on the licensee notice above the front door," she said smugly, just as the waitress appeared.

They ordered drinks – Carol, a white wine spritzer; the other two, long vodkas. Alice and Heather rummaged about in their bags and each handed Carol a couple of twenties. She groaned.

"Why is it always me who has the kitty? Can someone else not take it for a change?"

"You're the sensible one!" they chorused, laughing at her.

She grinned, not really minding. They were great friends to have, even if they did sometimes take the piss.

They'd chosen a table just off to the side of the dance floor and were still waiting for their drinks when Carol saw, out of the corner of her eye, the bearded man they'd been discussing walking towards their table. She nudged her friends to warn them.

"Ladies, ladies, welcome. I'm sure I'm not seeing you in before."

"We've never been in before," Heather replied, indicating Carol and herself, "but Alice was here last month." She was inwardly cursing herself for sounding so lame.

"We're always delighted when beautiful girls like you come visit our little club." He smiled and all three of them melted a little.

Impeccably dressed in a suit that said "money" but achieved a casual look at the same time, his voice had more than a hint of an Eastern European accent and he exuded a natural charm, despite his blatant smoothness. Undoubtedly, he was a good looking bastard; about six foot tall, with a slim physique that still managed to suggest an underlying hardness and a tinge of danger, but his eyes smiled when the rest of his face did and disarmed any feelings of threat or malice. "Has no one sorted for you drinks, yet?"

"The waitress is just coming with them; she took the order a few minutes ago."

"We can't have three lovely ladies sitting not with drinks." He casually nodded at a woman in a sharp tailored suit who was passing the table. "Anna, could you organise bottle of Prosecco for this table? One of good ones."

The woman, without smiling, nodded and turned towards the bar. She spoke to one of the barmen, waited while he placed a bottle and four glasses on the tray, then brought it over to the table. Still without a word, she placed the bottle next to her boss and dished out the glasses to the girls, giving him the last one. "Do you want me to open it?" she asked, her Geordie accent evident but not too strong.

He shook his head. "That's everything. You go now."

As she walked away, he turned to the girls. "My new manageress. She's bit abrupt sometime, but runs place like clockwork when busy and doesn't take shit from punters when get crazy. I have many staff to look sexy and be friendly with guests, so don't mind her showing some serious shit." It sounded as if he was making excuses for her and Carol wondered if she was more than just his manageress.

Not that she would have asked him, but he precluded any questions by popping the cork and filling their glasses from what Carol could see was an expensive bottle of fizz. The glasses were frosted around the top, which made her lips tingle when she took a sip. She was no wine buff, but she guessed that it was the best of stuff and hoped that it wasn't extortionate, as she half expected that they might end up paying for it.

That worry was immediately dispelled.

"My compliments, ladies. Here's good health and enjoyment at club."

They clinked glasses and chatted comfortably with him, asking about the club, and his background.

"Sorry about English. I learn quick, but sometimes not good. I came here from Albania about ten years ago and got work as barman in West End." Carol got the impression that he dropped the odd word and retained a slight accent for effect; there was no doubt that it fitted in with his appearance. His story was genuinely interesting and he told it casually and with humour, in a self-deprecating manner.

"After about five years, I was manager of club and getting good money, but I didn't spend much. Soon I bought small bar in not good area and got lucky, as students were just starting to rent flats close by. They liked tunes I play and cheap drink. Soon, I bought next-door shop and converted whole place to small club. It still does well and I have my little brother over to run it for me. It makes good money, but when I saw this building, I thought, Aleksander, this would make great club for rich people to come. Then I give to my brother other club."

He smiled, the girls hanging onto every word.

"So this wasn't always a club?" Heather asked, leaning over towards him.

"No, it was sort of warehouse, with small shop area at front. May have been small clothing factory long time ago, but used just as store for many years. Was good building. Just shell to work with. I borrowed lots of money from bank. Put in best of stuff. Now great club and expensive people come. Sound system cost hundred K alone," he told them, proudly.

"Why is it called Bloq?" Alice asked, curious.

He smiled. "When I come here first, I hear 'Eastern Bloq' this and 'Eastern Bloq' that. I ask what is this Eastern Bloq and they said it means all countries behind Iron Curtain, so I ask what this Iron Curtain and they say former communist states before wall come down. I tell them not all countries same, but they think we all USSR. When I buy club I think of name and make joke. I say will call it Eastern Bloq, but some friends say too long, so I decide Bloq. English people say should have letter 'c' but in Albania we have word *blloqe* nearly same, with letter 'q'."

They all laughed; it was a good name and it was even better when you heard the story behind it.

He recharged their glasses and his. "You should come often. Good place for young beautiful ladies. Meet nice people." He gestured around the room with his hand, as if to say *take your pick.*

"Are you single?" Alice asked, laughing.

"I have no time for ladies. Need to make money, pay bank." It could have been dismissive but he broke out that smile as he said it and they all knew that he didn't go short of female company.

"Do you ever go back home?" Carol asked, surprising herself and the others.

"This home now. But I visit my parents once this year for week. Anna and boys look after club very good. I meet all relatives; they see I do good. But would never move back. Well, maybe when very wrinkled old man, to sit in sun with other old men, drink raki and talk about old days." He laughed again. "I must go now. You're not only guests in

36

club tonight," he scolded them, grinning. "Enjoy bottle on house. Your other drinks will come when this finished."

"Thanks," they all chorused.

"My pleasure, call me Aleksander. I see you around." He held up his glass. "Gëzuar," he said, as he toasted them. "In Albania, means 'cheers'."

He got up and walked away, speaking to a person here and there, the odd hand on a shoulder, laughing and joking all the while.

"Wow!" said Alice. "Dangerous. But I'd do him."

"Alice, do you need to be quite so subtle? But I know what you mean. There's something *very* attractive about him." Carol smiled as she said it. They all felt his presence, even after he'd left.

"I wouldn't say no, if he asked, either," Heather said, "but we've no chance. Even if we did, he'd chew us up and spit us out when he'd finished," she added, rather more sharply than she'd intended.

"You're probably right. I'm sure he has his pick and I'd bet he doesn't stay with the same girl for too long," Carol observed.

"But what a night! It might just be worth it." Alice looked over as he mingled with a mixed group of very well-dressed, obviously moneyed, clubbers. "Look at the buns on him!"

"Alice, you always have to bring the conversation down to base level."

"Only saying what you're both thinking. He did show an interest, though. Which one of us do you think he'd go for? I think it's me. You two are too prudish. Especially if he's just after a shag."

"Alice!" the other two said simultaneously, but they all laughed and finished off the remainder of the bottle.

"Let's go and look round this place. We'll get our drinks later."

They made their way towards the main entrance; there were a couple of openings off to each side and a spiral stairway that led to a mezzanine level. They chose to go up the stairs and stood on the wide curved balcony that overlooked the dance floor, close to where they'd been sitting talking to Aleksander. More tables and seating occupied the upper floor, and Carol noticed that at this level it was mostly arranged in small booths suitable for two or four people. They scanned the dance floor below, noticing for the first time that there were a couple of semi-famous faces in, surrounded by hangers-on, fawning over their every word. They had a bit of fun identifying the more obscure of these celebrities until one of the waiters arrived with their drinks order. The waiter wouldn't take any money from them and when they looked down, Aleksander gave them a wave; they self-consciously returned it, mouthing thanks for sending up the drinks.

Carol was reluctant to sit her drink on the wide balustrade at the edge of the balcony until Alice pointed out the discreet but substantial net designed to catch any glasses, or possibly even bodies, that might fall towards the dance floor below. They sat in one of the booths adjacent to the edge and people-watched for a while.

"I told you I wouldn't have to buy a drink all night. I think he's definitely got the hots for one of us and I can't see it being either of you two."

"Shut up, Heather; it would be me if it was anyone," said Alice. "I think he must have noticed me the last time and decided to make a move. I don't know if I fancy him much, though. I think I'd rather have one of those guys down there," she said, pointing to a much younger group standing together at the end of the bar.

Carol laughed, accustomed to her two friends winding each other up. "I bet he buys drinks for any new girls coming here for the first time, to encourage them to come back. Everybody knows that it's the women who pull in the male clientele to nightclubs, so they'll do anything to get us to be regulars."

"You've always got to be fucking sensible, haven't you? Can you not let us have a fantasy for a moment or two, before you give us a reality check?" Alice groaned, but she was smiling at Carol as she said it.

When they'd finished their drinks, they returned to the lower floor and continued to look around the club. The door to the right of the entrance vestibule was marked *Private – VIP lounge only*, so they tried the door leading off to the left. It led into a wide but short corridor, with an identical door at the other end and they could feel the thud of a bass beat through the floor as they approached it. Seeing the shimmer and flashes of intensely coloured lights through the small round window in the upper half of the heavy door, they opened it and a wall of sound hit them, making them gasp with its intensity. A DJ stood on a platform in the centre, high above the dense crowd bouncing on the dance floor, the spectacular light show illuminating the dancers' faces eerily.

Heather leaned in towards her friends. "This is more like it. Let's have a fucking dance." Hardly making her out, Carol and Alice caught the gist of her words and they launched themselves into the melee, instantly part of the writhing mass of dancers responding to the DJ's manic performance. One track blended in with another and they must have been dancing for nearly an hour until, exhausted, they stumbled back through the double doors for a break. The music back in the main part of the club felt noticeably quieter now, after the crushing noise they'd just left.

"I can't believe how busy it is in there, and how loud. You can't hear it out here at all!" Carol exclaimed.

"I'm guessing he paid as much for soundproofing as he did for his speakers," Alice said, "and the lighting was pretty awesome, too. How does a guy who comes over here with nothing get successful quickly enough to be able to afford to spend that sort of money on a club?"

"If you've got the balls and the brains, and you're willing to take a few risks and flirt with the edges of the law, it's surprising how quickly you can make it big." Heather regularly interviewed young entrepreneurs for the paper. "It doesn't do any harm to be charming and have the gift of the gab, either," she added, "and your man here seems to have these qualities in spades, so it's not surprising."

"Or he may be the front for an Albanian cartel," joked Alice. "Those two bouncers at the door looked pretty thuggish and creepy."

Heather laughed. "Bouncers always look like that, that's why they employ them. But they prefer to be called doormen or security operatives nowadays."

After another couple of drinks and another spell in the "loud room", they were ready to call it a night. As they reclaimed their coats, Aleksander suddenly appeared at their side, from nowhere.

"Ladies, you are leaving so soon? Did you not enjoy my club?"

Heather and Alice tried to deny any form of dissatisfaction with their evening at the same time, drowning each other out. As they looked at each other in annoyance, Carol took the chance to tell him that they'd had a great night, but they were exhausted. "We'll definitely be back, though, and we'll tell everyone we know about it."

"Thank you, thank you. You are very charming ladies."

Again, the smile banished any arrogance from his face.

"Now let me get taxi for you. It's not good to wander round this place at night looking for cab. Some bad people out there." He motioned to the doorman, who spoke into a microphone attached to his earpiece, waving them over when he'd finished.

Aleksander surprised them all by kissing each of them on both cheeks before wishing them a good night and leaving them to be guided out by the doorman who, up close, seemed every bit as brutal as they'd remembered him, and with a much more marked Eastern European accent than his boss.

The doormen must have had direct contact with the drivers because there was a taxi sitting with its door open, ready for them, when they went outside. As it drove away, they could see what Aleksander meant about the area not being the best for a late night stroll.

"That's how he's got a club that size at his age. He was prepared to buy a property in a less fashionable part of town, probably at a fraction of the cost of a similar building somewhere classier," Heather said, as the cab sped northwards past the Elephant and Castle.

41

"He's been quite clever, as most people come by cab or car, so it's not necessarily an issue and anyway, I hear from those in the know that this area could be the place to be in five years' time."

Alice was quite often right with her predictions, but Carol was more intrigued by the man than by his money.

"There is something about him, though. A bit full of himself, but he just about gets away with it, somehow. And I think he's definitely got one of you two in his sights!"

Her friends laughed, but Carol could see that they'd come to the same conclusion and that neither would put up a fight if he made a move on them. As they crossed the Waterloo Bridge and the cab sped them back home to the north side of the river, a return to the club the following week was discussed with a feigned indifference.

-o-

Carol, surprising herself, felt a thrill of anticipation when her friends suggested returning to the club the following Saturday night. Neither Alice nor Heather would admit it, but both were intrigued by its charming and attractive owner. Although she would never have acknowledged it to the others, Carol was just as curious, if a little nervous at the thought of meeting him again, but she sensed that it wouldn't be a good thing if one of her friends did get involved with him.

It all added an extra edge to their night when they met up for a few drinks at their usual wine bar. When it was late enough to ensure that they wouldn't be arriving unfashionably early at an almost empty venue, they joined the scrum of revellers trying to hail a cab to take them over the river again. As usual it took Heather's aggressive competitiveness before they got one, which dropped them off as close to Bloq as the driver could get. Threading their way through the carnage of cars parked in every available square foot on both sides of the street, they made it to the door just before the queue was beginning to form.

It was a disappointment to all three when they got in to the club and there was no sign of Aleksander. When they asked Anna, the manageress, she told them, almost rudely, that he'd been away on business all day, but that he hoped to be back at some point in the evening. Carol wondered again if the woman was in a relationship with her boss, or wanted to be, because for a moment, her facial expression seemed designed to warn the three friends to stay away from Aleksander. If it was true, Alice and Heather hadn't noticed it.

They were soon joined by a few of the journalists who worked with Heather and Carol. Even Steve Evans, a seasoned columnist just escaping from his second failed marriage and a veteran of London nightlife, was impressed by the new club the girls had found.

It was almost the end of the night when Alice noticed Aleksander appear behind the bar. He might have been there a while; the staff were barely coping with the "last drinks rush" and their boss had stepped in to help until the drinkers waiting to be served thinned out to less than one deep. Small groups of clubbers were beginning to leave and Aleksander left the bar and spoke to some of those on their way out before approaching Carol and her friends.

Steve and the others were even more impressed when Aleksander quietly told them to wait until the majority had left and then to join him and a few friends for a private drink or two.

They waited until the exodus had dwindled to the last few stragglers and made their way to the entrance of the VIP room. One of the doormen had stationed himself outside, but he just nodded to Carol and her friends as they went through.

The room was much smaller than she'd expected; almost like an oversized living room, with a small bar at one end. There were perhaps thirty people present, relaxing in the opulent clusters of couches surrounding a small dance floor. The lighting was subtle and the music was quieter, with a smooth jazzy feel to it. Aleksander himself was dishing out the drinks and a couple of waitresses were carrying plates of nibbles for the guests.

Carol sat with her back to the dance floor, alongside Jenny, another of the interns, and Steve. Heather and Alice sat facing them, beside Dawn and Petra, a couple of young office trainees from the paper who were giggling excitedly, wondering aloud if it would be OK to talk to the three young West Ham players they'd recognised sitting at the next couch along.

Aleksander sauntered over and Heather introduced everyone while he took their drinks order. Most of them accepted the offer of a glass of fizz, but Steve ordered a whiskey sour in an attempt to impress the group. The nightclub owner returned to the bar to pour their drinks and a waitress brought them over. Aleksander, briefly talking to the young footballers on the way, followed her and sat beside them.

"This is really great of you to do this," Alice said, her words echoed by a few appreciative murmurs from the others.

"Not at all." Aleksander turned to Steve, Jenny and the two girls, who were still trying to catch the eye of the

44

footballers. "My three beautiful friends here are regulars; they bring me much new customers." He didn't seem embarrassed by this exaggeration and Heather, Alice and Carol basked a little in their colleagues' gratitude for being included in their privileged status, however unearned it was.

He definitely has designs on Alice or Heather. Carol didn't mind if it was the case; it was working to everyone's benefit. Steve was taking the chance to grill Aleksander about his rise from bar worker to club owner for a possible feature, and Carol and Heather cursed themselves for not thinking of it. The two girls from the office had plucked up the courage to talk to the three West Ham players, who weren't quite senior enough to be completely arrogant and seemed quite taken by Heather and Carol's young colleagues.

Carol didn't pay much attention to what was going on. Being completely honest, she was beginning to feel tired and was quite happy to make her drink last until the others were ready to go home, when she noticed Steve, Heather and Alice talking quietly with Aleksander. The next thing she knew, her two friends and Steve were each doing a line of coke on the table. It wasn't the first time she'd seen coke being snorted and she'd often shared a spliff with Heather and Alice, but she did feel a little uneasy at the sight of the three of them openly doing a line in front of her.

Aleksander leaned over. "You not want some?" he asked.

"No thanks," she replied, "I've never done it." She blushed at how naïve she sounded, but he didn't seem bothered.

"Fair enough. But let me know if change your mind. Is good if only use now and then. You try it before dance. Or make love. Best ever." He laughed, but she noticed that he hadn't taken any.

"Do you ever …"

"Yes, but not often and not when work."

Steve and Jenny had been talking together for a while before getting up for a dance, and the two trainees had moved along to sit next to the football players. It was the first time during the evening that Aleksander had the three friends together, alone.

"There's private party here next Thursday. Somebody slight bit famous. Do you want come to it?"

Alice and Heather looked at each other briefly and nodded. "Yes, we'd love to. Are you up for it, Carol?"

Carol wasn't sure. "I hate going out when I'm working the next day. I think I'll give it a miss, this time."

Alice was shocked. "You are joking, aren't you? You've got to come. How often will you get invited to something like this?" She turned to Aleksander. "Who is it?"

"Ach, that's secret. Girlfriend throw surprise party. Not know enough people to fill up club, ask me make look busy."

"Just come and don't drink too much. Or take the Friday off," Heather said to Carol. "When was the last time you had a day off work?"

Aleksander was, as always, diplomatic. "Let Carol make her own mind. You let me know by end of evening and I add you to list. It start sooner than normal night so you go home early if want to work next day. Work important. I now go work, too, keep other guests happy." He smiled at them and worked his way round to the bar, checking that everyone in the room had drinks.

Both her friends turned to Carol after he'd left.

"Come on, you can't miss something like this," said Heather.

"Don't be a dork. You'd hate it if we came back and told you all about us mixing with the celebs and you'd missed it," Alice added.

"I don't think it will be A-list, from what Aleksander said, but I'll come anyway, even if it's just to watch you two make arses of yourselves fawning over people who've been on TV for two minutes." She laughed.

Alice and Heather were delighted. "Right, that's settled. Let's have fucking dance, as Aleksander would say."

Heather and Carol giggled at Alice's impression of the club's owner, just as Steve and Jenny came back. They left them sitting together and had a couple of dances on the now busy compact dance floor. When they returned to their seats, the two other girls had disappeared with the football players and there was no sign of Jenny or Steve.

"Well, bugger me, so much for a night out with friends!" complained Heather. They laughed and agreed to call it a night. Aleksander saw them heading for the door and showed them out, once again making sure that his doorman had called a cab for them.

"Must go. Need to chase others now, too, or no sleep. You want come Thursday?"

He seemed pleased when they said that they were up for it and he left them waiting for the cab, which took no more than a few minutes.

"Hasn't he made a move on one of you yet?" Carol joked on the way back to her flat, where they were all staying.

"He's been the perfect gentleman to me. It's very disappointing." Alice did look a bit deflated.

"It's the same with me. Perhaps he needs to get me on my own," Heather said.

"You're bound to get a chance next Thursday. Maybe we should put bets on it." Carol found this hilarious, but the other two didn't join in with her mirth.

CHAPTER 3   LONDON

Bill awoke with a start. A little drool of saliva had trickled from the corner of his mouth onto his jumper and he quickly wiped it with a hanky, embarrassed despite there being nobody else present. For a brief second he wondered where he was, but that thought was brutally forced from his mind by the crushing recollection of why he'd woken up, cramped, in a chair in Carol's flat.

After checking the flat again for any clues as to Carol's disappearance and finding nothing of significance, he quickly left for the police station. He'd fortunately left his *A to Z* in the glove compartment the last time he'd been down to the flat, which now seemed to him like an age ago, and Kentish Town police station was relatively easy to find anyway.

Unable to find a space, he took the risk of double parking. A notice on the front door told him that due to critical staff shortages, there was no one manning the front desk until the 26th and that any enquiries should be directed to the neighbouring police station at West Hampstead or to Metropolitan Police Headquarters. He didn't fancy the trip over to Victoria and, irrationally, he thought the police might think his problem was too trivial for him to report it in the familiar and imposing Scotland Yard building that he'd seen so often on the news, when major crimes from the capital were being reported on the BBC.

Again the *A to Z* proved useful and he found West Hampstead police station with less trouble than he'd expected. If it hadn't been for his situation, he might even have enjoyed the reduced numbers of nose to tail buses, irritable taxi drivers and reckless cyclists that made it easier to travel across the city than through London's normally gridlocked streets. This time, he was lucky to find a parking space and he used his mobile to pay for the ticket.

Nervously, he stood in the crowded waiting room while a constant stream of people was dealt with by two bored looking officers standing behind a long counter. Bill looked around and saw the usual ethnic mix that always fascinated him when he was in London and, although his home city of Glasgow was fast becoming as multicultural as the capital, the sheer number of communities and cultures in London put it in a different league. Bill didn't feel particularly uncomfortable, even when his attempts to pass the time of day were rewarded with sullen silence, but he was pleased when it was his turn to approach the desk. He waited patiently for the officer behind the counter to lift his head from the sheet of paper he was reading.

"Can I help you, sir?"

Bill stumbled over his explanation of Carol's non-appearance, perturbed slightly by the lack of notes being taken, but he hesitated to comment on it so as not to antagonise the man. Eventually, when the officer had heard enough to realise that Bill's story was going to have to be recorded, he reluctantly, it seemed to Bill, selected a form from the rack behind him and asked Bill to repeat the information that he'd already given.

"We'll officially record your daughter as a missing person, which will mean that her name will be circulated around all the police stations in London and she'll be placed on the missing persons list in the nationwide database. In the meantime it would be better if you made your way home and we'll contact you when we hear something."

"I'm going to stay at her flat until I hear from her. I'll call back round tomorrow, if you don't mind." Even when he was annoyed, Bill couldn't help but be polite, although as a result of the policeman's seeming indifference, there was an edge to his voice.

"It would be better not to, sir. It gets pretty busy in here and we wouldn't want you wasting your own time or ours, would we?"

"I'll phone, then, if that's not going to put you out."

The officer looked at him as if trying to make up his mind if Bill's voice held a hint of sarcasm, but he let it slide. "That would be better, although you'd be best served by waiting till we call you, Mr Ingram."

Bill left, unconvinced of the prospect of the police exerting much energy in the hunt for Carol, and returned to the flat more dispirited than before.

Mrs Hamble, in her kindness, had made him some lunch, and as he ate the bowl of soup and sandwich at her kitchen table, with little enthusiasm, he updated her on the disappointing response of the police.

"Not to worry, Mr Ingram. I'm sure they'll get moving on it once they're fully staffed tomorrow. You should go and get some rest, after driving all night like that."

He thanked her for the food and, agreeing that a sleep would be helpful, he made his escape.

More to keep himself occupied than anything else, he retrieved his laptop from his bag and cursed under his breath as he realised that, in his haste to leave home, he hadn't packed the chargers for either the computer or his phone.

51

He fired it up anyway and, knowing that it was fully charged, he thought he'd go on to the Internet to find somewhere he could buy replacements.

It took him ten minutes to find the small card with Carol's Wi-Fi settings that allowed him to connect and a further five minutes to guess what her password was, but when he did, he quickly found two or three retail outlets nearby that might have chargers, if they were open. The most likely one was a Maplin store in Parkway, a few streets away. He walked, rather than taking his car, to clear his head and stretch his legs.

None of the shops in the row were open but he could see that, according to the notice stuck to the glass door, the Maplin store would re-open at 10 a.m. on Boxing Day for the start of the "New Year Sale". On returning to the flat, he restarted the laptop and retrieved the phone number and address for Carol's work, then found the contact number for Heather, one of her friends, in the family address book. Carol had given the girl's number to Bill when she'd first moved down.

Carol's office line re-directed him to an answering service informing him that her section of the paper was closed until the 27th. He rang Carol's friend next, but there was no answer.

When his phone rang a few minutes later, he jumped and grabbed it excitedly, knowing it would be Carol, but an unfamiliar woman's voice asked him if he'd called her number, and what did he want.

It took Bill a second to realise that this was Carol's friend calling back and he quickly apologised for phoning her.

"I'm sorry to bother you on Christmas Day, but I'm very worried about Carol. She didn't turn up in Glasgow for the holidays and I can't get in touch with her."

There was a pause and, when the caller spoke, it seemed to Bill that she sounded a little wary.

"I haven't seen Carol or spoken to her for months, Mr Ingram."

"I thought you worked together."

"We did, but Carol hasn't worked at the paper for ..." she paused again, "... oh, it must be at least two months now."

Bill felt a tightening of his chest and he struggled to breathe as he tried to come to terms with what he was hearing. "That can't be true. She never said anything. I don't understand."

"Mr Ingram, I'm sorry you didn't know. She lost her job. I thought she would have told you. I can ask around, if you like, to see if anyone's heard from her."

Before Bill could answer, he was cut off and he looked at his screen in dismay as the low battery message fizzled away with the last of the phone's power.

He quickly dialled Carol's friend back from the landline in the flat and explained that the call had dropped because his phone battery had died.

"I didn't realise you were down here, Mr Ingram," said Heather, recognising the number as Carol's. "I thought you were still at home. I think I should maybe come round to the flat and see you. There are a few things I think you need to know, but I'd rather not talk about it over the phone."

"Can you come round now? I'm really sick with worry and any information you can give me would be a great help."

"I'm on my way. It'll take me about ten or fifteen minutes."

While he waited, Bill, unable to sit and do nothing constructive, scribbled a brief summary of their conversation in his notebook and jotted down a few questions raised in his mind by what Heather had said. He went back downstairs and knocked on Mrs Hamble's door.

"Would you like a cup of tea, Mr Ingram?' she said, when she answered.

"No thanks; I'm waiting for one of Carol's friends to come round. She'll be here shortly. I just had a couple of questions to ask you, if that's OK?"

"Of course. Anything I can do to help."

"Have you noticed anything different about Carol in the last month or so? Was she about more often, especially during the day?"

Mrs Hamble thought for a moment. "No. Definitely not. If anything, I would say she's not been at the flat as much, of late. I just thought she was staying with friends. You know what young ones are like nowadays."

"Did she ever bring her friends here?"

"Not recently, come to think about it, but a couple of nice girls stayed over with her a while back, once or twice. They were never any trouble, noisy or the like."

"Did you ever see her with a boyfriend?"

"No, I can't say I did. She was dropped off a few times in a car, but it could have been a private hire, for all I know. I never saw who the driver was."

"Did you notice anything else, Mrs Hamble?"

"I'm not sure, because I saw less of her and when she was here, she always seemed to be in a hurry."

At that moment a taxi stopped outside and a young woman, who Bill assumed was Heather, stepped out and walked towards the house. He turned to the old lady.

"Thanks very much, Mrs Hamble, I appreciate your help. I'll let you know when I hear something."

Mrs Hamble peered around Bill to see the newcomer. "Hello, my dear," she said and, in a whispered aside to Bill, she told him that this was one of the girls who had stayed over with Carol a couple of times.

"Hi, Mrs Hamble; we met before. I stayed a couple of nights with Carol." Heather turned to Bill. "You must be Carol's dad. I'm Heather." She held out her hand and Bill shook it, surprised.

"We should go upstairs," he said, letting her pass and following on behind her, much to Mrs Hamble's disappointment.

As soon as she entered the flat, Heather turned to Bill, her face now pale and tense. "I should have contacted you earlier. I'm sorry."

Bill could see that she was fighting back tears and he reached out to touch her shoulder in support.

"Don't be down on yourself. It's always easy to know what to do in hindsight. Just tell me everything you know. Why did Carol leave her job? She loved it."

"She did, and she was really good at it; she would have gone far if she'd kept at it, but she lost interest and in the end she was asked to leave."

"You mean sacked?"

"In effect, yes, although not officially. I think they had liked her so much when she first arrived, they didn't want to make it impossible for her to get back into work again if she sorted herself out."

"What do you mean, *sorted* herself out?"

Heather started to cry and Bill handed her a paper hanky from the box on the table. "Take your time."

Between sobs, Heather managed to speak. "We think she has a drug problem …" She paused. "And there's this guy she's seeing …"

Bill was stunned. "What type of drugs?" he asked, sharper than he intended.

"Well, the last time we were together she did quite a bit of coke, but I'm worried that she was into other stuff as well."

"And you saw her taking this coke? That's cocaine?"

"Yes. I mean we all smoked the odd spliff now and then and we'd tried a line of coke once or twice, but Carol seemed to be getting more and more into it. I suppose that went with the club scene she was getting involved with."

Heather's eyes were rimmed with red and the little eye make-up she had on had started to dissolve and run down her cheeks in dark streaks. Bill gave her time to blow her nose on the hanky he had given her and wipe her eyes with another from the box. When she'd composed herself, he spoke again.

"And this man she's involved with. Who is he?"

Heather looked at Bill, a knot of guilt making it impossible for her to look him in the eye.

"It's because of us that she met him ..." She crumbled into deep sobs and Bill awkwardly put his arm around her, not saying a word. Part of him was angry, but he couldn't blame this young woman for not intervening. After all, he and Alison had noticed changes in Carol's behaviour since she moved down to London, but had said nothing

"What's this man's name?"

Heather managed to blurt it out, before breaking down again.

"His name is Aleksander Gjebrea. He owns Bloq, a nightclub Alice and I took her to. Carol said she could handle it, that she wouldn't let him hurt her."

"Tell me everything you know."

CHAPTER 4   EASTERN BLOQ

"We're on the list." Heather stared at the doorman. It wasn't the one who'd got taxis for them the last time.

"Just checking, miss. I've been told be extra careful tonight. Please bear with me."

Heather was fuming, but other than have a strop and say something to Aleksander later, there was nothing she could do without appearing petulant.

Finally they were allowed in, but for the first time, they'd felt as if they weren't quite welcome.

Once they were inside, the atmosphere changed completely. They bumped into Aleksander almost immediately and he escorted them through and sat them down at a table near to the bar but just off to the side, an ideal position from which to observe the birthday boy and his followers.

He apologised for having to leave them, but he explained that it could be a big night for him; attracting the type of people who would spend a large amount of cash on a regular basis was critical to his success. He promised that he would join them again when he could and they set about having a bloody good evening. They played a childish spot-the-celeb drinking game at which, for some reason, Carol and Heather seemed to excel, while poor Alice took a hit nearly every time. Carol called a halt to the game when she thought Alice was getting a little too loud and bought her a non-alcoholic cocktail to nurse for a while.

Anna, the manageress, noticed her buying it and gave Carol a nod; it had saved her the awkward job of asking Alice to tone it down a little. She spoke to Carol while she stood at the bar waiting for the other two drinks to be poured.

"I wouldn't get too close to Aleksander, if I were you." Carol was taken aback by Anna's warning. "He's out of your league and you'll only get burnt."

"I'm sorry, but why would you say that?" spluttered Carol, annoyed. "Are you and he together?"

"God, no. I'm just saying for your own good."

"In that case, if either of my friends did want to go out with Aleksander, I can't see why it should have anything to do with you." She said this in a low voice, although she was pretty sure no one else at the bar could hear what they were saying. The music was loud enough to make it necessary to lean close to be heard.

"It's not them he's interested in. Do what you want, but don't say I didn't warn you."

Carol's drinks arrived and, as she paid, she could see that the conversation was over. *Cheeky bitch.* But part of her brain was still trying to digest Anna's parting comment. *Is there any truth in what she said? There are no signs that he is interested in me.*

Back with her friends, Carol sat thinking while Alice sipped her drink, unaware of its non-intoxicating contents. Carol told Heather what Anna had said, omitting the bit about Aleksander's interest in Carol herself.

"Jealous cow," Heather blurted out. "Still, I suppose it means he's interested. I should really take advantage of

Alice being pissed, shouldn't I?" She laughed. Carol thought she was only half-kidding, but that it might be interesting to see what happened if Heather did try something on with Aleksander.

The next time he came over, she noticed that he made a point of sitting next to her, opposite her two friends, *but that was just where the spare seat was*. When he spoke, it was to all three of them and although he seemed to turn to Carol when he could, she wondered if she might be reading too much into it.

"So are you and Anna together?"

Carol was shocked when Heather blurted out what they were all thinking.

Aleksander laughed, not in the slightest put out by Heather's directness. "No, she bit of cold fish. Maybe she lesbian." He said this with a wide grin, disarming any offence they might have taken. "Don't have time and not my type. I like women with fuller figure. But she bloody good worker."

Had it been anyone else, they might have bridled at his comments, but all three silently assessed themselves and hoped they matched up to his benchmark.

As the party drew to a close, Aleksander left them to complete his host duties with the footballer and his fiancée, whose party it had been, but before he left, he gave the three of them a handful of Bloq's business cards.

"I'd most appreciate if you hand out these for me; give to people you think would like club."

Handing Carol her small bundle, he winked and smiled at her.

Later, in the cab, Carol idly looked at the card on top of the little pile she held in her hand and was surprised to see a phone number written on it, with "call me" scrawled below it. She hurriedly slipped the cards into her handbag, her pulse racing; a few scenarios ran through her head, but she couldn't see past the most obvious one. It *was* her that he was interested in and she wondered just what the hell she should do about it.

-o-

Aleksander usually picked her up from the flat. She still hadn't told the other two that she was seeing him. She'd waited three days after the private party to phone him, but he'd insisted on taking her out that night, and the following night, to what she considered obscenely expensive restaurants. On both occasions he had picked her up and dropped her back at the end of the road on her insistence, to save him driving up the narrow street with cars half parked on both pavements.

He never forced the pace, letting her be the one to decide to kiss him on the first night and encouraging his hands to wander a little the following evening. She knew it was only a matter of time before she was going to cave in and sleep with him, because she didn't care about the sense of danger that seemed to surround him or her suspicion that he would eventually move on and leave her an emotional mess.

She told Heather the next day that Aleksander had contacted her (true in the strict sense of the word, in her mind) and that they had been out on a *date* and were now seeing each other. Heather, after a few seconds of shock and a burst of jealousy that she immediately felt guilty about, laughed at her and Alice's presumption that it had been one of them that he'd been interested in. When she phoned Alice later that night to tell her Carol's news, she detected a similar note of envy in her friend's voice, but she couldn't blame her, because her own initial reaction had been the same.

But Heather also had a genuine concern for Carol, knowing that she was the most naïve of the three. Alice especially would have treated any involvement with Aleksander as a short-term affair to be enjoyed and discarded, and not cried over when it came to an end too soon.

A desire to give Carol and Aleksander their own space, and a horrible feeling that she would find it difficult to watch them together, led Heather to turn down Carol's invitation to go with her to Bloq that weekend, but she and Alice did cave in and go the following Saturday, and it hadn't been as bad as she'd feared it would be. Carol and Aleksander hadn't been overly demonstrative about their relationship and he had the good grace to appear embarrassed by the possibility that he had led the other two on in any way.

Despite this, and knowing that she'd become very close to Carol, Heather couldn't stop the unwelcome stab of envy when she realised that the woman she now considered to be her best friend was sleeping with a man who she'd half hoped to sleep with herself. It was hard to explain that for both her and Alice, rejection would have been easier to accept if, of the three of them, it hadn't been Carol who had been chosen by Aleksander.

That Carol and Aleksander had become intimate was obvious, despite the pair's attempts to hide it. And it had happened very quickly. On the third occasion he'd picked her up, it was with an invitation to have dinner at his home. She hadn't wavered for a second when he had suggested it and had coolly purchased some condoms on the way to work, knowing that he would probably be prepared anyway, but enjoying the decadent feeling that she was deliberately and unashamedly giving herself to him with undisguised pleasure.

His house had blown her away. It was brand new development in a very fashionable part of Islington. Even the address had a ring of class to it: *Mulberry Mews*. White, with lots of glass and cubes of wood, it was tall and thin; a modern town house, with a large deck overlooking a patch of sunken designer garden at the back. Everything about it spoke money to her, and plenty of it, but it was done with exquisite taste.

He cooked, as well. After showing her around, sweetly avoiding the bedrooms, they ate in the dining area adjoining the kitchen, looking out into the tastefully lit and exquisitely planted garden. If she hadn't seen him prepare the food herself, she might have been suspicious that he'd bought in a takeaway from one of the city's expensive restaurants and reheated it. She knew, just by looking at the bottle, that the wine they shared was probably of good vintage, and expensive.

Although wine might have lowered any inhibitions she had, it wasn't necessary, as she'd already long since decided that she would be staying overnight with him.

They both spoke of their backgrounds (his was much more interesting, she thought) and he made her laugh, and sometimes nearly cry, with stories of his first few years in London as an exile from his home in Albania, which he still loved with a fervour that she couldn't quite summon up for her childhood home in a comfortable, if somewhat boring, suburb of Glasgow.

Even his choice of music, from a hidden sound system casually turned on from his iPhone as they made their way up the stairs to one of the large modern L-shaped couches on the ground floor, was perfect. She wasn't a particular fan of classical music, but whatever the piece was that he'd chosen, it filled the whole house with a rich and seductive sound.

They had thrown themselves at each other almost immediately with a ferocity that was, to Carol, exhilarating and slightly frightening at the same time. Remarkably, another swipe of his iPhone made the glazing become opaque and they had sex for the first time on his very expensive antelope skin couch, neither of them willing to break off to make the journey upstairs to his bedroom.

Unsurprisingly, he was a great lover, but she'd known that would be the case. He oozed an animal arrogance that was only tempered by a sense of humour and occasional self-deprecation that saved him from being insufferable. And despite the fierceness of that first encounter, there were moments of tenderness and consideration that hinted at a caring nature beneath the hard and somewhat menacing shell.

He'd removed her clothes quicker than she'd thought possible, discarding his own, with her help, at the same time. After that, other than kissing her hard enough to almost hurt, there hadn't been much foreplay, but he'd stimulated her enough while fully clothed, hardly even touching her, to ensure that she came just before him. Even putting the condom on had been seamless; the packet appeared in his hand from nowhere and the contents were expertly applied with practiced ease, barely interrupting their progress.

Later, lying in his bed on the top floor, with floor to
ceiling views at both ends of the master bedroom, he'd
made love to her again, slowly and with a practiced
expertise that hinted at a breadth of experience that could
only have come from him having had a long line of
women sharing his bed, probably from an early age.
Fleetingly, it worried her a little that she was just another
sexual conquest in a life otherwise devoted to the
advancement of Aleksander Gjebrea's business career, but
the physical sensations he was triggering within her soon
banished any concerns she had. And although she didn't
see herself as a great or experienced lover, she sensed that
just responding to him, without inhibition, was enough for
him.

Afterwards, they showered in the large en suite wet room,
which they entered through an effortlessly pivoting door in
its glass wall. There seemed to be no privacy; the whole
room could be seen from the bed and she wasn't sure a
toilet visit would be an entirely comfortable experience
until he waved his hand in front of a faintly glowing glass
tile inset into the slate wall, and the clear wall, like the
windows downstairs, became instantly frosted. Another
gesture by him and the lights came on and were dimmed
and brightened by yet another motion of his hand. She
presumed that holding your nose in front of the sensor
would probably turn the fan on and pulling an imaginary
chain while sitting on the toilet would cause it to flush. He
laughed when she said so and showed her how the toilet
automatically flushed when you stood up after using it and
told her that the air in the toilet was constantly sucked out
by strong remote fans, whenever a person was sensed
within the room.

"The whole place ducted with air condition. Everything
automatic or remote control."

"What if you don't have your iPhone?" she joked.

"Always backup method to control everything, no worries."

As he gently washed her she half-considered how much all this luxury had set him back, but any thoughts of a financial nature were soon dispelled by his hands, slippy with shower gel, gently washing her breasts and following the stream of bubbles down her belly and between her legs. She wondered if there was a little nook where he kept a supply of condoms close to the shower, but she soon realised that his intentions, on this occasion, were for her pleasure only.

He dropped her off at work the next morning, after a surprisingly light and healthy breakfast. She'd heard him rise about six and had followed him downstairs shortly afterwards, clad only in a skimpy bathrobe that had been left for her on the chair at her side of the bed.

She'd descended two floors without finding him, but she could hear sounds of exertion from the basement below and realised that he had a gym down there, which he obviously used on a daily basis.

Not really a shock. She remembered the firmness and strength of his body from the night before and knew that he took keeping himself in shape very seriously. She returned to the penthouse bedroom and, looking into the large mirror hung on the opposite wall to the bed, she let her robe slip to the floor and tried to look at herself as critically and dispassionately as she could. *Perhaps slightly rounded in places, but not bad. Nothing a little working out wouldn't sort.*

He must have showered in the basement; when he returned, he smelled fresh and his hair was still damp. He had a towel wrapped around his waist, which he casually discarded, getting back into bed with her.

This time, he surprised her by being content to lie with his arm around her, answering her questions about the house. He'd lived in it only one year; he'd bought it off plan so as to have it done to his individual specifications and, no, he wasn't going to tell her how much he paid for it; not yet, at least.

At the office, she'd tried to appear as normal as possible, especially around Heather, not wanting to give any impression of smugness or self-satisfaction, but when Heather asked if she'd had a good time, she'd hinted just a little at how good it had been.

If Heather was jealous at all she hid it well, but Carol didn't give her any reason to think that she was gloating and she knew that they were still going to be friends.

On her own, she couldn't stop thinking about him and she had to firmly tell herself not to build up any expectations about their relationship. He seemed to her like a man who loved female company but was basically a loner, and she felt if she could always retain that thought, she would minimise the hurt she knew she would feel when it all came to an end. More than anything, she wanted to come out of it with her dignity intact and her heart as unscathed as possible.

Over the next few weeks, she stayed over at his place five or six nights, but never on the weekends. This suited them both. He needed to be at the club on the two busiest nights and she still had a social life with her friends.

She went home to see her parents for Christmas, even though she expected to be back up in Glasgow for her dad's birthday. When Aleksander told her that he was closing the club and having a private party for his friends and favoured customers to celebrate the fifth anniversary of Bloq's grand opening, she was delighted, especially as she would be the one at Aleksander's side all evening. He told her that she could invite a few friends and work colleagues, and she wouldn't have been human if she didn't enjoy her position as hostess. The fact that it was midweek didn't spoil it. She knew he was too much of a businessman to close the club to paying guests on one of his busier nights.

It came as a blow when she realised that her dad's party was on the same night. Despite never having missed one of his birthdays, she felt awful phoning him the day before to say she wouldn't be able to make it, made worse by keeping the reason from him.

Heather and Alice still made a weekly visit to Bloq with her, so they were delighted to get an invite to Bloq's fifth anniversary celebration. It was a hell of a night. Aleksander and Carol always kept any public show of affection to a minimum, which made it easy for her two friends to accept the fact that they'd been turned over by an outsider in their pursuit of Aleksander, especially one who'd made no effort in the contest.

Sometimes, curiosity got the better of them and Carol responded to their questioning by giving them vague details about their intimacy, but chapter and verse on their non-bedroom activity and his amazing lifestyle.

She made it clear to them that she knew where it was going.

"I'm not stupid; I realise that he's not the kind for long-term relationships. I'm just going to treat it like you two would: a bit of fun and a chance to live life in the fast lane for a while."

"I just hope you can do that. We'd hate to see you get hurt." Heather's voice held genuine concern and Carol touched her arm to reassure her that she could manage her own expectations.

"Think of it as a holiday romance," advised Alice. "Not that I'm saying it will only last for a fortnight," she hurriedly added, "but keep in mind that there's an end point."

"It's always possible that I'll be the one who he'll want to settle down with." Carol bridled, not enjoying her friend's dismissal of the possibility, despite her own conviction that they were right.

"Here we go,' quipped Alice, "she's planning the wedding already."

Carol laughed. "No, you're right. I was only saying ... I can handle it, I won't let him hurt me."

CHAPTER 5   HEATHER

"But she couldn't do that, despite all her talk about treating it as a bit of fun and going in with open eyes. She fell under his spell from the moment they got together. Over the next six months we saw less and less of her, and even at work, when she was there, she kept herself to herself. I overheard her editor saying that the quality of her work wasn't quite up to her usual standard."

The sadness in Heather's voice nearly broke Bill's heart; he knew that she'd been a genuine friend to Carol, but the guilt she felt about not intervening earlier was eating away inside her.

Heather could see the effect her words had on Bill. She'd almost told him the whole story, from her viewpoint. Most of the time he sat, head in hands, and she wondered if he was taking it all in. She continued anyway.

"It wasn't like that at first. Aleksander would drop her off at the paper if she'd stayed at his place and she definitely had a bounce in her step. She didn't say that much about their relationship, perhaps out of some misguided feeling that we might be jealous of her, but she did say a little more about the fancy places they visited and the type of people they mixed with. And she told us all about his house: some mega-expensive out-of-this-world town house in Islington."

Bill got up and started pacing around the room. "I'll just go and see her, now that I know where she is. I can persuade her to come home for a while and sort out her life."

"I'm not sure she'll listen to you. And then there are the drugs. They change people."

Bill tried to hide his anger but could hear himself shouting, "I'm her dad. I love her deeply. I know she loves me, too. I'll do anything I must to get her back."

Heather sobbed again and Bill felt awful, but she continued before he could apologise. "It's not that easy. She'll probably not be there. I don't think she's with him anymore."

"What do you mean? How do you know?"

"Alice and I went to the club a couple of weeks ago to try and reason with her one last time. She was normally there with him, but there was no sign of her. We nearly didn't get in, but Aleksander told the bouncer to let us through, to avoid a scene at the door, we thought. Once we were inside, he made no secret of that fact that he was with another girl. She was right there and, not giving a fuck that we were there, he went up to her and put his arms round her in front of us. He even fucking kissed her. I'm sure the only reason we'd been allowed in to the club was to rub our noses in it."

"The bastard. So where's Carol?"

"We asked him. He said she'd left him a few weeks before. Got angry when she'd thought he was with another woman and stormed out. Thought she might have gone back home to Scotland."

"And did you believe him?" Bill asked.

"Well, yes. I mean, there he was with someone else. It was easy to believe that Carol would have finished with him if she'd caught him with another woman. I didn't know your

71

address or phone number, so I couldn't check." She burst into tears again and Bill felt bad, wishing he hadn't been so hard on her.

"Listen, what's done is done. The most important thing now is to find her and help her, wherever she is."

"But I could have asked HR at work. They would have had her details. I could have contacted you when she was sacked. I can't believe now that I didn't."

Bill thought that Heather had been through enough and he figured that she'd told him as much as she was going to. He left her sitting quietly crying while he went through to the kitchen to make a cup of tea for her, but just as the kettle boiled he heard the door click and when he returned to the sitting room, it was empty.

He spotted a sheet of paper on the table. The note was addressed to him. It was an apology for leaving abruptly and for not having done enough, but saying she couldn't handle any more for now. He could contact her at any time if he needed any further information, or if he needed her help.

He didn't think he would, but made a mental note to send her a message thanking her for what she'd told him and for caring about Carol.

He would have gone straight to see this Aleksander Gjebrea, but Heather hadn't been able to give him the address, so he decided he'd go to the nightclub first. He thought he'd gain nothing by turning up during its noisy, nocturnal opening hours and doubted if it would be open on Christmas Day in any case.

Bill couldn't bring himself to sleep in Carol's bed, so he folded down the sofa bed that he and Alison had always

used on their visits, dreading that he'd spend the whole
night staring at the living room ceiling thinking about
where she was, but exhaustion once again got the better of
him and he slept soundly. He awakened to a precious few
seconds of time in his mind when Carol hadn't
disappeared, before reality crashed through and he looked
around to see the empty flat.

-o-

Although he didn't know why, Bill parked his car a couple
of streets away from Bloq; he felt it was just something he
should do. He made his way up a street lined with small
brick-built terraced houses, thinking to himself that the
residents must detest having a nightclub at the end of the
road; despite the street having seen better days, it looked
as if there were still residents who liked living there.
Turning the corner, he saw that the entrance did look
slightly seedy during daylight hours but, according to
Heather, it probably wasn't the sort of place that spilled
large crowds of noisy drunks in scant clothing onto the
street at three in the morning. There were probably no
groups of lads fighting or girls tottering in the sort of heels
that would have seemed like a good idea when they were
getting ready to go out, but were ankle breakers on the
end-of-night walk to the taxi rank.

The large black double doors were closed, each with a
wrought iron grille protecting it, and there was a small
sliding hatch in the right-hand door, which was closed. Bill
had no doubt that when the club opened its doors at the
ludicrously late time of 11 p.m. it could look quite
fashionable, but now it couldn't escape the usual rather
neglected look of a nightclub during daylight hours. He
walked round the back of the building, which had been a
garage or warehouse before conversion, through a yard
that served as the car park for the nightclub and the storage

area for its bins and those of the church next door. He was rewarded with the sight of two cars and a Transit van parked outside the nightclub's rear entrance. One of the cars was a large and ostentatious Mercedes; the other a smart car taking advantage of a miniature parking space created by one of the large wheeled bins jutting into it.

The black and silver Transit had dark tinted windows; there was a thin red line where the colours met, and it was emblazoned with the nightclub's name. Bill retraced his steps and rang the inconspicuous bell at the front door.

Nothing happened for a while, but Bill persisted and pressed the button a few more times until, eventually, the small sliding hatch snapped open. He could see a pair of eyes and a nose, with a few wisps of strawberry blonde hair, but he didn't have enough information to guess the gender of the person until a woman's voice asked him what he wanted.

Feeling a bit self-conscious talking to a door, he said, "My name's Bill Ingram. I'm here to ask about my daughter; she's gone missing and I have some information that she came here a lot. Can I come in and ask a few questions?"

"You'd be better off letting the police do their bit," the voice said, irritated. Bill thought he could detect a Tyneside accent.

"The police aren't taking it too seriously. They think that she's gone off somewhere on her own and simply doesn't want to be found, but I'm worried something's happened to her."

"We're closed just now. I'm only here today doing a little bookkeeping; I can't really see how I can help you; we get thousands of people through our doors every month."

"Yes, but they don't all have a relationship with your boss, do they?" Bill immediately regretted his outburst, expecting the hatch to slide closed, conversation ended, but nothing happened and the voice behind the door remained silent for a few seconds.

"What did you say her name was?"

"Carol. Carol Ingram."

"Bill, was it? Listen, you never got this from me, but she did come here a lot and she was with Aleksander Gjebrea for a while, although she's not now. I haven't seen her for a few weeks."

"Is he in? Can I have a word with him, please?"

"I'm not sure if he would talk to you even if he was in, but he's not here today."

Bill hated being taken for a ride. "Then whose is the Mercedes parked round the back, then?"

The voice behind the door hardened. "He isn't here, I told you. He has two cars and always keeps the Merc here. He takes the other one home. It's a Porsche," she replied.

"Sorry, I didn't mean to …" He faltered, but knowing that her patience was wearing thin, he continued. "So where does he live? I can get it from public records, you know," he said, not knowing if it were true, "so you might as well tell me."

The disembodied voice hesitated again. "I'll tell you, but I never spoke with you, right?"

Bill agreed and she gave him the address, which he quickly wrote down before he forgot it.

"You'll probably find him there today. I hope you find your daughter. Good luck."

This time the hatch did slide shut.

Bill started walking back to his car. As he turned the corner, the rear door of the club opened and Anna, the manageress, stepped out and got into the smart car. She edged out into the street and drove towards the crossroads where Bill had disappeared. She drove on past, but saw Bill walking away from her down the side street on her left. She turned left at the next junction, then left again. She pulled in to the side of the road and watched for a few seconds as a car, driven by the man she knew as Carol's father, appeared from the other end of the side street that he'd walked down. It turned towards her and she cursed, swinging the sun visor down to hide her face. As the car passed her, she quickly drove past the junction, reversed into the street and then followed Bill's car, trying to keep a safe distance from him without losing sight of his vehicle.

The Boxing Day traffic was heavier, so Bill made slow progress crossing northwards across the river. He nearly screwed up when he reached the Euston Road, and had to cut across two lanes to avoid being shunted down a one-way street into the Congestion Charge zone, almost hitting a cyclist and incurring the wrath of the drivers of two buses and a black cab. Anna shook her head and cursed Bill for being forced to make an equally insane manoeuvre to keep him in view.

The exclusivity of the area and the house prices increased as Bill headed north, following the satnav's instructions. It let him down at Highbury Island when he got into the wrong lane, which sent him up Holloway Road with the sound of "Turn around at the next junction and take the first exit," ringing in his ears. He was almost at the London

Met before he managed to turn right, and let the satnav readjust. Keeping the Emirates Stadium on his left, he eventually managed to reach Highbury Road, sweating and frustrated.

He headed into the affluent streets of Islington and drove down Highbury Grove, past the opening into Aberdeen Lane. He parked a hundred yards further on and returned on foot to the entrance to the lane, walking up as far as the exclusive cul-de-sac where the bastard lived. Checking out the black Porsche parked across the *keep clear* markings at the entrance of the mews, he paused only for a second, then made his way through the narrow opening which led to a double row of ultra-modern three-storey conjoined houses that made up Mulberry Mews, each offset a different distance from the landscaped courtyard.

Anna, who'd somehow succeeded in staying behind Bill, had seen him enter the mews but didn't follow him. She parked the smart car up the street from Bill's and stared in the rear-view mirror to watch for him to reappear.

Bill checked the numbers as he approached Aleksander Gjebrea's house. He wasn't sure what he was going to say, but he knew that he had to confront the man who seemed to be at the root of his daughter's downfall.

He rang the doorbell and waited for the door to be answered. Instead, a speaker at the side of the door crackled and a foreign sounding voice asked what he wanted.

"Could I possibly have a word with you, Mr Gjebrea?" Bill asked, hoping he hadn't mispronounced the name too badly.

"OK, you talk to me now already, but what it's about?"

"I think you know my daughter and I hope you can help me find her."

"Who is daughter? Why you come here?"

"Her name is Carol Ingram and I've been told that you had a relationship with her that ended recently. Now she's gone missing."

"Ah, Carol. We split up few weeks ago. I have not seen since."

"Don't you have any idea where she could have gone?"

"No. Have you tried flat in Camden?"

"Of course I have; that's the first place I went." Bill's exasperation was beginning to show. "I've been to the police, you know. They are looking for her, too."

"That very good. Police best idea. I tell them same if come here."

"Listen, Mr Gjebrea, I'll not rest until I find her and if it comes to light that you've harmed her in any way, I'll make sure that you get what you deserve."

"You come my house, threaten me, Bill?" The tone in Aleksander's voice had changed and, although he knew Carol would have told him her dad's name was Bill, it still felt chilling to hear him use his first name.

He continued. "It not good to do that. Not my fault that Carol not want to see you. Perhaps she go holiday somewhere. She was upset we split up; maybe needs break in sun to cheer up. Best you go home and wait, not give trouble to nice people. If cause a scene, I phone police myself. This good area, not want to annoy neighbours."

The speaker clicked off, even as Bill was about to shout an answer. He stood staring at the door for a few minutes, then turned and walked away from the house, tears of rage nearly blinding him

He paused at the start of the path leading back through to the lane and looked back. A woman was standing in the window of the house he'd just left and for a moment, through his blurred eyes, he thought it was Carol, but she turned to look at him and he realised he'd been mistaken.

As he exited the courtyard, he almost collided with a woman walking towards him.

"Sorry," he mumbled.

"Are you OK?" the woman asked, concern on her face.

"Yes, I'm fine." Bill turned away, not wanting the woman to see his tears.

"I don't want to pry, but you look upset."

Bill had always found that, in general, people in London didn't involve themselves with strangers, so this conversation took him by surprise.

"I could be anybody. Why are you asking?"

"Look, I'm sorry. I shouldn't have said anything." She went to turn away, but Bill put his hand out to stop her.

"No, it should be me who's apologising. I'm upset because my daughter's missing. Do you live here?"

"Yes, I do. Do you want a cup of tea?"

Bill smiled at her offer of the universal panacea for comforting those in distress, but he didn't want to involve her in his struggle with Aleksander Gjebrea.

"Thanks, but I don't want to get you on the wrong side of your neighbour. He's not the sort of person you want to fall out with."

"Mr Gjebrea. Is that who you're talking about?"

"Yes. How did you know?

"Everyone is too frightened to complain except me. He has a reputation, but I don't care. I live here, too. I mean, look at his bloody car. He parks it there all the time." She pointed to the black Porsche. "The local parking warden never books him. And the noise! No one minds a party, but his go on all night and he doesn't limit the noise. The people he invites: some of them wouldn't look out of place in a Moscow gangster film."

Taking into account that she'd probably spent at least one and a half million on her house only to find out she had the neighbours from hell, Bill dismissed his feeling that she was maybe a bit snobbish, and showed her a picture of Carol.

"That's my daughter. She had a relationship with him. Now I can't find her and he just laughed in my face."

"I'm sorry. I recognise her. She's a pretty girl, and not as brash as the rest of the girls who come and go. I only spoke to her once. She seemed very nice."

"When did you last see her?"

"Oh, it must be a month or more. She's better off out of it. I hope you find her."

"I'll do my best. Just watch yourself. He's got some sort of involvement in drugs, I think."

"Don't you worry about me. And good luck with your daughter."

He thanked her and made his way back to his car. It wasn't until he was nearly back at the main road that he realised he hadn't even asked the woman her name.

Anna saw Bill come out of the lane and started her engine as he got in his car and drove off. She followed three or four cars behind; he wasn't driving fast. She nearly lost him at a set of traffic lights, but had caught up with him by the next junction.

He parked on double yellows outside the police station and went in. *Good luck*, she said to herself. She waited until he came out, wanting to know where he was staying, and was rewarded for her patience when he drove to a flat in Camden. *This must be where Carol lived. He's using it as a base, which makes sense.*

Pausing only to write down the name of the street and the flat number, she drove past, turned at the next available inlet and headed out on to the main road and back southwards again.

-o-

Realising he'd forgotten, Bill nipped out to the Maplin store and purchased the extra chargers for his phone and laptop and returned to the flat. He sat alone, drained and exhausted. Aleksander Gjebrea's casual indifference about his daughter's whereabouts and his disdain for Bill's threats to go to the police had unsettled him, especially

81

when his gut feeling told him that the nightclub owner had been instrumental in Carol developing her drug habit and had abandoned her after he had no further use for her.

His humiliating and hurtful experience on his return to the police station that day had left him bruised and battered and his faith in the British police had taken a significant dent.

It was unfortunate that he'd had to reveal his new information to the very same officer who had been so offhand the first time. When he had recounted Heather's story and told of his own visit to the nightclub and the house, the policeman had again listened politely, taking a minimum of notes.

"Well, sir. If we had to arrest every man who's done wrong by a woman, the prisons would be full to overflowing, even more than they are now."

Bill had tried to argue that he wasn't asking for an arrest; only that it would be worthwhile for him or his colleagues to question the nightclub owner. His requests had been gently but firmly rebuffed.

"We don't have the manpower to go around questioning people just because an anxious member of the public asks us to. We follow a set procedure on a case-by-case basis, so I'm afraid you'll just have to be patient, sir."

"And exactly what procedures have been put in place so far, if I'm entitled to ask?"

"I'm sorry. Once we've passed the details on to CID, we have no information on how the investigation is progressing."

"Could I speak to someone in CID, then?"

"I'd imagine someone from CID will contact you in due course. At the moment, I'm sure that they'll all be out investigating crime, and we wouldn't want to pull them away from their inquiries, would we? You did leave a contact number, didn't you?"

"Yes, I left my mobile number and the number of my daughter's flat, where I'm staying at the moment."

"Well, I would wait until they contact you."

Bill had insisted that the officer make a note of his request to speak to someone in CID and had left, with no option but to trust that something would eventually get done. Now, sitting in Carol's living room, he was resigned to the fact that he was on his own.

CHAPTER 6   ALEKSANDER

Aleksander was right. Sex after doing a line was fucking phenomenal. He'd never pushed for her to try it, but it was always around, at the club, at any parties or functions they went to, and at his home. He didn't take it often himself, and it was probably seeing how easily he controlled his own consumption that persuaded her to try it.

At first, they'd only see each other twice during the week, but she always stayed over and he would see a little of her when she went to the club with her friends. Free entry and VIP treatment made it inevitable that this was the three young women's Saturday night venue of choice and, because the club was always busy, Aleksander only spent a short while with them, so it still felt like the usual girl's night out for them all.

The first time Carol went to the club with Aleksander alone, it was on one of their midweek nights at his home, four or five months after they'd met. He was called in because Anna had phoned in sick; a twenty-four hour vomiting and diarrhoea bug had floored her and she didn't want to risk passing it on to any of the other staff, or the punters.

Aleksander had apologised to Carol and told her he would drop her off at her flat on his way to the club unless she wanted to go to there with him and stay over at his place as normal.

Not wanting to miss out on a night with him, she sat at the bar and chatted with him when his managerial duties would allow it, but by about eleven she was tired and bored. After a drunk divorcee on a night out with a group of friends tried to pick her up, she asked Aleksander if she could use the VIP room to have a quiet seat to herself away from the clamour of the bar.

"Someone in VIP room. You don't want go there for quiet time." An upmarket stag do had booked the room and he knew that the expensive strippers he'd hired for them would be putting on an explicit show that Carol *definitely* wouldn't want to watch. "I do better than that," he said, taking her hand and leading her through the door behind the bar into the staff-only area at the rear of the club. She'd never been back there and was curious to know what exactly went on behind the scenes. The corridor he led her down was dimly lit to reduce complaints from staff that bright lights hurt their eyes after working in the subdued lighting of the bar area.

He showed her the large storeroom, with stocks of any drink you could think of, plus everything else, from packs of spare emergency clothes for clubbers who'd had a drink, or worse, spilled on them, to a box of overpriced red roses which was changed every few days on the rare occasion that they weren't purchased by a forgetful guest who'd forgotten their partner's birthday.

The kitchen was surprisingly small, but he explained that all the food they served was cooked off site by a friend's catering firm; they only needed facilities in the club for re-heating it and plating up, and for making the odd snack for the staff.

There was a general office, which housed the usual plethora of desks and a filing cabinet, and three large screens, each showing multiple CCTV views that, between them, covered most of the club, including the VIP room. Aleksander, aware that Carol was watching the screens with interest, switched off the feed that showed the stag party with a few clicks of a mouse, before the strippers warmed up and did their girl-on-girl act. Carol had seen enough to guess that that type of entertainment was available to order in the club, for those groups that could afford the hefty price tag of the private room.

In any case, she was more intrigued when Aleksander took out a set of keys and unlocked a door at the rear of the office and told Carol to have a look.

Puzzled, she entered what she'd thought was a cupboard only to find a set of narrow stairs that led upwards, with another door at the top. She followed him up and, once he'd unlocked it, they passed through the upper door into what was a compact but luxurious suite comprising a sitting and dining area and, through a second door, a king-sized bed that all but filled the small room it was in.

"I hope this is not for the customers," she half-joked, slightly concerned that she'd discovered that professional sexual services were also on the club's menu.

He laughed. "No. Strictly for me to use. When club first start, before house ready, I stay here all nights. Now just use odd occasion."

Part of her wanted to ask how many girls had made their way up the narrow stairs with him, but it annoyed her that the thought had even crossed her mind. *What does it matter? He's with me now.*

There was no kitchen – "Use the one downstairs if you need anything," he said – but there was a small fridge in the corner which contained some bottled beer, a few bottles of wine; one red, one white and a bottle of Prosecco. It also held bottled water, a selection of fruit juices and, in the freezer compartment, some bags of ice.

A small shower room with a toilet completed the accommodation. Carol was impressed. *I could live in here quite comfortably.*

"Help yourself if you want drink," he told her, then showed her where the TV controls were and left her to it.

She opened the bottle of white and poured a large glass. She idly flicked through the channels, finding nothing that attracted her. She pressed what she thought was the off button, but the screen flickered for a few seconds, then filled with a grid of black and white CCTV images, mirroring the screens on the system she'd seen in the office.

Curious, she navigated around the grid using the arrow keys on the remote and used the select button to choose the view from the camera situated in the VIP room.

The stag do was just getting into full swing; the strippers had just started their performance, which she could see was going to be somewhat interactive.

She watched the two girls approach the prospective bridegroom, sitting on a chair in the centre of a circle of his friends. One of the girls danced round behind him and, grabbing his hair, pulled his head back into her cleavage and wiggled her chest from side to side, slapping the sides of his face with her large silicone-enhanced breasts.

The other girl stood in front of him and straddled his legs, her torso almost touching his chest. As the circle of his friends moved in to watch, she lost sight of the three protagonists in the melee of excited men. Any concerns for the girls were soon alleviated when one of them emerged from the crowd triumphantly waving the stag's trousers around her head, followed by the other, who repeated the performance with his boxers.

As the group followed the girls to the bar, obviously cheering and clapping, she eventually caught sight of the naked victim, tied to the chair by his shirt, with one of the girl's thongs over his head, the small triangle covering his nose and mouth like a mini gimp mask.

His friends left him there for a while to suffer. He could only watch as the girls continued their show on top of the bar. She cringed when she saw the level of audience participation the girls encouraged, but it stopped just short of actual sexual intercourse.

She noticed that the bar staff were all male and that one of the evil-looking bouncers was present, standing near the door, presumably as a precaution against any of the guests going too far.

Not impressed, but not quite naïve enough to expect that this sort of thing didn't go on in clubs all over the city, she decided she would say nothing to Aleksander. But she'd seen enough and flicked the channel back over to Sky, to try and find a film worth watching.

About midnight, she suddenly felt hungry. She realised that not having a kitchen was the one flaw with the little flat. Still clutching her wine glass, she descended the steep stairway and found the club's kitchen, cursing the dim lighting. She was relieved when she switched on the bright lights of the kitchen; the shadows of the corridor had creeped her out a little. *Idiot. You're quite safe here.*

She made herself a slice of toast and found some smoked salmon and cheese that she didn't think he would mind her using. A little bit of salad and a few tomatoes completed her snack and she picked up the plate, turning out the light as she left. As she wandered back to the office, she felt the hairs at the back of her neck prickling. *There's someone in the corridor*. She whirled round and dropped her wine glass, letting out a scream.

In the poor light he looked like her worst nightmare but, with relief, she realised that it was Dhimiter, the biggest and, if she was honest, the most nasty looking of Aleksander's security staff.

He still hadn't moved, or said anything, his face expressionless.

"Shit, you gave me a hell of a fright. I was just down getting a bite to eat." She bent to pick up the shards of glass, but realised she'd need a brush and shovel. The bear of a man still hadn't moved, which unnerved her, but she got up and went back to the kitchen, relieved to switch on the light again.

Putting her plate on the counter, glad she hadn't dropped that, too, she rummaged about in the cupboard under the sink until she found a small dustpan and brush, and lifted a cloth from the worktop. By the time she went back out into the corridor, he'd gone. *Creepy bastard.*

She quickly gathered up the remains of her glass and wiped the floor with the cloth. She deposited the smashed glass in the bin and hurried back upstairs, plate in hand.

There was a lock on the door at the top of the stairs, so she turned it, instantly feeling safer. She was annoyed with herself for having been spooked so easily. In the cosy surroundings of the flat, it didn't seem quite as scary as it had been at the time and she laughed at herself. *You're not a little girl anymore.*

Probably because of the fright she'd had, she drank a little faster than she would have normally and before she knew it, the bottle had gone. *I spilt a large glass. It wasn't a full bottle.* But she did feel the effects of the alcohol and the long evening catching up on her.

She awoke with a start, lying on the couch. Aleksander was bending over her, smiling.

"The sleeping beauty! Handsome prince wakes with kiss." He laughed.

She smiled at him and made to get up, but she nearly fell over and started to giggle.

Aleksander looked at the empty bottle of wine on the bedside table and the empty glass, and smiled.

"How did you get in?" she asked him. "I locked the door."

"I have spare key." He dangled it from his fingers for her to see

He went through to the fridge and fished out a bottle of Prosecco, grabbing another wine glass as he did. He poured them each a glass and downed his in one, refilling it immediately.

"I need catch up. Only one drink all night."

He kissed her gently, smoothing her hair with his hand. She was still tired, but felt herself respond. *Christ, will I ever get bored with him?*

"You fancy try coke? Make extra special."

Part of her said no, but she was tired and a bit drunk. Besides, she'd seen him do the odd line from time to time and it hadn't done him any harm.

And he was right. Besides the astonishing kick she got within a second or two of her first sniff, their lovemaking

90

was incredible – every sensation was heightened and they seemed to pleasure each other in a way she'd never have believed possible.

It must have been good for him, too, because, even afterwards, he couldn't leave her alone. It must have been after four in the morning when they finally lay together, spent and exhausted, on the thick rug on the floor. He grabbed the throw from the back of the couch and covered them in it, his arm on her belly and hers on his chest.

She felt surprisingly good in the morning; rising from bed, where they'd moved to sometime during the night, only a mild residual headache from the wine reminded her of the evening before, but sleeping until almost lunchtime had helped her avoid the tiredness she'd maybe deserved. *No worse than smoking a joint. Just keep it for special occasions, though.*

Downstairs, she found Aleksander at his desk in the office, a pile of business papers on one side and a copy of *The Sun* on the other. Not sure if he was relaxing or working, she walked round behind him and circled his neck with her arms. He was reading *The Times*, but he assured her that he'd done a couple of hours of paperwork before Josef had handed the papers in and he'd taken a break to catch up on the news. He poured her a cup of coffee from the jug stewing on the machine and filled his own cup, too. Seeing his newspaper made her feel guilty.

"I'll need to phone in sick," she told him. "I was supposed to start at nine."

Using Anna's vomiting and diarrhoea bug as an excuse, she phoned in and told her editor that she wouldn't make it in to work that morning, but hoped to return the following day. For a while she watched Aleksander work, enjoying just hanging out with him, a change from their usual rush to get her to the office before he headed to the club, often via the cash-and-carry or a meeting over coffee with some business associate.

He dropped her off at her flat before the club opened. She thought he might have stayed over with her if Anna hadn't had to take a second night off. The disappointment was tempered by the thought that her body might have struggled with two nights in a row like the one they'd just had.

CHAPTER 7   MORGAN FAIRLEY

When Bill returned to work after Christmas the associate director called him in to his office. He guided him to the chair in front of the desk, taking his own seat behind it.

"I hear your daughter's missing."

The evening before, Bill had phoned Jack Armstrong, a fellow engineer at Morgan Fairley & Partners, and told him the story. He figured that it would save him having to painfully repeat the details to a large number of people at the office and it seemed to have had the desired effect. One or two of his colleagues attempted a word of support or comfort, but most left him alone and nobody pried, already knowing as much as Bill wanted them to.

And obviously his boss had been told.

"Yes, she didn't turn up on Christmas Eve."

Bill repeated the account of Carol's disappearance that he'd told Jack Armstrong. He considered Christie McAlpine to be a good boss; he'd always let Bill get on with his work with little interference, knowing he could trust him to get the job done, but he was always available if any issues needed clarifying. He was also a good listener.

Christie let Bill finish, then asked him if there was anything the firm could do to help.

"Well, I was going to ask for some time off to search for Carol, but I know the M74 contract is putting us under pressure."

Morgan Fairley were subcontractors for the new motorway link running across the south side of Glasgow.

"First of all, we all have children, and none of us would want to be in your situation, so you must do what you need to do, but I'm going to say something as a friend, not as your employer. Would you not be better leaving it to the police?"

"They're just not interested. I suppose down there people go missing all the time and for perfectly understandable reasons, but I know Carol's in trouble."

"How do you know that?"

"I found out some things when I was down that I'd rather not talk about, if you don't mind."

"No, that's all right, Bill. If you need to be in London, that's what you must do."

"I'm sorry, but I just can't leave it to the police. I've got to find her, and soon. I had a few days booked off either side of New year. I was going to take her away for a break." Bill made a mental note to cancel the holiday, then scolded himself for even thinking like that.

"I've got a suggestion and it's as much for your own self as it is for the company. How about working flexitime? That would give you more of an opportunity to look for Carol."

"What do you mean?"

"Well, if you could work some extra hours Tuesday to Thursday you could be down there four days a week. I could clear it with security for you to work late or early, or both. And we could bring in one of the graduates from the Velodrome contract to take some of the load off you."

Bill considered his boss's offer. In his heart he wanted to be down in London walking the streets every day of the week looking for Carol, but he was intelligent enough to know that he had to keep a bit of normality in place, for his own sanity, so he agreed to try it.

"I can easily do all my hours in three days," he said, "and with a graduate to help, it shouldn't impact too much on the work. I'll be available on the mobile if he needs anything when I'm away."

Bill thanked Christie and left to work out what parts of his brief he could hand over to the young engineer who would be assigned to him.

As it turned out, the arrangement only lasted for seven weeks. Bill would pack a bag and take it to work on Thursday, leaving the office at four-thirty; he was usually at Carol's flat by midnight, or just after. Starting at seven each morning, working through until eight-thirty at night, and cutting his lunchtimes to half an hour, he was still cramming in around thirty-five hours at the office and Adam, the young engineer Christie McAlpine had sent him, turned out to be more than capable of anything that Bill threw at him.

Bill's weekends were spent pounding the London streets, looking in bars and clubs for any sighting of Carol. He had a pile of flyers printed, which he handed out on street corners and posted on billboards.

He contacted all her workmates and most of her friends, but they couldn't add much to what Heather had told him and she'd supplied little extra information when he'd met with her again.

He had the painful task of changing all Carol's household bills over to his own name, or risk sanctions. It felt like a betrayal; an admission that she was gone for good.

Every time he was in London, he jumped on the Overground and visited the police station in West Hampstead. It did no good, but it gave him a perverse feeling of satisfaction to make a nuisance of himself. He knew that they must hear a story like his many times in a day but, to his mind, there was no excuse for appearing to do nothing at all. He didn't take his car down. Driving and parking in the city was horrendous, and the resident's parking permit had expired; to continue using the car in London, he would have had to renew it for a whole year.

In his search for information on Carol's disappearance, he even spent an evening at Bloq. He'd brought his newest suit down from Glasgow with him and he purchased a fresh shirt; a trendier one than he was used to, like those he'd seen the majority of men wear when heading to the restaurants and bars of the city while he stood on street corners, handing out leaflets with Carol's picture staring out from them.

He still felt grossly out of place, but no one would have noticed a reasonably dressed single middle-aged man in the club if he hadn't gone around from person to person showing them Carol's picture and asking if they'd ever seen her in Bloq. Even then, he might have gone unnoticed if he'd limited his inquiries to the clientele.

It was one of the staff who told Anna that there was a strange man upsetting the customers and asking awkward questions. He'd been asked by Bill if Mr Gjebrea was going to be in the club that night and if he'd ever seen Carol with him. The barman had immediately found the manageress to let her know.

Anna knew that Aleksander was due in any time and she didn't want him to have to deal with Bill, so she contacted Dhimiter, Aleksander's "chief of security", on the two-way radio to have him ejected. Bill was duly approached by Dhim, as he was known by everyone at the club, and the other large black-suited doorman, Josef, who professionally and with as little fuss as possible manhandled him out of the door. Bill protested vigorously that he'd paid his admission fee and should be allowed to stay until the end. The men just laughed at him and told him that if he appeared again at the club, they'd call the police.

Bill was tempted to do just that, but realised that it would do more harm than good and so made his way wearily back to the flat.

When he had no success publicising Carol's disappearance, Bill started calling at drug rehabilitation centres, hostels for the homeless and finally women's refuges. He covered miles, checking each bundle of clothes and cardboard that housed London's street dwellers, wondering if she was one of them, and why she would choose to live anywhere other than her own flat, if she was still alive.

He sometimes felt he was doing nothing more than wearing out his shoes, but he couldn't bring himself to stop looking. To do that would have been to admit defeat and he refused to give up on her.

Mid-February, sitting in Carol's flat on a Monday night and preparing to leave for Euston to catch the train back home, he suddenly realised it was Valentine's Day. He had a thing that he'd done every year since Carol was about eight. It had started when she came home from school crying because she was the only girl who didn't get a card.

The next year, Bill had purchased a valentine card for her and posted it to the house.

He'd done it every year since and it had become a standing joke every February the 14th.

Just before he caught his train back to Glasgow, he bought a card at WHSmith in the station, along with a book of stamps, and posted it to her flat with his usual message. *To a very special girl.*

-o-

The next day, he was called in to see Christie McAlpine.

Sitting once more in front of Christie, Bill could see that the older man was troubled.

"What's wrong, Christie? It's not some news about Carol, is it? Have they—"

Christie interrupted him. "No, no, nothing like that. I'm sorry I gave you a fright." He hesitated again. "Bill, I don't know quite how to say this, but—"

This time it was Bill's turn to cut in. "If it's about last Tuesday, I phoned in and told them I wouldn't be in until mid-afternoon. The West Coast main line was shut due to a derailment. I had to go via Newcastle and Edinburgh, and it was a nightmare getting on a train at all. I made up some of the time last week and I'll catch up with the rest this week."

"No, it's nothing like that. If anything, you seem to be cramming more in than you did before and you're ahead of where I expected you to be at this point, which is a testament to your determination, I must say, but ..." The partner looked down at the table and then brought his eyes up to look straight at Bill. "I think you should take a leave of absence."

Bill opened his mouth to speak but Christie put his hand up.

"Hear me out. The sad thing is, your work is fine but I've had a number of the other staff come to me and say that they're finding it increasingly difficult to work with you. I know it's wrong, but I can't afford to lose half of my team at this point. And Steven Kincaid has finished on the Stena Loch Ryan project, so he can take over from you as soon as."

Bill was stunned. "Who's complained? I've not said anything that would have upset anyone."

"I'm not going to say who it is, but it is quite a significant proportion of the staff. If you must know, it's partly because you don't talk any more, other than the bare work-related essentials, and also that you're frequently morose and irritable. And they all say that the biggest thing that bothers them is the atmosphere in the office. They feel that they can't laugh and joke any more, that there's no banter, because it would be inappropriate, given your situation and your mood."

"At no point have I ever said anything to them about Carol, and I've never stopped them having a bit of a laugh."

"Bill, put yourself in their shoes. Would you laugh and joke in the presence of a man who was desperately searching for his missing daughter? To be honest, if you did occasionally talk about Carol it might be better; if they knew what was going on, they could deal with it, but they say you keep it all to yourself; you never say a word about how you're getting on."

Bill said nothing, so Christie continued.

"We've always had a relaxed atmosphere in this firm; some might say too casual at times, but we think it works for us. I'm not going to jeopardise that, even though I have the utmost sympathy for your predicament."

"And what if I don't want to go? I mean, you are talking unpaid leave, aren't you?"

"Well, yes. But you can come back when it's over. We'll keep the position open for you."

"You mean when I give up searching, or they find Carol's body, is that it?'

"No, it's not," he said sharply, but his eyes told Bill differently. For a few moments, Christie said nothing, then he seemed to come to some sort of decision. He opened a folder sitting on his desk and extracted a sheet of paper from it. "If you don't want to come back, I've been authorised to offer you a package. It's generous and it will allow you all the time you want to try and find Carol." He pushed the sheet of paper across the desk to Bill. "Have a look at that and see what you think."

Bill picked it up and stared at it. "I'll need to look at this in detail and I'd want to sleep on it. I'll let you know tomorrow." He looked straight at his boss, disappointment etched on his face. "You do realise that I could have just taken sick leave to get the time off I needed and Morgan Fairley would have had to live with it, but I'm not that kind of person. I always cared enough about my job and the firm to do my best for you." With that, he got up and walked out of the room.

The older man sighed and shook his head; hard as it had been, he told himself that he'd had no option.

Bill walked out into the main office, looking at his fellow workers, wondering which ones had stabbed him in the back. Most of them had their heads down, intent on their work, or keen to avoid Bill's gaze.

He ploughed through his work for the rest of the day and left late, as normal, but the next morning he knocked on Christie's door as soon as the older man was in.

"I'll take early retirement, but I need better terms."

Christie didn't bat an eyelid at Bill's belligerent response.

"OK, Bill. What exactly are you looking for? I thought our offer was generous enough."

Bill detailed what it would take for him to leave. Christie knew that an industrial tribunal would have a field day with the way he was being forced to deal with Bill and, in the grand scheme of things, Bill's severance package was largely irrelevant to the finances of the firm – especially weighed against the importance of having the rest of the staff happy and efficient. Of course they would miss Bill's expertise and attention to detail, but he wasn't irreplaceable.

He agreed to Bill's terms. In a way, it had made it easier for him that Bill had taken a hard-nosed stance against the firm, but he shook Bill's hand with genuine respect.

"I think it's better if this comes into effect immediately," he told Bill, who nodded in agreement.

Bill left to organise handing over his work to his junior engineer, who would handle it until the company had appointed Bill's replacement. The young man surprised Bill by thanking him for everything he'd learned in the short time he'd worked with him. A few of his fellow workers came over and sheepishly said their goodbyes, but Bill knew that most of them were relieved to see the back of him, and he was sad that his long association with the company had ended like this.

In a way, he was as relieved as they were. He had been struggling to cope with full-time work and the search for his daughter, and he was happier that he could now concentrate fully on looking for her, with no worries about keeping his employers happy, and with the freedom from financial constraints that packing in his job would have entailed.

CHAPTER 8   ANNA

For the first time, Bill sat in the flat and didn't have a single idea about what he was going to do next. In the three months since Carol had gone missing, he'd exhausted every single avenue that he could think of, but he couldn't go home. It would have felt like he was giving up on her and, while there was a possibility she was still alive, he would keep trying. Despite his determination, in his increasingly frequent darker moments he began to admit to himself that she might be dead. A phone call from the detective inspector at CID hadn't helped. The police had eventually visited the club and asked Aleksander Gjebrea and his staff about Carol. Nobody at the club, including Aleksander, had denied that Carol had been in a relationship with the nightclub owner, or that she spent a fair bit of time at the club, but everyone interviewed said that they hadn't seen her since the couple had split up. The DI had continued.

"Mr Ingram, everyone we've spoken to has told us that Carol had a heavy and spiralling drug problem. We've talked to her employers, her work colleagues and her friends. I know it's hard for you, but your daughter is a drug addict and it's very common for them to fall off the grid. We know you've spoken to all these people as well. Surely you must have realised."

"Yes, I have. But that shouldn't stop you looking for her. She's still my daughter and she's still missing."

"We will keep looking for her in the respect that if she shows up on our radar, we'll contact you immediately and let you know. It's just that we don't have the resources to look for everyone that doesn't want to be found. I'm sorry, but that's the reality of the situation."

"So unless she turns up in a hospital, a morgue or a police cell, I'm on my own?"

"It's not quite as stark as that."

"Oh, I think it is. And what about Mr Gjebrea's behaviour? I'm convinced he's to blame for my daughter's addiction. Is he immune to the law of this country? That's the way it looks to me."

"We have no substantiated complaints against Aleksander Gjebrea or his club, but we will be keeping a close eye on them."

Bill doubted that would last long, but he'd said nothing and ended the call.

He put the remains of last night's curry into the microwave and pressed the start button twice, to give it a minute. He watched the plate turning for a few seconds, then turned on the TV to catch the news, which barely interested him, but was better than sitting in silence.

Bill had never been a big drinker, not since college days, but when the news finished, he had a sudden urge to get drunk. He knew there was nothing in the flat; he'd found nothing but empty bottles when he'd cleaned the flat on the first day he'd arrived to look for Carol.

He'd got into the habit of getting by on takeaway curries and microwaveable meals-for-one, and by eating at the pub twice a week. Even though he never spoke to anyone other than to order his food and a pint from the bar staff, it made him feel human again just to listen to the sound of other people around him, laughing and joking with each other, chatting about their daily lives and about football, TV and how bad the government was.

So when the newsreader handed over to the weathergirl, Bill put on his coat and left the flat for the ten minute walk to the Elephant's Head in Camden High Street. Since Carol's disappearance Bill had lived in a bubble and, as he walked down along Chalk Farm Road, under the railway bridge, he was unaware that someone was following him. Deep in thought, he crossed the Grand Union Canal; if he'd looked, he would have seen his shadow do the same thirty seconds later.

He reached the pub and, it being a Monday night, had his choice of seat. He sat at a corner table towards the back, which allowed him a view of the TV screen and the chance to observe the other punters, few as they were. An old couple sat two tables away; him sipping at his pint, his wife nursing a sweet sherry and regaling him with a mundane list of all the gossip she'd heard during the day. Her husband nodded at the appropriate moments and Bill reflected on just how much he missed Alison at these times.

A group of older men sat at two tables that had been pushed together and turned out a box of dominoes, with a loud clattering on the polished surface. One younger man sat with them and, when one of the group took out a pencil and pad of paper and started to sort out his companions into pairs, Bill realised that this was the dominoes team and there must be a match on.

Sure enough, within ten minutes, the opposition arrived en masse and the pub began to get noisy with their cutthroat mockery of each team's inadequacies. Bill had been in once before on darts night and, while he could understand the players getting carried away with the skill and excitement of a game of arrows, he was left bemused at how a group of men could take what he thought of as a child's pastime so seriously.

But it passed the time and Bill watched the wins mount up for both teams until the young man faced the opposing team's star player in the deciding end. By this time, Bill had made the short journey to the bar four times for a pint. He was beginning to mellow a little and almost enjoy himself. He even had a short conversation with one of the dominoes team, who explained that this was a top-of-the-league clash and was effectively the title decider at this late stage of the season.

Just as Bill was getting engrossed in the conclusion of the match, he realised, to his annoyance, that his bladder was full and it urgently needed to be emptied. He made his way past the throng clustered around the two players, the sound of one of them "chapping" ringing in his ears, and found the gents. Glad of the relief, he washed his hands and, exiting the toilets, decided to have one last pint before leaving; he wanted to see who was going to win the dominoes before heading back to the empty flat. Approaching the bar, he noticed a woman sitting by herself and, after he'd ordered his pint, she surprised him by speaking to him.

"Hello, Bill."

He was shocked when she used his name, but something about her seemed familiar.

"Do I know you?" he said.

"I'm Anna, the manageress at Bloq, the nightclub."

Bill remembered her immediately, her voice more recognisable than her face. She looked different, but he'd only noticed her fleetingly on his one night at the club and had seen even less of her on his first visit to Bloq, during the day.

"Can we talk somewhere?" She spoke quietly, looking around as she did.

"I've got a flat; it's about ten minutes away."

"No, definitely not."

Bill's first thought was that she'd taken his offer as a sleazy attempt to pick her up, but she continued.

"It would be dangerous for me to be seen at your daughter's flat. You've been getting up some ruthless people's noses."

Bill was shaken. *How does she know it's Carol's flat?*

He pointed over to where he'd been sitting. "What about here?"

She nodded and followed him back to his seat. He held the chair for her and she sat down.

"Do you know something about Carol? Is that why you're here?"

"No, I'm sorry if I got your hopes up; I've got nothing specific I can tell you about Carol, but I might be able to help."

"Anything you tell me will go no further. I'll keep your name out of it completely."

"It's not as simple as that …" She paused, taking a large breath. "I'm going to trust you here, Bill. If Aleksander

Gjebrea or any of his associates ever finds out, my life will be in danger."

Bill thought she was being a little overdramatic, but he was prepared to give her the benefit of the doubt.

"OK. I'll not do or say anything that would jeopardise you in any way, I promise you that."

She opened the small shoulder bag she'd placed on the table and handed Bill a photograph.

"Who's this?" Bill asked. "She's very pretty."

"That's my sister, Susie. Well, to be honest she's my half-sister, but we never think of each other as anything but sisters. She's been missing for over eighteen months and I've no proof, but I think that she was involved with Aleksander Gjebrea before she disappeared."

"But you work there; how ... why ...?" Bill stammered, unable to grasp what Anna was saying.

"I only started working there to try and find out what happened to my sister. I met Carol a few times and she seemed nice. I think he did the same thing to your daughter as he did to my sister."

She said this in a flat monotone, but Bill could sense that was the only way of dealing with it without falling apart. He looked around the pub to see if anyone was looking at them, but the old couple had left and the domino match was about to come to an exciting finish. The din surrounding the two combatants was reaching a crescendo, which was good; there was no chance of anyone overhearing Bill and Anna's conversation.

Just as Bill was about to speak, the match ended and the room erupted as if the home team had won the FA cup or the Ashes.

As the players from both teams moved towards the bar, amidst much clapping of backs and rueful expressions, the noise subsided enough for Bill to make himself heard.

"Do you know what happened to them?" Bill tried to keep desperation out of his voice.

"No, not for sure. But I have my suspicions that the bastard seduces pretty middle-class girls, has some sort of relationship with them, introduces them to drugs, then, when they are in too far to get out, he discards them to a life of drug addiction, and probably prostitution."

Bill gasped for air, but it was as if he couldn't breathe. He wondered if he was having a heart attack, but there was no pain.

Anna reached out to him. "Are you OK?" she asked, her face a mask of concern.

Bill nodded, recovering slightly. "How do you know?" he managed to blurt out.

"I just pieced together all the little bits of information I could find out about Susie, then watched him with your daughter Carol and filled in the blanks."

Bill was incensed at Anna's thoughtlessness and said so. "You *watched* this man with my daughter, knowing what he did to your sister!"

Anna looked around, terrified that Bill's raised voice would attract unwanted attention. Shocked by Bill's anger, she wasn't able to keep the emotion out of her voice. "I tried to warn Carol and her friends, but they wouldn't listen. I did try, please believe me, Bill."

Bill, horrified at his ability to reduce women to tears when they were only trying to help him, tried to limit the damage his outburst had caused. "I'm sorry. I shouldn't have lashed out at you, but it's devastating to hear your worst fears confirmed."

They sat in silence for a few moments. The crowd at the bar was thinning out and they had a large part of the pub to themselves.

"Tell me about Susie," he said.

CHAPTER 9   SUSIE

"Susie was five years younger than me and was, in a lot of ways, my complete opposite. She was outgoing, confident; a bit of a party girl. She dropped in and out of jobs, never staying too long in the one place. Travelled a hell of a lot. She spent a year and a half in Australia, backpacking, and I went out for two weeks to spend some time with her while she was there. I was surprised but pleased when she came back, because she loved it. Now I wish she hadn't."

"You were quite close, then?"

"Yes, despite the age gap, we were very close. Oh, we each did our own thing, but since my mum died, we've always looked out for each other."

"What about your dad?"

"Mum never told us who mine was and Susie's dad fucked off when we were small; Susie was only a baby. We've never had any contact with him. Susie and I would talk two or three times a week on the phone and, depending on where she was, we would meet up regularly. There were lots of spells when she would crash at my flat for weeks at a time between jobs or boyfriends and she was forever borrowing money from me when she was short." She smiled. "She always paid it back. Susie was a bit of a free spirit, whereas I went into nursing straight from school, earning cash in the evenings and at weekends in bars and restaurants to pay my way through university. I worked my way up to ward sister while she was enjoying herself partying halfway around the world."

Even when Anna paused, visibly upset, Bill didn't interrupt.

"I didn't mind. I was happy that she always knew she had somewhere to go if she needed it and I knew she would settle down some day. Fuck, there were times when I wondered which one of us had it right; she seemed to get more out of life than me."

Bill looked at his watch but there was still at least an hour until closing time.

"I hope I'm not boring you," Anna said, bristling.

"No, not at all." Bill hurriedly pulled his sleeve down. "I was just checking how much time we had before last orders. Are you sure you'd not rather come to the flat?"

"No, it's too risky. I don't think he has any doubts about me, but he might be watching you. I checked you weren't followed here earlier."

"Except by you, it seems." Bill smiled.

"I had to be sure you weren't being watched and I needed somewhere I could approach you without attracting attention."

"I think that would be difficult; a young woman like you talking to an old guy like me in a bar."

"They'd think I was your daughter. I'll throw a 'dad' or two in for effect." She saw a shadow cross Bill's face. "I'm sorry, that was stupid."

Bill shrugged. "No, you're all right. But what I wouldn't give to be sitting here with Carol ..." He took a sip of his pint. "Go on. Tell me more about your sister."

"Well, just over eighteen months ago she told me she'd met someone but she was, for her, pretty quiet about it. I didn't think anything of it; she wasn't the type who always insisted on introducing the latest love of her life to you, but she didn't usually hide them either.

"Nothing much changed for quite a while and she seemed very happy. We met up on a weekly basis, sometimes more often, and she had a steady job for as long as I ever remember her having one, in an advertising agency. She mentioned that the guy she was seeing owned a nightclub and I briefly saw him once when he dropped her off at my flat one evening, but apart from his fancy car, I couldn't have told you much about him.

"About two years ago, she started acting a little strange; subdued and withdrawn, she missed meeting up with me the odd week and, on a couple of occasions, she snapped at me when I commented on her moods. I knew she'd moved in with this man, but I still hadn't met him and I didn't even know his name at that point. Every time I asked she would clam up and I so regret now that I didn't find out more about him and about their relationship."

She was trying hard to stifle a sob and Bill could see that it was painful for her to talk about Susie.

"I feel the same. Carol was different the last few times she was home and I never tackled her about it. I keep going over every minute we had and telling myself there were so many times when I could have spoken to her, but I didn't. If anything's happened to her I'll never forgive myself for not intervening."

"You're right. It'll be with us for the rest of our lives." Anna paused and then continued with Susie's story.

"We'd only met up once in the last couple of months before she went missing, but we still phoned each other two or three times a week. I just thought it was her settling down with this guy and moving on, becoming independent from me. I did feel a bit hurt about it and it bothered me that she didn't seem to want me to meet him and be part of their life, but I was in a new relationship at that point and particularly busy with my nursing. I was also doing a part-time master's degree, so I let it slide until, all of a sudden, I never heard from her at all for four or five days. I phoned the police, but missing adults seem to be a low priority unless there's suspicion of foul play.

"I kept phoning and phoning her mobile, but it was always unobtainable. I couldn't remember what her boyfriend's club was called, but she'd told me it was near the Elephant and Castle and the only thing I remembered about its name was that it was short, so I looked up all the nightclubs within a mile and there were only two. When I saw the name 'Bloq', I was nearly sure that was the one, but I checked them both out on Google. The other nightclub that could have been an option was owned by a woman."

She glanced at Bill, who was looking at her with a puzzled expression on his face.

"I know what you're thinking." she said. "How did I get into the position where I didn't even know who she was with or where they lived? I've asked myself that question so many times and it's never an easy answer."

"I wasn't judging you. I'm just as culpable; I didn't even know Carol was with this man. I only found out from her friend Heather."

She smiled at him gratefully, even if his attempts to make her feel better were clumsy at best. She carried on.

"I phoned the club but no one would admit to ever having known Susie, and I spoke with the manageress and Aleksander Gjebrea himself. I was still sure that I'd got the right place, so I thought I'd take a bit of a look. I went to the club one night when it was busy and asked around the punters and some of the bar staff. They described Aleksander with a girl that sounded like Susie. I took a risk and showed a couple of clubbers her photo and they confirmed that that was her. I couldn't see any advantage in confronting him and when I spoke to the manageress, she told me that she was leaving and that they were going to be looking to recruit someone to replace her. I'd done a fair bit of bar work over the years, so I made up a CV and dropped it in. I was given an interview within a few days. I packed in my nursing job right away. They must have been desperate to get someone, because they offered me the job there and then."

"But were you not afraid of being recognised, or linked with Susie?"

"Anna's not my real name; it's Jill. I'm using a false surname, too. I get paid cash by the nightclub; I insisted on that when I started. Aleksander thinks I'm on the run from an abusive partner."

"You've taken quite a risk there. What if he finds out?"

"I'd still be OK; Susie had her dad's surname, Bryant; I had my mum's. Also, I'm not really from the North East, although we did live there for a couple of years, so I knew I could do the accent. She surprised Bill by lapsing into a middle England dialect.

"My real accent is pretty nondescript. We moved about so much, it's a bit of a mish-mash, really."

She switched back to her Tyneside brogue.

"I need to stick with speaking like this; it makes it less likely that I'll slip up at the club and give them a reason to be suspicious. And I've got to stay there a bit longer. I haven't got enough to go to the police with yet, although I did manage to find out that Susie was on hard drugs and working as a prostitute; she'd been moved on to a brothel that I think Gjebrea's cousin runs for him, but I'm sure the bastard himself is the money behind it. Unfortunately, I don't have any proof of their involvement or know where it is, but I'm still looking. There's no sign of Susie anywhere; she might not even be in London. They could have moved her on to another part of the country. I think they run more than one place in London and there could be others elsewhere. The other possibility is that she's been killed and disposed of, like some piece of meat." She choked out the last bit, sobbing again.

"Even if I go to the police with what I've already got," she continued, pulling herself together once more, "the most he'd get done for is keeping a brothel used for prostitution. He uses his thugs at the club to supply the drugs, mostly coke, so if it did get raided, one of them would take the blame; he would come out with some crap that they were dealing without his knowledge and they would get well rewarded when they'd done their time."

"There must be something we can do. I'll not stand back and let him get away with it."

"He thinks he's above the law. There's obviously a flood of cash generated by all his businesses, but on the surface, Bloq is the cleanest of the lot. Apart from my wages, everything else goes through the books."

"Why do you think he agreed to employ you on a cash basis?"

"I don't know. He's cash heavy and I think he was struggling to get someone else quickly. Sometimes he just likes the look of people. I've seen him do that a couple of times. He's arrogant enough to believe that his instinct is infallible."

"What would you have done if he hadn't taken you on?"

"I don't know. Perhaps I would have risked using my real name."

"So what made you approach me?"

"I've been watching you, since you first turned up at the club. To be honest, I sent you to see Aleksander Gjebrea on purpose, to see if you'd shake him up a bit. I'm sorry about that, it was wrong of me to use you."

Bill gave a shrug. "I'd have gone anyway. Not that it did any good. He didn't even seem to care when I threatened to get the police involved. He thinks he's invincible."

"I had you thrown out of the club on the night you were there asking questions. You weren't as subtle as me and I didn't want you to get caught at it when Aleksander came back. He's a very dangerous man and I didn't want you getting hurt."

"He wouldn't have dared. The police would have been down on him like a ton of bricks."

"He's not frightened of them. The police came and questioned everyone at the club about Carol. I wasn't in that day. As far as I know, they believed Aleksander when he said they'd split up and he hadn't seen her since. The rest of the staff backed him up. He didn't even need to ask them to lie for him, apart from the three thugs he used as security, perhaps."

117

"I knew the police were there. CID phoned me. From what they say, I'm pretty sure they'll not do much more. As soon as they found out that Carol was a drug addict, they more or less washed their hands of her, so I'm on my own."

"It was the same with Susie. Once they knew she was heavily involved in drugs, it was like turning a switch off." Anna took a deep breath. "Will you work with me?"

Bill looked at her. For some reason he liked this young woman and, despite having only just met her, he felt that he could trust her.

"What can I do that you haven't already done?"

"Are you in?"

Bill only paused for a moment. "Yes, I'm in. What do you want me to do? I've been struggling to know where to turn next. It's been like hitting my head off a brick wall."

"If Susie's still alive, she's in a brothel somewhere and, I'm sorry, but so is Carol. I think you should start going round these places to try and find either of them. I can't do it, obviously, but you could."

"You want me to start going to prostitutes?" Bill said, taken aback at her suggestion.

Her voice hardened. "You want to find Carol, don't you? I'm not asking you to have sex with any of the girls, but it's a way for you to get in, if you turn up as a punter."

"All right, I can see now why you needed me. How do I find these places? They're not exactly in the Yellow Pages, are they?"

"I've asked around and looked on the Internet. Plus, you'll see adverts everywhere for personal services; even in the Evening Standard. Most are just single girls working on their own, but they're of no interest to us. The rest are organised; I've made a list to start you off. I'll get it to you."

"How do we communicate? Where can we meet up?"

"This place is as good as any, but let's make it a different weeknight each time we meet; we'll be less likely to get noticed. Have you got a computer?"

"Yes, I've got a laptop."

"Open up a *Gmail* account with a random girl's name and send an email to this address." She handed him a slip of paper, which he pocketed. Make sure you put a good password on your account. I'll email back with a date to meet up again, with the list attached. Once you get it, start visiting some of the places. Ask for girls who're a match for Susie or Carol, if you can. When you get with a girl, just say you want to talk while they strip or something; you don't have to touch them. Offer them some extra cash if they'll look at the photographs."

"I can't say I'll find it easy, but I'll do it." He thought for a moment. "What should I call you? Jill or Anna?"

"Stick with Anna. It's easier for both of us and it's safer; just in case we're ever in earshot of someone from the club."

Anna looked at Bill for a moment. She felt a twinge of guilt involving him in her pursuit of justice for Susie; naïve, trusting and seemingly fearless, he was entirely motivated by his own daughter's involvement and, like her, had a focussed intensity that she'd observed while watching him investigate Carol's disappearance.

"Bill, before we do anything, I feel it's only fair to warn you how dangerous these people are."

"I know what they're like. I've seen them."

She shook her head. "You don't know the half of what they're capable of. They beat up an old tramp last year for simply raking through the recycling bin for bottles with dregs of alcohol left in them. I saw it all on CCTV and grabbed one of the waste baskets to empty as an excuse to go out. They stopped when they saw me, but didn't make any attempt to hide what they'd done. Aleksander saw it all and didn't try to prevent it. They just left him lying there. By the time I went home that night, he'd gone.

"The second time, they might even have killed someone; I don't know. It was a young black lad; no more than twenty, I'd say. They caught him selling drugs in the club at New Year. Dhim and Josef, the two nastiest bouncers, marched him through to the back. I was in the office when they brought him in. Aleksander had a few words with him; very controlled and reasonable, but the stupid arsehole was mouthing off, trying to act tough. Aleksander didn't touch him. He just turned to Dhim and told him to get him out of his sight and make sure he didn't come back.

"The last time I saw him, he was being bundled into the van and driven away. Aleksander turned to me and said that we wouldn't be bothered by him anymore. It was the cold way he said it that made me think the worst. I looked in the papers for a few weeks afterwards, but there were no reports of a body being found that would have matched him, but ..." She shrugged her shoulders. "Both times

Aleksander didn't lift a finger, but he definitely gave the orders."

Bill listened, but she could see that her words weren't going to scare him off. *Now he can't say I didn't warn him.*

"I'm still in," was all he said.

CHAPTER 10   CHARLIE

It took less than two months for Carol to be hooked on coke. At first she used it just for sex, and even then not every time. But it was always available and when she was offered it in the nightclub after a few drinks one night, she went with the crowd and did a line. From then on, there were few nights out when she didn't take it at some point and Aleksander would join her in a line or two when he wasn't working, making it even easier for her to think of it as normal.

And there were more than enough nights out; whenever Aleksander wasn't working, which was at least three nights a week, they would be at a party in some exclusive development, visiting an art gallery opening, taking in up-and-coming bands and DJs, or meeting a seemingly endless series of his friends and acquaintances for trendy food in Michelin-starred restaurants.

Added to that, Heather and Alice would still come to the club on a Friday or a Saturday and there would be charlie available for them, too. Both her friends were surprised that Carol had started using coke, but as occasional users themselves, they were happy to take advantage when it was free.

There was a core crowd who were there every week; some were Aleksander's friends or acquaintances, but others were simply long time regulars at Bloq and had been absorbed into the "in crowd". As Aleksander's girlfriend, Carol was naturally included, and so were her friends.

At first, Heather and Alice were impressed by their new social status, but as they got to know Carol's new friends, they found that they liked them less and less. They fell in to three groups: those that were shallow good-time hangers on, mostly with too much cash, who loved to be seen hanging about with the second and more dangerous group; mainly male and who also had cash, but who didn't hide the fact that at least some of their earnings came from the greyer areas of the entertainment and leisure industries. The latter generally attracted the third group; very beautiful young women from often humble backgrounds who saw their own looks and sexual promise as a way to a glamourous lifestyle with no money worries.

Sadly for them, Heather thought, they'd traded one load of anxieties for another; a constant battle to be attractive and desirable replacing the fight for the next pound that their parents and siblings still waged. The only members of the in crowd who were true to themselves in any way were the hard men, but Heather and Alice did their best to keep out of their way. It wasn't a fear of violence; neither felt under threat on that score. It was more the way they were both scrutinised intimately, with sexual potential as the only consideration. The one saving grace was that they were deemed to be too intelligent to be taken seriously. These men didn't like their women to have minds of their own.

When Carol told her friends about her mum's illness, and that she'd have to go home every weekend, Alice and Heather cried with her and said that they'd do anything they could to help; she only had to ask.

For a few weeks they continued to go to the club regularly each Saturday, but without Carol, the people they hung about with seemed even harder to tolerate and, in Aleksander's case, there was something that made them uneasy. There were no overt signs from him, but they both, independently of each other, got the impression that if they'd given him any encouragement or indication that they were available, he would have taken the opportunity while Carol was in Glasgow.

He was still very good to Carol when she was there and she never had to buy cocaine; even the small amount she needed to get through the weekends at home appeared without her having to ask. When she was in London, she rarely used her own flat. She'd virtually moved into his house, although they stayed at least once a week in the suite above the club.

The sex was still amazing. He gave her sensations she hadn't thought possible and taught her to do the same for him. She sometimes cringed at work when she imagined what people surrounding her would think if they knew what she was like in bed with Aleksander. Still shy on the outside, the drugs and his coaching had made her feel comfortable with sexual practices that she might have considered slightly questionable or even humiliating before she met him.

"Wait till try coke on condom," he'd said one evening on their way home from a fundraiser for some Albanian charity that she wasn't quite sure was completely above-board. The cast of characters at it had made her feel slightly uncomfortable because the majority of the company had been men, and most of the conversation surrounding her had been in Albanian. Even Aleksander had spoken more often than not in his mother tongue, leaving her feeling very peripheral at times.

But the direct effect of the cocaine when he was inside her made up for it, when once again, his knowledge and ability made her forget any of the negatives that went with a relationship with Aleksander Gjebrea. Being honest, she had to admit that the sense of danger she got by being with him gave her a thrill that she'd rarely ever felt.

Occasionally she told him she felt uncomfortable with something he suggested and he always apologised and made a joke of it, like the time he'd heavily hinted at anal sex and had got as far as using some of her own lubrication to gently push his finger into her anus during his usual exploration of every part of her.

She hadn't initially reacted; he'd given her so many new experiences, she was willing to see if this was another one, but as he started to press a little more firmly, then attempted to insert a second finger, she froze, and he immediately asked her if he'd hurt her.

"No, but I don't really feel comfortable with that. I'm sorry."

He hadn't removed his finger immediately.

"Have never had sex like that?" he asked her.

"No, I haven't, and I don't think I could, Alekski." She had her pet name for him and she used it to let him know that she wasn't upset.

"OK. I don't want make you not happy."

He'd gone on to make her feel the usual fulfilment that being with Aleksander Gjebrea meant to her.

Away from him, she was unhappy. Her mum was deteriorating fast, despite a mastectomy, radiotherapy and chemotherapy. The surgeons had warned Bill that his wife's treatment would only buy her a bit of time, if any at all, and he thought it only fair to tell Carol, not wanting to build up any hopes she might have of Alison recovering.

Carol saw Heather at work, but they weren't quite as close as they had been and there weren't that many opportunities for Carol to speak about her mum with her. What didn't help was that Heather and Alice, on one of the few weekends that Carol was in London, had separately said to her that they were worried about who she was hanging out with, how much coke she seemed to be doing and how involved she was getting with Aleksander. Predictably, Carol thought they were just jealous of her, but didn't voice these thoughts.

Over the next few months she gradually distanced herself from them, made easier in Heather's case by the number of days Carol was missing from work. Everybody knew that her mum was dying and most people, even her employers, were sympathetic and tolerant of her absences – but Heather knew there was more to it than that.

When Alison died, Carol took a couple of weeks off to help Bill with the arrangements and the aftermath of her death. She tried her best to cut back on her coke use and to a certain extent she succeeded, but when she returned to London, satisfied that her dad was going to cope, she could sense a difference in Aleksander's attitude to her.

Hoping for some affection and sympathy, she was shocked when he never even asked her how she was, how her dad was, or how the funeral had gone. When she arrived at his house, instead of the quiet night in with him, talking, that she'd been expecting, she found to her dismay that he'd invited a few of his Albanian compatriots around to discuss, in their own language, various business arrangements that she wasn't privy to. During the evening the four of them, including Aleksander, became increasingly loud and intoxicated and by the time they left, at two in the morning, she'd already been in bed trying to sleep for over an hour.

She heard him coming up the stairs and tried to feign sleep, but he switched on the light and the music player, with the volume turned up higher than she thought was appropriate for that time of night. He sat on the edge of the bed next to her and spilled a small packet of coke onto the bedside cabinet. He was pretty drunk but he managed to arrange it into two straight lines. He snorted one himself, then shook her roughly and told her to do the other one.

"I'm too tired, Alekski. Can you just hold me tonight?"

"Come on. Just one line then we make love." He laughed.

Carol started to cry, everything suddenly heavy on her shoulders: her mum dead; her dad on his own, and now her boyfriend, boorish and insensitive when what she needed was for him to hold her tight, tell her he loved her and that everything was going to be all right.

He put his hand on her shoulder and squeezed it gently. She smiled weakly and reached up to touch his face. Instead of kissing her hand, as she'd expected, he grabbed it and pulled it down to his crotch.

"C'mon, baby, you been away too long time. Alekski want much to love you."

Carol wasn't in any position to move away, as he was now lying on top of her. His other hand found the bottom of her nightie and pulled it up, reaching for her breasts. He kissed her hard on the mouth and when she didn't respond, he pulled away and reached for the rolled up twenty he'd used earlier.

"Here, you need take sniff and wake up a bit."

"I don't really want to, Aleksander; I'm upset."

"I give you coke all time, even when away. Now you home you don't want? Maybe I look for new girl."

"Don't be like that. I've just buried my mum and I've had a really bad time of it. Please be nice to me."

"I want be nice to you." He squeezed her breast suggestively. "Your mum die is best thing. You say yourself on phone. No pain now. Just me and you now."

She could see he wasn't going to take no for an answer, and anyway, the line of coke was looking more attractive to her, as she felt awful.

She leaned over and snorted the remaining line. She hadn't had any for a couple of days and it worked its wonders quickly, with more of a rush than normal. No sooner had she turned back round to him than he had his hand between her legs, searching for the moistness and the spot that normally turned her into jelly, to do as he liked with, but though she was wide awake, she still didn't feel any response to his unusual clumsiness.

He gave up trying to stimulate her with his fingers and moved down her body with his mouth and tongue, pushing her legs firmly apart as he reached her pubis. She tried to bring his head back up, but he was too strong and she gave up, letting him move his tongue around and inside her, wetting her with his saliva, his hands under her, lifting her roughly up to his lips.

When he thought she was wet enough, he moved up again. Kneeling between her legs, towering over her, his hands moved to grip her forearms and, leaning forward, he entered her more roughly than he'd ever done. Even when their lovemaking was at its most passionate and violent, there was always an element of gentleness, of her taking him in, so unlike this forced submission, which she'd never before experienced.

She gave a gasp; not so much of pain but of shock. He didn't give any sign that he'd noticed and, still pinning her arms to the bed, he continued to thrust repeatedly, pressing her into the mattress with every stroke.

He finished eventually. She'd lain still the whole time, hardly moving, a steady stream of tears rolling down from the corners of her eyes. Glad it was over, she waited for him to roll off her, but instead he withdrew from her and knelt alongside, then, with little apparent effort, turned her onto her front.

He pushed one knee between her knees, then moved her leg to the side with one hand while cupping the other around her belly, and lifted her towards him.

No, not that. A groan escaped her lips. Perhaps taking that as encouragement, he guided himself into her again and started to move. Relieved as she was that he hadn't tried to use her anally, she continued to weep silently as he ground away behind her, oblivious to her shock and grief at his conduct.

She knew deep down that this was what she'd heard called date rape and she vowed to leave first thing in the morning.

Spent again, he had the gall to lie beside her, his arm circling her protectively. Hardly sleeping for the first few hours, she eventually dozed off into a fitful and restless dream, until she awoke in bed alone in the morning.

Just as she glanced at the clock, Aleksander strode into the room carrying a tray with a full breakfast on it. Suspicious, she sat up in bed and took the tray from him.

"You stay bed a while. Aleksander look after you."

She stared at him, confused. Had last night really happened? She was sure it had, but she couldn't see any guile on his face.

He kissed her forehead and sat on his side of the bed while she ate.

"I go in late today. Drop you off at work on way. Pick you up after and take somewhere nice."

"Why are you doing this, Aleksander?" she asked, incredulous that he thought he could change what had happened like this.

"I drunk last night. Not nice as should be. Make up today."

She began to question in her own mind if she'd overreacted, or if it had been the drugs. He hadn't hit her and perhaps she hadn't really said no. With him being drunk, maybe he'd read the situation all wrong.

Even as she tried to rationalise his behaviour, a voice deep down told her she was wrong, but seeing him back to his usual charming self, being as nice as ever to her, she decided to give him a chance.

-o-

For the next few months, Aleksander almost made her forget that he'd ever been anything other than loving, attentive, patient and kind. Their life swung back into its old routine; only the occasional visit back home to check

130

that her dad was coping interrupted the constant social whirl that was her life with him.

In between a short break in the south of France, where they mixed with the super-rich without unease or any feeling of being out of place, and a trip north to the Edinburgh Festival, they spent a lot of time together in the capital, mostly in the company of others, but often alone. Their relationship seemed to deepen, she thought, and she was gradually coming to terms with the loss of her mum.

Beneath it all, there were still problems. By the autumn, although her absences from work dropped, an increasing dependence on coke to fuel her social and personal life led to a deterioration in her ability to work well when she was at the office. Colleagues who noticed it put it down to her having a hard time getting over her mother's death but Heather, out of them all, knew that bereavement was only a part of Carol's problem. She approached her one morning and coaxed a reluctant Carol to go out with her for a bite to eat at lunchtime.

Even in late October it was warm enough for them to sit out at their favourite lunchtime spot. Halfway through their starter, Heather broached the subject of her friend's drug use.

"Carol, I'm only saying this because I think we're still mates, but you really need to get some help."

Carol made to get up but Heather put her hand on her arm.

"I know you've had the hardest time imaginable with your mum and everyone thinks how you are at work at the moment is down to that, but I know there's more to it. We've all been guilty of doing some coke, but Alice and I can take it or leave it. I look at you every morning you're in work and it's obvious that you're hungover and still wasted from the night before."

Carol shrugged her shoulders. "It was you two that took it first. I don't know how you can be so high and mighty about it. And anyway, it's not every day. We only do a line a couple of times a week."

"It's more than that, and you know it. And I wish we'd never gone near Aleksander or his club. He's no good for you."

Carol was furious. "Who are you to tell me who's good for me? You're just fucking jealous."

Heather blushed. "Maybe at the start. Not now. Aleksander and his crowd have changed you. You're not the Carol I knew six months ago."

"Maybe I like this Carol better. I've seen and done things you could only dream of. I didn't ask you to be my minder. I can look after myself."

Heather got up. "I've tried my best. If you won't listen, I can't help you. Let me know when you see sense and we'll talk then. I'm sorry."

She dropped a twenty on the table and left the restaurant, visibly upset. Carol sat for a while nursing a glass of wine then, instead of returning to the office, she got a taxi to Bloq.

The club was closed, but Anna, the manageress, let her in. They talked for a couple of minutes, but the woman had the cheek to warn her again about being one of a long line of Aleksander's sad conquests. *Did everyone have something to fucking say about their relationship?* She had a good mind to tell Aleksander what his staff were saying about him, but she knew she wouldn't do anything in case he sacked the interfering woman, as she chose not to have that on her conscience.

She didn't want to hang about the club listening to Anna give her more unwanted advice so she slipped up the stairs and switched on the TV, pouring herself a glass of wine from the bottle in the fridge. Opening the small freezer compartment, she reached in behind a bag of ice to the spot Aleksander had showed her, and pulled out a small packet from the plastic bag of cocaine he kept there.

She left it out on the table to thaw and, feeling guilty about work, phoned in and told the office manager that she had a migraine, an excuse that she'd used more and more, recently.

He told her that she was to call in and see him the next day as it was necessary to discuss her medical problems. Pissed off that everyone seemed to be on her case, she poured another glass of wine and waited for the coke to thaw out.

It didn't take long. It was so dry, by the time she'd finished her third glass, she was able to tip it on to the coffee table and arrange it into two lines. She did both, then filled her wine glass up again. She looked at the almost empty bottle and the remnants of dust on the tabletop and a small part of her knew she hated all this, but then the coke kicked in and she giggled at a fat woman sitting in her bra and pants and being harangued by the audience on the Jerry Springer show.

Aleksander still hadn't returned by eight. She'd started another bottle of wine, but the alcohol was making her lonely and miserable, coming down off the coke. She

133

looked at herself in the mirror and was glad her parents couldn't see her now. She started to cry, wanting more than anything for Aleksander to come and make it all better.

She thought she heard sounds of someone in the office downstairs and, looking at her reflection, she realised that she looked a mess. *He mustn't see me like this.*

She cleaned off the smudged mascara and applied some fresh make-up, then brushed her hair. She had to steady herself on the way down the stairs, but she'd more or less got herself together when she opened the door of the office, expecting Aleksander to be sitting at his desk.

"Oh, it's you," she said, surprised to see Anna in Aleksander's chair. She had a pile of papers in front of her and was holding one of them in her hand. Even though Carol was pretty drunk, it passed through her mind that there was something a bit furtive about his manageress. She passed it off as her imagination, admitting to herself that she didn't like the woman much.

"Hello. I'm just looking for an invoice. We're getting low on wine glasses and I need to find out if the order went through last week."

Anna sounded matter-of-fact and her usual hostile self.

"No sign of Aleksander yet?" Carol asked, trying not to slur her words, acutely aware of prompting the other woman's contempt if she thought she'd been drunk and loaded all afternoon.

Anna placed the invoice back in the pile and crossed to the filing cabinet.

"No, I haven't seen him. I'm surprised; I would have expected him in by now. There's quite a crowd in, including a few of his friends. You should go through and join them; they're in the private room. I'm sure they'd love to see you."

Carol couldn't work out if she was making an attempt to be friendly or just being sarcastic.

"I might just do that. Aleksander will be here soon."

She left the manageress to her filing and hurried through to the VIP room, hoping it was some of the less fearsome members of Aleksander's crowd who were in.

Behind her, in her boss's office, Anna exhaled slowly, willing her heart rate to return to normal.

Too fucking close for comfort.

-o-

Only one of Aleksander's more scary associates was in and he was distracted by a particularly vapid and superficial blonde who was doing everything but a lap dance for him in an effort to get him to spend the night with her.

The room was only half-full, but there was the pleasant buzz of people determined to enjoy themselves and not caring how much they had to spend to do it.

A group of girls, who Carol knew reasonably well, shouted her over, offering her a drink from a bottle sitting at the side of the table in an ice bucket. She joined them and a glass appeared almost instantly, conjured up by an alert waiter who'd spotted her coming in.

"Let me pour that, Miss Carol," he said, smiling at her. It was one of the things she liked; the deference of some of the staff to the boss's girlfriend, but she still felt a little self-conscious about it.

The girls, nice as they were, soon bored her. She wished that Heather and Alice were here, then remembered Heather's unwanted interference earlier and made an effort to be friendly with her current companions.

Carol motioned to the waiter and spoke to him quietly when he came over. About five minutes later, one of the doormen came in and spoke to Carol, shaking his head.

Angry at his refusal to get some coke for her and her companions, she ordered another round of drinks for them. She wished Aleksander was around to give his security staff a talking to, and she resented his absence.

She flirted a little with the waiter, just for fun, and because she was annoyed with Aleksander. He was young, good-looking and just cocky enough with it, so all the girls took her lead. It whiled away an hour with lots of laughs and giggles, and some lewd and suggestive comments from the four of them, deflected charmingly by the waiter who saw the possibility of a large tip at the end of the evening but knew that a liaison with any of the guests, especially Carol, would mean instant dismissal at best.

By the time she looked at her watch and saw it was nearly midnight, she was tired, fed up with her new friends, and still pissed off with her old so-called friends and the patronizing manageress, plus the fact that Aleksander hadn't shown up, especially as she'd sent him a text earlier.

She asked his gangster lookalike friend if he'd heard from him.

"He was at the opening of Miriam someone-or-other's exhibition tonight. Why he supports arty crap like hers, I don't know. It's shite." He laughed. "He said I was welcome to bring Melinda here; he promised he would catch up later, but I might have to take a rain check. I'm not sure I can wait much longer." He looked at his companion, rubbed his hand up her leg and winked at Carol.

Carol smiled. *What a dick*. She felt slightly nauseous.

Shortly afterwards the pair left, his hand on her barely covered arse the whole way out. "Sorry, girls," he said, looking over his shoulder, as if they couldn't contain their disappointment.

"Yuk," Carol said to her friends, who giggled at her.

-o-

Aleksander didn't appear. By two in the morning the staff were trying their best to encourage the remaining clubbers to leave.

"Where are we going to go now?" Ella, one of Carol's new aquaintances, asked.

"Come back to Aleksander's house. There's plenty booze and some coke." Carol felt a bit reckless. *Fuck him.*

"Wow, that would be great, but won't he mind?"

"I live there, too. He'll be fine."

On the way back in the taxi, Carol had a few sudden doubts, but was still annoyed enough with him not to care.

The taxi dropped them off and they noisily meandered through the mews to the house. She looked up at the windows, puzzled, as they approached. Most of the lights were on and she could see a couple standing at the upstairs window. She recognised the man as one of Aleksander's inner circle of friends but she'd never seen the woman before.

She unlocked the front door and entered, shouting Aleksander's name as she motioned for her companions to follow her in.

As she took their coats to hang up in the small cloakroom off the vestibule, Aleksander came down the stairs, two at a time. She thought a look of annoyance crossed his face, but she might have imagined it because he beamed at the three girls with her and kissed them on both cheeks.

"Welcome, ladies, to my house. Make yourselves at home."

He turned to Carol and, putting his arm around her back and pulling her towards him, kissed her on the lips.

"Sorry not to text you. Doing some business then come back for few drinks. Expect you here. Were you out with Heather and Alice? Where they now?"

"No, I went to the club. I thought you were there today. I spent the evening with Ella, Mandy and Martine. We thought we'd come back here for a few drinks."

"Not worry. Good you now here. Come up and meet boys."

He bounded up the stairs and they followed, more carefully, to the smaller and more intimate sitting room on the first floor.

If the guy at the club had looked like a gangster, he was minor league compared with the men sprawled around on Aleksander's ample couches. For the first time that evening, Carol felt quite uncomfortable and wished she hadn't brought the others back.

There were three of them. Each of them made her feel uneasy; there was something malevolent about them all.

The guy she'd seen at the window was Prek Dushku, a close friend of Alekski's from home, and she was familiar with his cousin, Ilir. She didn't know the third man; he was older and Aleksander introduced him as Pjeter.

"He my best Russian friend," Aleksander said, grinning, his arm around Pjeter's shoulder.

Carol thought the girls they were with looked like escorts. There were five of them; a niggling worry briefly pierced the haze of alcohol. *What might have gone on if I hadn't turned up?* There was certainly some sort of party in progress, judging from the nearly empty bottle of *Stoli* which she knew was full when she'd last looked.

Aleksander found some shot glasses for the new arrivals and a round of Albanian and Slavic toasts saw off the last of the vodka. She looked around but, unusually, there were no wraps to be seen. The room felt crowded; it was smaller than the downstairs lounge but there were still seats for everyone if you allowed for the girl sitting on Ilir's lap.

The host disappeared downstairs and returned with another bottle of Stolichnaya vodka in one hand and a hookah in the other. His fellow Albanians cheered and slapped each other on the knee as he placed the large and lavishly decorated opium pipe on the table.

Taking a cube of solid opium from an ornate wooden box, Aleksander loaded up the hookah and lit the small burner at the base. As smoke began to appear in the glass chamber the hookah was placed in front of Prek. Holding the flexible pipe extending from the neck and looking from side to side at his expectant audience, he placed the mouthpiece between his lips and sucked.

The water in the glass bulb bubbled as he inhaled deeply. At first his pupils contracted, then dilated as the opium hit home. Ilir was next to take a pull from the pipe, followed by the Russian. Two of the women took short drags as it was passed along the couch, ending up in front of Carol. She glanced at Aleksander, who smiled and nodded.

On a family holiday to Morocco she'd seen men of all ages gathered in the middle of the day in the cafés of Tangier, smoking opium from the traditional sebsi pipe, never thinking that one day she would be in the position of having to decide whether or not to inhale opium fumes herself.

She hesitated for a moment, but feeling Aleksander's supporting hand on the back of her neck, being intoxicated with the exotic danger of it all and having her inhibitions obliterated by the alcohol, she let out a long sigh and breathed in her first hit of a drug which surpassed cocaine on so many levels.

She watched, detached, at her fellow smokers as a profound euphoria seemed to well up from deep within her. She sensed that these people were lifelong friends as a sensation of mellow contentment washed over her.

She felt Aleksander's touch sear her skin with a warmth and tenderness that was painful and exhilarating at the same time. She needed to be naked and lying with him, but she couldn't move. He must have taken a draw from the pipe because he lay beside her, equally immobile.

When he finally did move, it was to somehow carry her up to the bedroom. She was vaguely aware as she left the room that the remaining guests were either smoking from the still bubbling hookah or in intimate contact of various degrees with each other, in full view of the other residents of the mews, if any of them had been awake and watching.

Aleksander's last act before leaving the room had been to switch the glazing to its opaque mode, to spare their blushes. He did the same on entering the bedroom, before laying Carol gently on the bed.

The sex was as different again as it had been on coke. They lay side by side, barely touching or moving, him just inside her, but even the slightest brush or gentle ripple of movement seemed to unlock waves of almost overwhelming intensity, reaching out all over her body from each point of contact.

She clung to him afterwards, even when he'd finally fallen asleep. Nothing had prepared her for the depth and range of experiences that this man had given her and she was willing to live with any of the negatives, just for those moments.

-o-

She didn't make it into work the next day and when she finally showed up at the office on the Monday, there was a brown envelope on her desk. Looking around, aware of a few glances from her fellow journalists, she opened it.

141

It was a final written warning. According to the letter, she had already been given two verbal warnings about her timekeeping and absenteeism and, although she couldn't specifically remember them, she could recall a couple of mid-morning lectures from her manager when she'd been suffering from the after-effects of alcohol, coke and sleep deprivation from her frequent midweek sessions.

The letter further stated that, in the absence of any medical information she should have supplied to the management, she would be well-advised to seek advice from a health professional regarding her current problems.

She had a dull headache and felt slightly nauseous, but she took the letter and immediately knocked on the manager's door. He showed her in with what she assumed was a sarcastic remark.

"Carol, I'm glad you could make it. Have a seat and I'll be with you in a second."

He made a point of typing for a minute or so on his terminal, making the odd note on a scratchpad in front of him while she sat waiting, feeling like a child in front of the teacher, waiting for punishment.

"Carol, thanks for coming to see me," he said, finally turning to her. "We seem to have a problem, don't we?"

"I'm sorry, but I've not been great since my mum died. It's been a very hard time for me." Even as she said it, she hated herself for using her mum as an excuse.

"Carol, although we sympathise fully and realise you were very close to your mother, it's been three months now, and I'm not convinced that's the only issue here."

Carol bridled. "What do you mean?"

"Well, did you go to bereavement counselling, as I suggested?"

Carol couldn't meet his eyes and she stammered a reply. "Well, no, but … I mean, I was going to, but I just couldn't bring myself to talk about mum to a complete stranger."

"Carol, however difficult it would be for you, that's what these people do; they're very good at it." He paused. "I think you should make an appointment as soon as possible, if you are going to get back on track. We are trying to help here; we think you have great potential as a journalist if you can sort out your problems."

Carol could feel the prickle of tears in her eyes and angrily tried to fight them. She swallowed and forced herself to be apologetic. "I'm sorry. I'll make sure I do that this week."

"I also think it would be advisable if you took medical advice on your lifestyle choices."

Carol was shocked and angry. "Excuse me," she snapped, "what are you trying to say?"

It was his turn to look uncomfortable. "Do you want me to spell it out for you?"

Feeling sick, she decided to brazen it out. "Yes. Yes, I do."

"OK. A number of your colleagues have approached me. They had strong suspicions that, on some of the days when you actually turned up for work, you may have been under the influence of drugs; prescription or otherwise."

She sputtered. "I don't know what you're talking about. I may have taken tablets to help me sleep, but that's all."

"Were those prescribed by your doctor?"

"Yes, but in any case that's a private matter between me and him," Carol said, the lie coming easily.

"Not if it impacts on your employment."

"I've had the odd absence but I've always phoned in with a reason."

"Do you know how many days you've had off in the last two months?"

"Two or three at most, but I haven't counted."

"Eleven days. Now, we don't want to go down the route of having to investigate your case independently, but unless you are willing to work with us on this, we may have to."

"And what if I don't?" Carol said, indignantly.

"Well, we would probably have to dismiss you, which would very much prejudice your future employment applications elsewhere."

"And if I left now?"

"We would give you a reasonable reference. None of this is documented as of yet."

"You just want me to leave, is that it?"

"Not if you can sort yourself out and return to being the promising and conscientious employee that you were up until a few months ago."

Carol could feel a dull ache in her bones and would have given anything just to get out of the building and back to the club or Aleksander's house and have a snort or a smoke.

"I can't work in a place that has no concern for their employees' health. Here, you can have my resignation, if that's what you want." She picked up a sheet of paper, scribbled a note and threw it down on the desk.

He picked it up and shook his head but before he could say anything, she'd stormed out of the room, slamming the door behind her. Several of her colleagues looked up as she marched down the office to her desk, grabbed a couple of personal items and made for the stairs.

She was just disappearing down the first flight when Heather stepped out of the lift.

"Carol!" she shouted, but her friend had already reached the next floor down. Heather turned to one of the copy girls at the front of the office and asked her what was wrong.

"I think she's just been sacked."

Heather rushed down the stairs after Carol, but by the time she got to the front door of the building, she was gone.

-o-

"I packed my job in. The bastards were going to sack me anyway, but I got the promise of a good reference if I went quietly. They said I haven't been performing well enough since my mum got ill. I mean, talk about insensitive."

Aleksander could see she was fuming.

"Well, not to worry. I see you OK."

"Thanks. Is it OK if I work at the club till I get something else?"

"No. You are girlfriend. You not work in club. I give you money until you get new job."

"Alekski, I can't do that. I have savings I can use. Why don't you want me to work at Bloq?"

"It not good for my girl to work in club. Other workers get funny about it."

"Oh, I never thought. I'll get a job quickly, though."

But she didn't. Aleksander gave her a credit card, which he kept topped up, and although she didn't abuse it, she very quickly got used to not working and still being able to spend money when she needed to. Aleksander liked her to wear nice clothes and underwear and he encouraged her to pay a bit more for it than she would have done if she was using her own money.

She would rise just before lunch and eat a bit of breakfast. Very few days went by when she wouldn't do a line of coke in the morning to get her going, and she would smoke her first pipe of opium by five o'clock, most days. It was always available and Aleksander never commented on how much she was using. If anything, he seemed to encourage her. She assumed it was because with the drugs, she was extra special to him in bed. She didn't care, because to her, he was all that mattered.

She hardly saw her dad after she'd left her job. On the phone it was easy to lie to him about her employment status, but it took a lot of effort not to give it away on the odd weekend she did manage to travel up to see him. And she struggled when she was home to keep her drug addiction, which she barely admitted to herself, from her father. Just a few days after her late October visit, she was already dreading the next time she was due to go up to Scotland, which would be over Christmas. Nevertheless, she booked a seat on a Christmas Eve train to Glasgow and sent a text to Bill letting him know her expected time of arrival.

The following evening she'd been drinking with her vacuous friends in the VIP room, but when she asked Aleksander for their usual, instead of opium, he provided a wrap of brown powder for each of them.

"All out of opium," he said. "This better."

She knew it was heroin but she was only smoking it; it wasn't as if she was going to inject it.

And he was right – it was better. Her three friends and a semi-famous musician, who was hanging out with them, had heated it up in the usual way, in silver foil, using a lighter; she only used a hookah when she was at the house. The hit she got almost blew her away and she looked around expectantly to see if Aleksander was there, wanting her, but the club was exceptionally busy and he couldn't spare too much time, not even to have a chat.

By midnight, she and her friends were completely wasted and she asked Aleksander to take her home. Instead of that, he got annoyed and rather unceremoniously half-carried her up the back stairs and put her to bed.

Out cold, it only barely registered when the bed creaked and a hand snaked around her, feeling for her nipples beneath the flimsy bra she still had on. Something felt strange, but she knew she was still fried from the drugs she'd taken.

Another hand removed her panties and she felt fingers probing. She moved and groaned, knowing his touch would soon have her ready, but an unfamiliar clumsiness,

147

unlike his usual lightness of touch and finesse, alerted her that something wasn't right and she tried to turn round.

"Don't worry. We just have extra fun tonight."

It was Aleksander's voice, but it was directly in front of her. She opened her eyes. He was naked and already had an erection. As he kneeled beside the bed, expecting her to go down on him, the sudden realisation cut through the fog of heroin and alcohol that there was another man in the bed with her and she was expected to service both of them at the same time.

Her sexual experiences with Aleksander had broadened considerably over the previous few months; she'd even eventually allowed him to have anal sex with her. It hadn't been as bad as she thought it would be; with his hands and fingers reaching round in front of her, he'd made sure she got full enjoyment from it, but she couldn't say it was something she would actively seek out with him. He had at one point jokingly suggested including one of her new friends in their sex life for a night, and although she'd turned him down flat, a small flicker of curiosity had made her wonder if she'd also give in, over time, and try that as well.

But a threesome with Aleksander and another man had never been discussed and she would have felt violated if he'd even suggested it. And here she was, completely smashed, with two men, one of them the man she loved, attempting to have sex with her.

She tried to resist, but the chemicals in her blood had floored her and the roughness with which they responded to her attempts to push them off made it simpler for her to comply with their wishes.

When they had both finished, they changed places and it all started again. Afterwards, they left and she wept quietly when she finally heard the door being locked behind them.

In the morning, when she awoke, there was a foil by the side of the bed, a wrap of heroin beside it and a lighter standing close by. She looked at it for ten seconds. There was a pain deep within her and, instinctively, she knew that the only way to banish it was to light up and let the smoke give her the relief she craved.

But it didn't stop her thinking of what had happened the night before. As the pain subsided with every breath of the drug, she knew she needed to confront him and tell him she was going to leave.

She searched for her phone, but she couldn't find it. *I must have left it in the club last night.* She tried the door, but it was locked. Losing the fight to stay awake, she fell into an unsettled and unsatisfying sleep, lying across the bed.

When she heard the key in the lock, she couldn't say what time it was. She'd been floating in a twilight world for hours and was just starting to come down. She half-rose as Aleksander walked round the bed.

"Alekski," she pleaded, as he approached the bed, "why?"

"I like bit of fun and so my friends do also. You not like two of us?"

"I love you. Why would you want to share me with somebody else? You must have known I wouldn't want to." She sat up, turning to face him.

"You love drugs, love lifestyle, love me have sex with. But don't love me. Not know me."

"How can you say that? What have I done to make you be like this?" Tears washed streaks of last night's mascara down her cheeks.

"Look at yourself. You fucking mess, right?"

Carol rocked back and forth, hugging herself, unable to take in what Aleksander was saying. She could hardly catch a breath to speak; a vice-like panic gripped her chest and her throat burned with swallowed tears.

"Dhimiter will take you back to house. You get stuff. He drop you off at flat. Don't come back club."

He turned and left the room. Carol dully gave in as Aleksander's self-styled security chief motioned for her to get dressed, not making any pretence of looking away while she did so. She turned her back to him, scrambling for last night's discarded clothes, covering herself as best she could. She lurched into the toilet and made herself decent, although she knew she still looked a mess.

She felt something hard in her jacket. Realising it was her phone, she slipped it into the back pocket of her jeans.

She walked through the door ahead of Dhim, down the stairs and through the club. On the way, he motioned for his sidekick to join them and said something to him that Carol couldn't quite catch. The club had a side door into the yard, accessed from the other end of the corridor from the opening through to the bar area. It was meant to be a fire escape, but they used it to put rubbish out in the bins and for staff to get in and out when the main club doors were closed.

The black and silver nightclub van had been parked outside, with its side door open. The two men roughly shoved Carol through it, into the back of the van. Dhim, by

150

far the larger of the two, tossed the car keys to his subordinate and got in beside her, pulling down the two "jump" seats bolted to the bulkhead that separated the body of the van from the driver's cab. He gestured for her to sit in the one furthest away from the door, which he slid shut.

The van drove for about twenty or thirty minutes. She couldn't tell the direction or distance, but something made her think that they weren't heading for Aleksander's house, or her flat. Halfway there, her phone vibrated in her jeans pocket. Touching against the steel of the seat, it rattled and buzzed noisily.

Before she could completely fish it out, her escort had reached over and grabbed her arm and, twisting it round towards him, wrested the phone from the tight grip she had on it.

He looked at the screen and smiled. She thought it might be a text from her dad, but she watched in dismay as her captor held her phone between his forefinger and thumb, dropped it onto the floor of the van and ground it under his heel, smiling at her as he did it.

When the van stopped, the driver let them out and the thuggish pair manhandled her roughly in through another doorway. She didn't even have a chance to see much of the exterior of the place, but she got the impression that it had been one of those seedy and decrepit hotels that were so common in parts of the east end of London.

Inside, it wasn't badly decorated, if a little old-fashioned. She was bundled up three flights of stairs into a small locked attic room, furnished only with a bed. There was a toilet and dingy shower cubicle in a space that looked more like a cupboard, at the back of the room.

151

She was told to sit on the bed. Dhim nodded to his underling, who stood by the door. The big man grinned.

"You're going to be staying here for while. If you want drugs, you do what told."

He pulled out the kit she needed to smoke and showed her it. "I have four of wraps here. But you need earn it, say Aleksander."

She looked at him, stupidly. He started to undo his belt. Her eyes widened and she began to cry again. He held up the small pieces of folded paper containing the drugs, passed them to his companion and motioned for her to get undressed.

Something deep within her tried to resist, but the intense painful craving that was gnawing at her insides was more powerful, and she reluctantly did as she was told.

He didn't even take his trousers off; letting them fall to his ankles, he told her to lie back on the bed then entered her, using a spit of his own saliva on his hand as a lubricant. When he finished, he wiped himself on the bed sheet and gave her one of the packets, and her kit. He watched, disgusted, as she fumbled to pour the powder into the foil "bowl" she'd fashioned and tried to spark a flame from the lighter to heat it up. He grabbed it from her clumsy and impatient fingers and lit it, handing it back to her.

She lay down on the bed as the soothing fumes entered her lungs and into her bloodstream; a comforting and soothing balm to the torture that the day had been. The gorilla chucked the three remaining packets of heroin onto the bed beside her and left. Glancing out the door, making sure his superior had gone, Josef, the less malevolent of the two, took two strides towards her, reaching behind him. She flinched, expecting him to assault her as well, sexually or otherwise, but he pulled a few twenties from his back pocket and put them into her hands.

"Hide this. First chance get, make run away. Sorry. It's all can do."

Locking the door behind him, he left.

-o-

"Ilir, I need to speak with Aleksander. There's been a big mistake. I need to go back to my flat."

Aleksander's cousin smiled at her.

"You no go anywhere. Aleksander send you to me. You do good sex, you get plenty powder."

"With you?" she said, incredulously.

"Not me. Just sad men who can't fuck woman without pay."

"I can't. You won't make me a prostitute," she shouted.

He hit her once across the face, with the back of his hand.

"You do as I want, or get punish and no drug."

"I'll not do it." This time she whimpered and flinched as he moved towards her, but he knew that the threat of a smack to the side of the head was just as good as than the real thing and he didn't want to damage her too much; *what punter want badly bruised whore?*

He left, taking what remained of the heroin.

By the time he returned six hours later, Carol was screaming in the agony of withdrawal. Again he silenced her with a slap and gave her another wrap.

As she desperately set up her kit, he spoke to her.

"Tomorrow, you'll get first customer. If you give him good time, you get much as need," he said, dangling the small paper parcels in front of her. "If don't, you get a bit of this." He touched her face with the back of his hand. "Now, seeing as I need check stock out, give blow job."

-o-

Carol's days didn't vary much. From midday onwards, she was taken from the room and moved to one of the bedrooms downstairs. Even if she'd been able to make a break for it, there were always two people at reception, the only way out. The doors to the fire escape were chained and locked.

The other girls were a broad mixture of British girls who had, in the main, come to London with the intention of making it big, but failed and ended up hooked on drugs and on the game, and trafficked girls from the Balkan states and the Far East. Most of the British girls lived off-site and came to work every day, but all of the Slavic and Asian girls were accommodated in the small annex at the back of the hotel, four or five to a room, and strictly controlled.

On average, for the next seven months, Carol had to perform some sort of sexual act with at least five men each day. On an easy Monday, it might only be three and two of them might be hand-jobs, but at the weekend she

154

sometimes lost count of the men who used her body in the course of the day.

She tried her best to stay safe, and condoms were always available, but the heroin sometimes made her forget and, anyway, some of the punters paid extra to fuck her bareback.

None of the other girls became anything like friends, but a few of them tried to help her in little ways; she grabbed these small displays of humanity with a pathetic gratitude that would have shocked her a few months earlier. After she developed a cough from all the smoking and struggled to inhale, one of the other girls showed her how to cook up and inject herself, and from then on she would only use heroin intravenously.

In mid-June she saw an opportunity to get away. They must have believed that she was broken and could be trusted. The door to her attic room had been left unlocked for a few evenings; even in her loaded state, she managed to slip down three flights of stairs and out the front door, but her strength and focus failed her and she'd only stumbled a few hundred yards when Ilir and his assistant, Stan, caught up with her, tipped off by one of the other girls trying to ingratiate herself in the hope of receiving preferential treatment.

Careful not to break any limbs, they'd taken her up to her room and beaten her horrifically, warning her that they wouldn't be anywhere near as lenient if she tried it again. She lay in bed in her locked room for three days with only water and, surprisingly, a supply of heroin that had been left on the floor with her foil and lighter. She figured out by the third day that it was the easiest way for them to keep her quiet and compliant, and during the time her bruises were healing she almost enjoyed the respite from servicing the endless stream of men who used the establishment.

As her hunger for food eventually kicked in and her body's defences, weakened by the drugs, poor nutrition and abuse, failed to fight off the bacteria and viruses that should have been neutralised by a healthy immune system, she succumbed to a kidney infection and viral pneumonia, which weakened her even further.

The last thing she could remember was collapsing in the cramped toilet; lying slumped on the floor, wedged between the sink and the lavatory bowl.

CHAPTER 11   VICE

Returning from his tenth visit to a brothel, Bill, as usual, had a shower before he did anything else. He was no prude, but he felt dirty and seedy each time. It wasn't so much the girls; he could only feel pity for them and he couldn't see why men would pay to have sex with a girl who, implicitly in the transaction, was only yielding her body to him out of financial necessity. During his marriage, other than in the early years, Bill knew that Alison sometimes made love to him because she thought he needed it and not because of a great desire on her part. Because of that, Bill didn't particularly enjoy those occasions, but so as not to upset his wife, he tried to muster as much enthusiasm as he could. Looking back, he knew they were both pretending to a certain degree, but compared to what it must be like with one of these young women, he now recalled those times with fondness.

The whole transaction at every place he visited couldn't have been better designed to extinguish any desire he might have had, even after an extended period without sex, stretching back to the last occasion he and Alison had managed it, when she was quite ill. She'd asked him to make love to her one last time, partly just to feel human again. It had been difficult and awkward and he had been terrified of hurting her frail body, but to him it was a memory he would always cherish.

From the painted and disinterested woman on reception, through the hovering doorman-cum-minder, to the faded decor and cheesy music, he knew that these were no high end bordellos.

Asking at each place for a particular type of girl, his job was sometimes made easier by being able to browse through a photo selection of those available. Every time he scanned through, his heart was in his mouth; part of him didn't want to find her in that sort of place, but every time he didn't see her photograph by the time he'd reached the last one, he was gutted because at least a positive match would have meant she was alive. In the first place he'd been to, he hadn't been offered this visual menu, but he got lucky when the girl he'd been offered felt sorry for him when he told her he didn't want sex.

"My wife died this year and I just want to talk to a woman without having to get to know somebody. This is her." He showed the young prostitute a picture of Alison first, then the photos of his daughter and Anna's sister. "And these are my daughters, Carol and Susie."

He was watching closely but he couldn't see the slightest flicker of recognition cross her face.

"They both look like your wife, although I can see a bit of you in that one."

She pointed to Susie's photograph.

Bill had smiled to himself at the irony and, after chatting about Alison and Carol for a while, being careful to include a few embroidered details about his other "daughter", he gave her an extra ten pounds, which she hid in one of her shoes.

"Thanks. They used to search us, but hardly any of the punters give extra here, so they're pretty lax about it now."

Even in the places with pictures of the girls, Bill gave them the same line and showed the photographs as well. It was a good cover story for not wanting sex and it also had the outside chance of unearthing a girl who had come across Carol or Susie in passing, but most times, the girls were unsympathetic and were more worried that Bill not having sex with them might annoy the management. Bill always told them that he wouldn't say a word and would prefer it if they didn't, either, to save him embarrassment. This seemed to placate them and they usually shrugged and listened to him with poorly disguised boredom. The last thing Bill wanted was for word to get around that there was a man visiting brothels and not getting the sex he had paid for; it might raise suspicions about him.

They got their first break after Bill had visited five or six establishments. The prostitute who Bill was allocated didn't react to Carol's photo, but Bill saw a frown of recognition on her face when she looked at Susie's picture. At first, when Bill questioned her, she denied having seen Susie at all, but Bill took a risk, explaining that he was searching for his daughter and that there would be a couple of hundred pounds in it for her if she could provide any information.

The girl hesitated, eyeing up the money Bill had produced, then seemed to make a decision.

"She was here for a few months; pretty fucked up, she was. Then all of a sudden she was gone."

"Can you remember when that was?"

The girl began to have second thoughts.

"You're not the pigs, are you?"

"No, just a desperate father looking for his daughter."

"I believe you. You look like the kind of poor bastard who would try and save their kid from a life they don't approve of. You do realise it'll probably not matter a fuck, don't you?"

"I've got to try, haven't I? I don't care what I have to do. Don't you wish there was someone who would do that for you?"

"Listen, fuckface, the only person who ever looked after me was me, so don't give me any of your pity, or try to make me feel sorry for you, either. Another hundred quid would work better."

Bill handed over the extra cash. She pocketed it in her tight jeans with the other cash.

"It was about eight or nine months ago. Her name wasn't Susie, though, it was Marcia, but a lot of the girls use different working names."

"Any idea where she went?"

"Nah, we didn't get a chance to talk before she left, and I didn't know her that well."

"There's nothing else you can tell me?"

"Fuck, you like to get your money's worth, don't you?" She flipped down her top to reveal a small pale breast, with a pierced nipple. "Sure you don't want a shag as well?"

Bill ignored her. "Listen, this is important. I need your help, but if you can't be bothered, I'm out of here."

"Chill, fuckwad. Take a pill." She looked at Bill again and he thought she was going to push for more money, but she carried on.

"There's only one thing; it might be nothing, but I was off the day she disappeared. I was talking to a couple of the other girls when I came back and they said that they'd come in for work on the day I was off and they were sent home; told there had been a raid."

"Does that happen often?"

"Nah, but when it does, they're always very careful for a few days afterwards, and this time they weren't. Also, the other girls who were in earlier that day; they were sent home, but none of them would tell me nothing."

Bill didn't pull her up on her double negative. "Perhaps I should have a word with them. You could ask them for me. Tell them there's some money in it for them; you as well."

She laughed. "You've fuck all chance of them talking to you if they won't say anything to me. I don't think you know the type of people you're dealing with."

"Who is that? Who owns this place?"

"Even if I knew, you wouldn't have enough money for me to spill. I've told you too fucking much already."

She turned her back on him and lit a cigarette. "I think it's time you left or they'll think you're a fucking stud," she said, a jaded sneer in her voice.

Bill could sense he'd got as much out of her as he was going to, so he left without saying any more.

Bill and Anna usually met up somewhere after each one of Bill's brothel visits. They'd used the pub at first, but Anna had soon become nervous, so they'd started to vary their meeting place. Bill would send her an innocent email stating a spot close to their intended meeting place and a time two hours before he wanted to meet her, finishing with an innocuous girlie comment. This gave him the chance to check out the location for any observers, in case Anna's cover had been compromised, and it meant that she could find him without having to search too far.

When Bill told Anna the details of his conversation with the girl when they next met, she was distraught but strangely resigned about it.

"She's dead, Bill. I knew it anyway and this confirms it. She would have somehow managed to contact me if she were alive. If she is dead, I hope it was an overdose; at least that way she wouldn't have suffered. It would be harder for me to take if she was killed by someone."

"She might not be dead. There's no hard evidence for that. I know it's difficult, but try to keep your hopes up."

"Thanks for trying to help, but I'm beyond hoping now. I'd just like to find her to know what happened and say goodbye."

Bill resisted putting his arms around her – she hated any form of contact that might get them noticed – but he did cover her hand briefly and gave it a squeeze. She didn't object, but pulled it away after a few seconds. She gave a Bill wan smile of encouragement.

"But you shouldn't give up on Carol. She's still alive, I'm sure. Just keep looking. We *need* to find her to get evidence against the bastard who put them both there."

"I'm not stopping now. I still have another ten or twelve places to go to." He hesitated. "Should we tell the police now about what we've found, or wait to see if we find Carol?"

"They've not bothered their arses when we've gone to them before; why should now be any different? I'd leave it. It's not as if it happened recently, so I doubt they'd find anything, even if we could get them to take an interest in it."

"OK. I'll carry on doing what I'm doing and we'll keep in touch. When do you want to meet up again?"

"We take a risk every time we're seen together. Don't contact me unless you find something and I'll do the same. I'm trying to see if there are any records at the club for any of the other properties he owns. If we can tie him to one of the brothels, the police would be forced to investigate. I'm also gathering information about his financial dealings, but the stuff I've found so far only seems to be concerned with the club. I'm sure there must be more somewhere but I have to be careful and I don't get that many opportunities to ferret around in the files."

"Be careful, Anna. Don't take any silly chances and as soon as we get anything useful, we'll go to the police."

-o-

When Bill received an email from her the following week asking for a meeting that afternoon, he thought the worst about his daughter, but when he saw Anna's face, he knew it was Susie.

"They've found a body on a building site in Greenwich. They think it's Susie. I've been asked to go and identify her this afternoon."

Not caring if anyone was watching, he clumsily wrapped his arms around her, feeling the dampness on his shirt where tears coursed down her cheek, soaking him.

"I'm so sorry, Anna. I don't know what to say."

"You don't need to say anything," she sobbed, "I knew it was coming. In a way it's a relief, if that doesn't sound awful."

It did to Bill, but he said nothing.

"Will you come with me?"

Bill was surprised. She was normally so careful about them being seen together.

"I've no one else. I don't think I can do it on my own."

Bill's heart went out to her. "Of course I will."

-o-

They met at the entrance to the Royal Free Hospital and made their way to the mortuary. She warned him to make sure to call her Jill and told him her real surname, Miller, just in case. Bill decided it would be safer not to mention her name at all, unless it was absolutely necessary.

Anna seemed to get some peace from seeing her sister, but to Bill she looked terrible; nothing like the young woman in the photograph he'd been touting around. She was drawn and pale, as if the fluid had been sucked out of her, and there was some bruising and cuts to her face. Her hair was matted with blood from the wounds on her skull and her skin also had a strange texture, as if she had some longstanding dermatitis or psoriasis. Bill wondered if it had something to do with the drugs.

But she was recognisable. Anna confirmed that the body was that of her sister and they weren't shown any more than her head and neck. The mortuary assistant told them that due to the dryness of the burial site and the coolness of the temperature of the ground under the pile, her body hadn't decomposed as much as it would have normally.

The following day, after the post-mortem, they met with Detective Inspector Keith Kirkland, who was working on Susie's death. He confirmed what they had suspected from the way she'd looked and from what Bill had learned at the brothel:

"Susie had been severely assaulted, with extensive injuries to the head, chest, abdomen and all four limbs. She had three fractured ribs, a fractured left elbow and the right humerus was also fractured, but she would have nearly certainly survived if she'd received medical attention. The actual cause of death was bacterial complications of the fractured ribs and a punctured lung, which eventually led to a severe pleuro-pneumonia."

"So she was beaten up then left to die?" Anna asked, cold as ice.

"Yes, that would sum it up. We are treating it as murder."

He paused, apprehensive about telling her the rest.

"She also had both ankles broken; one of her feet was almost chopped off, but," he added quickly, "that was done after she was dead."

Bill suddenly realised that he was gripping Anna's hand, so he squeezed it a little tighter. He couldn't remember taking hold of it; had she taken *his* hand at some point?

"Do you know why they did that?" Anna asked, her voice small and fragile.

"We presume it was to make it fit into something for transport to where she was buried."

"I thought she'd been found in a building site," Bill asked.

"No, it was a storage yard for a demolition company. She was found when they cleared a large heap of loose rubble that had been dumped there. We were lucky, really. The site manager told us that the pile could have sat there for years, but a construction company requiring a few thousand tonnes of bottoming had purchased the whole lot and it was cleared down to the level. A bucket loader driver noticed a bit of polythene sticking up and when he pulled it he could smell something decomposing, so a couple of the site staff got a spade and investigated. They stopped when they found her foot and called us in."

"Was she on drugs?" Anna asked.

"Not at the time of her death, but she had needle marks on her ankles. That's quite often where prostitutes shoot up because it's easily hidden with a pair of boots, so she may have been involved in prostitution. We reckon she died a few days after her assault, so she could have been taking drugs up to the point of her attack."

"And her skin condition; was that drugs related?" Bill asked.

"Skin condition? There was no mention of a skin condition." The policeman looked puzzled and a slow comprehension dawned on his face. "That was post-mortem change – she was lying under a mound of rubble, but the stuff she was buried in was much less coarse. Even so, her skin was marked by the small pieces of grit and gravel that surrounded her."

When Bill and Anna stayed silent, he handed them his card and told them to contact him if they had any more questions.

166

As he turned to go, Anna realised they hadn't told him what Bill had found out.

"Just a second, we have some information about where she was probably attacked."

The detective looked extremely sceptical. "We're always interested in information that would help the investigation, but how did you come about this information and why haven't you come forward with it before?"

"I reported Susie missing nine months ago. When the police learned that she was a drug addict, they did nothing about it. I found out that she might have become involved in the sex trade and my friend Bill here gave me a hand to look for her in some of the areas where the girls work."

She gripped Bill's hand hard as she said this and he had to try hard not to react, realising that she was trying to warn him not to say anything about her involvement at the club, or about Carol. He knew why: it would spell the end of her ability to search for material behind the scenes, and the police already thought that Bill was an irritant to them.

The policeman apologised for not doing enough, if that was the case, but he strongly admonished them for putting themselves at risk.

Bill told him the name of the brothel he'd visited and although he couldn't remember the name of the girl he'd talked to, he described her to him and recounted his conversation with her, excluding the part about Carol.

"We'll follow this up today, but please don't go off doing this sort of thing again. Leave it to us."

Almost as soon as they'd left the police station, Anna turned to Bill.

"I know what you're going to say. We should have told them about Aleksander Gjebrea and the club. And Carol. I'm sorry."

"I was shocked for a few seconds, but I know why you did it and I think you're probably right. Otherwise I would have gone ahead and said something, no matter what you thought, because Carol might still be alive."

"Thanks. It would have meant the end of me being able to work on the inside to find out how Susie died and where Carol is."

In agreement, they parted, with their usual assurances to contact each other if something of relevance cropped up.

-o-

Bill had forgotten about the funeral. When Anna emailed him with nothing but a street address and a time, he'd had to look it up on Google maps and only when he saw "crematorium" did it dawn on him that Anna had, on her own and in virtual secrecy, arranged her sister's funeral.

They were only three extra people at Susie's second funeral. Of the six people present, four of them were professionals: the detective who'd talked to them and the undertakers. Although he'd never met her, Bill was surprised that he felt almost as much pain for Susie as he had when Alison died. It may have had something to do with a young life cruelly wasted or perhaps it was merely that his and Anna's shared burden led him to empathise strongly with the two sisters.

The service was brief and poignant, with a single flower on top of the coffin as it rolled through the curtain. Afterwards, they sat in silence for a while in the crematorium garden until Anna's voice suddenly cut through Bill's thoughts like a knife through flesh.

"I'm going to kill him. I don't know how, but the bastard's not getting away with this."

Bill looked round, hoping no one was close by. "Anna, watch out. Someone might hear you."

"I don't care. I'm not going to stand by and see her death go unpunished."

"Let the police deal with it, and in the meantime keep on looking for evidence against him. But you can't kill him. Even if you managed to do it, your life would be ruined; you'd spend at least fifteen years in prison."

"He's ruined my life anyway and the police aren't much better."

Seeing his puzzled expression, she explained.

"Sorry, I haven't told you. The police phoned this morning, today of all days. They found nothing at the brothel. None of the girls knew anything; nobody matched the description you gave and a search of the premises found nothing at all."

Bill gasped. "They must have found something."

"No, the room she'd been in had been gutted and most of the girls were gone."

"They can't just stand by and not do anything."

"Oh, the brothel will get closed down; he said vice are on the case now, but he told me that none of the girls admitted to recognising Susie, and some of them had been there for years."

Bill listened with utter dismay. No wonder she was upset.

"Without the girl they've got nothing, unless anyone saw them burying Susie down at Greenwich, but so far, no one's come forward. We've got to find Carol. She's our only hope."

"I've been to another three on your list. Nothing doing. That's why I didn't contact you. I'm beginning to think that it's all been pointless. Carol could be anywhere."

"Don't give up on her, Bill. I still think there's a chance that you'll find her. Think how long they kept Susie alive for."

"I'm sorry. Here I am wallowing in self-pity while you've lost your sister, with little chance of getting justice for her."

"Concentrate on keeping the search for Carol going and I'll keep working away at the club. I'm convinced there's something there that will nail the bastard." She looked at Bill. "I'm relying on you. Keep in touch."

Bill watched her walk away, wondering at her inner steel, on the worst day of her life.

CHAPTER 12   ROYAL FREE

Bill's investigations had become so disheartening and
mundane that it came as a great shock when he found
Carol. He had almost reached the end of Anna's list when
the young prostitute he was with recognised Carol when he
showed her the photograph.

"She's here," she told Bill, in a monotone voice, "but she's
not working at the moment. Is she really your daughter?"

Bill had to resist grabbing the girl. "Yes, where is she?
Can you take me to her?"

Too late, the girl realised that she'd given away too much
without having screwed Bill for some additional cash.

"I'll need some money before I do anything."

Bill took out his wallet and gave her two hundred pounds.
She greedily eyed his wallet for more as she grabbed the
pile of twenties he gave her, but something about Bill's
stare made her continue.

"She's ill. They have her in a room on the top floor. It's
one they don't use for the punters, but there's no way I'm
taking you there."

"All I ask you to do is keep quiet. Does anyone walk
around checking on the girls?"

"Nah, they're too fucking lazy. We have a buzzer we can
ring if there's any hassle."

"Right, listen. If you do exactly as I say, there's a decent amount of cash in it for you."

"How much? I'll have to make myself scarce. You've got to make it worth my while."

"A couple of grand, if I get her out. I'll meet you afterwards and give you the money then."

"How do I know I can trust you? I might never see you again."

Bill sighed. "You'll just have to believe me. I've got to trust you, haven't I?"

She looked at him for a second then seemed to come to a decision.

"OK. You look all right. Go back to the stairs and take two flights up. Then go along to the end of the corridor. Open the door at the end and take the stairs up to the attic. The door at the top will probably be locked, but the key might be in it. This time of day is fairly quiet, so there shouldn't be too many punters about."

"Right. I'll come back here once I get her. Don't move."

Bill carefully opened the door a crack and peered out. The corridor was deserted. He slipped out and closed the door behind him. Having reached the stairs without meeting anyone, he stood at the bottom and listened. Not hearing anything, he climbed both flights, two steps at a time. He could see the door she'd told him about at the end of the corridor, but he could hear voices in one of the rooms. He tried to walk as casually as possible, in case any of the occupants came out, but he made it to the door without being seen.

He could feel his heart pounding in his chest, partly from his sprint up the stairs but mostly through the fear of what he was going to find when he got to the top of the narrow flight of stairs in front of him. The girl had been right. When he got to the top, the door was locked, but there was a key in the lock as she'd suggested. He unlocked it and, taking a deep breath, burst into the room.

It was dim. The curtains were drawn on the small dormer window on the right-hand side. He opened them to reveal a poky little attic room with an unoccupied and unmade single bed jutting out into the middle of the floor, and very little else. There was a smell to the room and he could see some sort of dried bloody discharge on the bedsheets. There was no sign of Carol. There was a small door at the other end of the room and he thought he could hear a few quiet sounds behind it.

He stepped around the bed, cursing under his breath as he tripped over a small electric heater that fortunately wasn't plugged in. He tried to open the door, but it was locked from the inside. He could now hear the sound of someone crying softly coming from the other side of the door, so he put his shoulder to it and pushed.

The flimsy bolt gave way easily, allowing him to open the door a crack. He could feel a weight on the other side as he pushed and could only open it far enough to get his head through the gap. Slumped in the corner between the toilet and the wall, under the small sink, he could distinguish the dark shape of a person, but he couldn't make out any detail in the semi-darkness.

Before he did anything else, he went over to the room door, removed the key from the outside, then locked it from the inside.

Pushing the toilet door again, he tried to get into the small room but the gap was just too narrow. He noticed a light switch cord hanging from the ceiling and tugged it.

Even with the light on, he still couldn't see if it was Carol in there, but it was a girl with blonde hair. She was dressed in some sort of dressing gown, with the hood up.

"Carol," he hissed, "let me in; it's Dad."

She didn't answer, but she stirred just enough, bringing her knees up to her chin and hugging them, to allow Bill to wriggle through the gap.

The moment she turned her face to him, he knew it was her, but the change in her shocked him; she was thin and pale, and like Susie, she had multiple bruises and lacerations, including a burst lower lip.

He got his arms around her, under her armpits, and with a struggle managed to heave her to her feet. Tears streamed down his cheeks and great racking breaths burned his throat as he held his little girl tightly, almost overcome to have found her alive.

Bill allowed himself a minute to recover his composure, then swung Carol round and sat her on the toilet while he opened the door fully. Pulling her to her feet again, he half-carried, half-dragged her over to the bed, where he laid her down. He looked around and spotted a half-empty teacup on the floor, which he rinsed out and filled with cold water from the tap. He splashed some on Carol's face and was pleased to hear her groan, then see her open her eyes.

It was hard to tell if she recognised him, but she gripped his arm and clung to him for a few seconds. She attempted to pull herself up from the bed using his arm to hold on to, but her head slumped forward, and she nearly rolled on to the floor. After a brief struggle, and with her help, he finally managed to get her into a sitting position.

He tried to support her while scanning the room for something for her to wear. All he could see was a filthy pair of jogging pants and an old T-shirt, so he removed her dressing gown, leaving on the almost see-through nightie that was under it. He tried not to look at the bruises on her breasts and ribcage that, like the ones on her arms and legs, were various shades of black, purple, green and yellow.

With difficulty, he dressed her, tucking the nightie into the sweatpants and putting the T-shirt and the dressing gown on top. The only footwear he could find was a pair of flimsy pumps, so he lifted her feet one at a time and put them on.

She was now sitting unassisted, though slumped forward. She still hadn't acknowledged that she knew who he was, but at least she was functioning at a basic level. He left her on the bed and unlocked the door. Making as little noise as possible, he descended to the bottom, pushed the door a little ajar and peered along the third-floor landing. It was deserted, but he could hear the sounds of a couple coming up the stairs at the far end. He waited in silence as a young prostitute guided her next client along towards him and entered one of the rooms on the left-hand side. Bill waited a few seconds to make sure nobody else was coming.

Returning back up the stairs, he paused only to plug in the electric fire by the side of the bed. He lifted Carol up, encouraging her to stand, and helped her across to the door. Half-carrying her down the stairs, he sat her down on the second bottom step and made his way back up to the attic room. He gathered the sheets from the bed, stuffed them into the toilet pan and flushed it. He repeatedly plunged the sheets into the full bowl until they were well soaked, then wrung them out into the sink.

On his way back through the room, he dumped the sheets on top of the electric heater, arranging them so that they covered it completely. Leaving the door open, he went back down to help Carol.

Bill supported her as best as he could and they made slow and painful progress to the main stairway, where he paused only to get a better grip of her, before proceeding down the stairs as fast as they could without risking a fall. As it was, she slipped three steps from the bottom and he only just managed to avoid them both landing in a heap on the first floor.

The girl who'd told him where to find Carol was watching for them and waved to Bill to hurry. He could hear voices in the foyer below and the sounds of a man and a woman starting to climb the stairs. Half staggering, he hauled Carol the last twenty yards and through the door held open by the young prostitute, who was making sure that she was going to have a chance to collect her money.

She turned to Bill as she closed the door. "How the fuck are you going to get her out past reception? Marie never moves from there and either Stan or Ilir will be at the door."

"Is there a fire alarm anywhere?" Bill asked, still supporting Carol.

"At the far end of the corridor from the stairs; on the wall. You have to be right at it before you can see it." She looked at Bill as if he was stupid. "They'll never fall for that, though. Only one of them will come and investigate."

"Just wait a few minutes. There should be some smoke soon. If no one sets off the alarm upstairs we'll do it here, but we'll wait until there's enough smoke to make it look like a proper fire."

"You haven't set alight to the fucking place, have you? There are thirty or more people in here. You'll kill them all."

"I just put some damp cloths on top of an electric fire. It'll create a lot of smoke, but it won't cause the place to go up in flames. In the meantime, have you got a coat that you wear home?"

"Yes. It's here." She picked it off a hook in the corner and handed it to him.

He removed Carol's dressing gown and clumsily got her into the coat. "Get rid of this during the confusion," he said, giving the young prostitute Carol's dirty gown, "and make your way out before us. Shout 'fire' a few times and scream, just to add to the general panic. Meet me tomorrow at Westferry Circus, on the riverside overlooking the pier, and I'll give you your coat back. We'll never forget you helped us today."

The girl looked at Bill strangely, but when the first wisps of smoke began to appear in the corridor, it was she who set off the fire alarm and ran down the stairs, shouting and screaming as Bill had asked her to.

A number of things happened simultaneously. Bill watched through the small gap in the doorway as two men rushed up the stairs, shouting for everyone to get out, but even before that, people in various states of undress were already opening doors and rushing down the corridor. Bill wrapped a towel around Carol's face and watched the melee heading towards the stairs. Girls still in their skimpy underwear, and men desperately trying to pull on their shirts and jackets, were fleeing down the stairs from the smoke- filled upper floors, impeding the progress of the two brothel employees trying to get up to the source of the fire. One of them carried a fire extinguisher, making it even harder for him to make his way against the flow of panicking people.

Bill waited until the point of maximum chaos then shoved Carol out into the corridor. As they pushed towards the stairs, quite a few of the other girls had scarves or pillowcases held to their mouths and noses, because of the smoke, and Bill tried to keep the towel in place over Carol's face, making it less likely that she would be spotted leaving.

The woman Bill took to be Marie was desperately trying to put all the takings from the till and the safe into a leather bag, so they passed through the foyer and out into the street without her noticing them. As they rounded the corner, Bill saw their accomplice standing with a group of the other working girls, looking up at the smoke billowing from the roof. *Clever girl.* Bill was glad she'd realised that she would be under much less suspicion if she hung around, but it was a brave thing for her to do, to fight the urge to make herself scarce.

On Bill's last view of the building, he noticed a flicker of flames at the attic window where Carol had been held and hoped it wouldn't catch hold and set the whole building alight, even if it was owned by Aleksander Gjebrea.

-o-

Anna came to the hospital as soon as she got Bill's email.

I've found just what you've been looking for. Meet me this evening where we last saw your sister.

The morgue was closed when Anna got there, but Bill was waiting and had watched her arrive. She waited a few hundred yards away, as she always did, to let him check whether she'd been followed.

When she finally approached Bill she was in tears, until Bill told her that Carol was alive and in one of the wards.

"You bastard!" she said, punching him on the arm. "I thought she was dead when I got the email."

"I'm sorry. I thought it was safer for Carol if I didn't mention where she was and I knew you'd be able to work out where to come. I didn't realise until now how bad it sounded."

"I've so many questions, but how is she?"

"She's in a bad way on a few fronts, but there's hopefully nothing that can't be sorted. She's got some physical trauma, but nowhere near as bad as Susie had. They ran some tests and they say she's been on heroin. She has some sort of kidney infection and a high temperature; the doctors think it might be pneumonia. She's also had at least one abortion. They did a scan and they can't rule out the possibility that it could affect her future ability to conceive. They haven't told her that yet."

Anna put her hand on Bill's arm. He gave a grateful smile of sorts.

"She's on a drip and they're doing all sorts of other tests."

"Christ, I hope she's OK. Has she said anything?"

"Not much. Yesterday she didn't speak at all. I wasn't even sure that she recognised me at first. Today we've talked a little, but I didn't press her."

"How did she get out? Were the police involved?"

"No. I found her and managed to get her out myself. Oh, apart from a bit of help from a girl that worked with her. That reminds me, I'm meeting her in half an hour. Can you sit with Carol? I told the hospital that you're a family friend. I briefly explained to her why you're here, so she doesn't get a shock, thinking Aleksander might have sent you, but I don't know how much she took in."

"Sure, I can do that. What ward is she in?"

"I'll take you up. Then I'll go."

Anna looked puzzled. "Why are you meeting this girl? Is that not dangerous?"

"Because I promised her I would. I need to give her coat back to her; she lent it to Carol to get her out unnoticed and I told her I'd give her some money if she helped Carol get away."

Anna realised that Bill would never go back on his word, no matter the risk. She accompanied him to the single room Carol was in, on the sixth floor. Bill introduced her to the nursing staff and took her in to see Carol.

"I told Carol that you were on her side, but I don't know if she took it in."

Carol was asleep, so Bill left Anna with her while he went to meet a young prostitute for what he hoped was the last time. He stopped off at the bank on the way and withdrew the money that he'd promised her, placing it in a small gift bag that he'd bought at the hospital shop.

He arrived before her to check out the paved viewing area looking out onto Canary Wharf Pier, but it looked clean of any watchers. He knew the spot from when he and Alison had been in their sightseeing phase when Carol had first moved down. When the girl appeared, only a few minutes late, Bill was as confident as he could be that she wasn't being followed.

They sat down and Bill handed her the gift bag and a larger bag containing her coat. She briefly glanced at the contents of the two bags then placed the small one inside the larger one.

"You can count it if you like. There's three thousand there. I thought you earned it."

Her eyes widened, but just for a moment.

"Thanks. You turned up, so you'd hardly cheat me now. I wasn't one hundred per cent sure you'd be here."

"So why did you do it?"

"Mostly for a chance that you'd turn up with the money. But …"

"But what?"

"Nothing, but I'm glad she's safe."

He didn't push her.

"Was the place badly damaged? I didn't think it would go up like that."

"Nah, Stan and Ilir put the fire out quite quickly. Only the bed and the carpet were thrown out, but the place still smells a bit smoky."

"What about you? Did they question you?"

"They grilled all the girls. Most of the punters disappeared immediately, but I hung about with everyone else to see what would happen."

"Yes, I saw that. I thought it was brave of you, and clever."

She looked at him dismissively. "It would have been fucking obvious I was involved if I'd left. They're pretty pissed off that Carol got away. They think she got out herself, in the confusion, only …"

"What?"

"They don't know how she got the door unlocked, they can't work out why the toilet door was busted in, and they don't have a clue who set off the fire alarm. They assumed that must have been one of the punters. Whatever you do, get her as far away from here as you can. For just being one of the girls, the way they reacted when they found out she'd gone was over the fucking top."

"What will you do now?"

"I'll wait a week then tell them I'm packing it in. Head off down the South Coast. Rent myself a flat and get some decent clothes."

"Get a bar job or something, don't stay on the game, please."

"You'd like that, wouldn't you?" She got up to go.

"Don't waste this chance," Bill shouted.

She didn't turn around, but Bill smiled, watching her hand slide up her back, giving him the bird.

-o-

When Bill returned, Carol had woken up. When she saw Bill, she gave a strained smile then started to weep silently when he crossed to the bed and put his arms around her. Anna got up to leave the room, but Bill motioned for her to stay.

When Carol turned her head to the window, Bill mouthed a question to Anna, asking her if Carol had said anything. Anna shook her head and whispered to Bill that she'd mostly slept, but when she'd woken, it seemed to her that the best thing to do was to tell her the whole truth, about herself, and Susie.

Bill spoke quietly to Carol, making sure she knew that Anna was a friend, mentioning the help Anna had given to find her. He told her that she could take her time telling them as much as she felt she could and that at some point, they would need to get the police involved.

Bill had told Anna on the way up to the ward that he hadn't contacted the police immediately because he didn't think Carol would be strong enough for at least a few days. Anna had argued that if he called the police in, Carol would at least have some protection, but Bill had been adamant: Carol wasn't going to face being questioned until she was able to cope with it; mentally and physically. He also reasoned that because he and the nursing staff would be with her most of the time, she'd be safe; it was unlikely that Aleksander Gjebrea or his associates would try anything in the hospital, with so many witnesses present.

In the hours after her rescue, Bill had questioned why he hadn't called the police the moment he'd found her. In truth, it hadn't even crossed his mind in the brothel to phone them, and he figured that, subconsciously, he must have lost so much faith in them that they weren't even a consideration.

At Carol's bedside, when she'd fallen asleep again, Anna spoke to Bill for a moment before leaving to go to work.

"I don't think she knew who I was when she woke at first. She started to panic, but then she seemed to remember you telling her I was a friend. I said that I was helping you and I told her a bit more about Susie, which calmed her down a bit."

Bill looked relieved but she went on.

"I can't visit again; it's too risky. Even if they don't do anything to Carol, they'll want to find her and keep an eye on her, so they might be searching the hospitals for her."

"That's why I brought her here and not the Royal London, even though it was nearer. I wanted to take her away from London all together, but I was frightened when I realised how ill she was."

"I still think you should call the police."

"I will. Just give me a day to speak to her and let the doctors do their bit. I promise I'll phone them after that."

"OK. You'll get no Wi-Fi in here and no mobile reception, so I'll phone the ward if I need to get in touch and leave a message as Carol's *Auntie Margaret*. If you need to get in touch with me, phone my mobile. I may not be able to answer, but I'll get back to you." She gave him her number and entered his into her phone as *Billie*, which would look innocuous if anyone at the club saw it.

She walked down the corridor and Bill was sad to see her go, but he knew that she needed to stay at Bloq for a while longer, gathering evidence in their determination to see that Aleksander Gjebrea and his organisation were brought to justice.

"Dad, I've been so stupid; I'm sorry I've let you down."

Bill's heart was breaking. Carol spoke in a quiet, slurred voice, through tears and shame.

"Carol, it's finished. You're safe now; that's the main thing."

He'd been holding her hand almost continuously for thirty-six hours as she drifted in and out of sleep. She was on a drip and the doctors had given her low doses of methadone to bring her down off the heroin gradually. Even so, she'd had a bad night. Restless and sweating, she had muscle spasms and vomited twice, Bill holding the bowl and wiping her face afterwards.

As morning had broken, Bill, standing at the large window, could see the light creeping over Hampstead Heath in the distance. He hadn't slept, always alert to anything Carol needed, from wiping away the rivers of sweat that threatened to soak the bed, to stroking her hair and talking quietly to her when she was at her most distressed. By daybreak, she seemed to have improved and was less agitated and more settled. She awoke briefly at nine, and managed to eat a little porridge, which she kept down, and promptly fell asleep again.

Bill took the opportunity to catch a little sleep in the chair and he woke about twelve to see the nurse cajoling his daughter to take some soup from a bowl she held in front of her. She struggled to finish all of it, but it was a start. When the nurse left, she seemed to want to stay awake and talk.

That heartbreaking apology, the first thing she said, haunted Bill, and he knew his reassurances probably meant little to her at this stage. She spoke in a low monotone, in short bursts, sometimes slurring her words, and he had to lean close to her to make her out at times.

"He was so nice at first, and exciting. It was all new to me and we did so much; it was like a different life. I thought I could handle the drugs; Aleksander managed, and so did my friends. And it was only coke at first; nearly everyone did it. Except, I couldn't. I just wanted it more and more. Aleksander encouraged it, I can see it now, but we had an absolute ball. I never wanted for anything."

She looked at Bill to see if there was any sign of understanding on his face. He tried to be as sympathetic as possible, but he couldn't quite comprehend how an intelligent girl like her could be drawn in by a man like that, and to the drug culture he pushed her in to.

"After a while, I started to see another side to him. I loved him, but it was as if he was trying to push me to do things that I wasn't comfortable with to see how far I would go for him. And Mum was dying and he didn't care. I'd go up to see her and it was so hard; when I came back I'd want to talk about it with him, but all he wanted was for me to be there for him and his needs."

She burst into tears and Bill held her close, murmuring her name, stroking her hair. He felt the sobbing subside as she slowly regained her composure.

"I was trying to be so strong for Mum and you, but I dreaded coming home, seeing her slowly disintegrating in front of me at every visit. Even so, I grew to hate the thought of going back to London, but I wanted him so badly at the same time. I started missing work, and blamed Mum ..."

Carol broke down again. Bill said nothing, recognising that letting the words pour from her was the best thing he could do for her.

"I felt awful. Most days I missed work it was because I was wasted; nothing to do with Mum. I should have left London, packed in the job and stayed at home, but part of me didn't want to let you both down."

This time it was Bill's tears that were wetting the bedclothes.

"You wouldn't have let anyone down. I wish now that we'd said something that would have made you come back home. We were so worried, but we didn't want to interfere and we assumed you would have told us if there was anything seriously wrong."

"And I thought I'd hidden it well." She gave a half-smile at that.

Bill waited, knowing that she'd want to get the rest of it off her chest, no matter how painful the telling might be.

"I think the hardest part was when Mum was in the hospice. When it came to her dying, I felt as much relief as pain. Even then, I had to get out of the house and find somewhere to do a line of coke. I was terrified that you would find my supply, but of course you never even suspected any of it."

"No, I'm ashamed to say that it wasn't until Heather told me that you couldn't handle the drugs that the penny dropped. But I knew something was up; all those weekends you came up after your mum died, you weren't the same girl that I knew. It was as if there was a shadow over you. I'll regret not asking you what was wrong for the rest of my life."

187

"Dad, you and Mum were always great at letting me make my own decisions, and my own mistakes, so don't blame yourself for this. I had plenty opportunities to ask for your help but I didn't, because I was a fool. I still loved Aleksander, despite everything, and I was too proud to admit that I still needed you."

Bill got up from the bed and walked over to the window.

"You can see for miles from here, but all this is only a tiny part of London. People get lost down here; it's a different world. You just bumped into the wrong people and got caught up in something that was evil and beyond your control. It's not your fault. You would see good in anyone and miss the signs that they're not who they make themselves out to be."

"He was a beautiful man, Dad, and he made me fall in love with him. I thought he loved me, too, but he didn't; he just used me for sex. I'm not too ashamed to say it; you've seen where I ended up. I just want you to know how I got there. I sometimes wonder if I got hooked on the danger of it all. Even when I was in that place, being used by other men, I still wanted to go back to Aleksander, although I knew he didn't love me and would probably be bad to me again."

She could hardly look at him. He sat down on the bed again and lifted her chin up to look at her.

"Listen, you're my only daughter and I don't care what you've done. I will always love you and I will do anything that I can to fix this. You don't have to tell me everything, but if it helps, I'll listen and not judge. That's not to say that I'll find it easy to take in, but never again should you feel that there's something you can't talk to me about."

"I'll tell you most of it, but there are things I can't say. I'm too ashamed and they're not things that it would be fair for you to hear. It's not that I don't want to be honest with you."

"I told you before, tell me only what you want to, but I'd like to know the truth about what that bastard did to you. I'll not rest until he pays for it."

"Dad, don't go near him. You don't realise how dangerous he is. He's the head of an organisation that's involved in everything from prostitution to people-trafficking to money laundering. I've seen it. I thought he was just a very successful businessman with an up-and-coming nightclub. You've no idea the glamourous lifestyle he leads and the people who flock to him. I don't know why that's not enough, but he seems to be greedy and ruthless, and he surrounds himself with hard and terrifying people, too, mostly working away in the background, far from the respectable front he puts on."

"I think we should contact the police tomorrow. I can't protect you from these people. And there's got to be a way of stopping him." Bill hesitated, then decided to tell her more about Anna and Susie. "Do you remember the woman who was in the other day? Anna."

"Yes, I knew her from the club. It gave me a bit of a fright. She explained a little about her sister."

"She thinks Aleksander Gjebrea did the same to Susie as he did to you, but in the end he as good as killed her."

"She once tried to warn me off him. I wouldn't listen."

"It's easy to see the truth in hindsight," he said. "She was working at the club to try and find out what happened to her sister. Since March, Anna and I have been working

189

together to try and find enough evidence to put him away. The police haven't seemed to be interested up until now, but when they hear what you have to say ..."

"I don't think the police will be able to protect me and it's just my word against his. I've put you in danger, too. I've really screwed up, haven't I?"

"Yes, you made a big mistake, but you've fucking paid for it." He hugged her tightly, her body shuddering again. He wondered how long a person could cry for.

Carol stiffened. She couldn't ever remember her dad swearing, but Bill had never been as angry and she hadn't even told him the worst.

"He forced himself on me a couple of times when I refused to do things for him that he asked me to, but the most horrible thing, the thing that made me realise that he was evil, was the time he made me do things with him and a friend of his, then he sent me away." She looked straight at Bill. "I tried to leave him, just before Christmas. I sent you a text."

"I know. I got it. I met the train. When you weren't on any of the later trains, I knew something was wrong."

"I never got the chance. They took my phone and locked me up. He let one of his gang – his chief of security – rape me, and his cousin forced me to do things for him, too."

Bill forced himself to listen, storing all his anger for later, understanding now the vow that Anna had made to kill Aleksander Gjebrea. He could easily add the man's vicious employee and his cousin to the list.

"By that time, I was completely addicted to heroin; I'd thought I was OK if I didn't inject, but it was just as bad.

190

Ilir, that's his cousin, took away my supply until I would have agreed to anything. And I did. I traded sex for drugs, Dad. I'm a prostitute."

He gripped her sobbing body tightly and, for the first time, he was glad that Alison wasn't around. She couldn't have coped with the knowledge of what Carol had gone through.

"Listen, it won't help now, but I truly believe you will recover from this. You'll be a different person than you were before; you can't go through something like this and come out of it unscathed; but you can be happy again and have a normal life, no matter how black it seems at the moment."

She said nothing for a while, happy to hold on to him, knowing that he loved her unconditionally and would die protecting her. When she did speak, Bill realised it was probably as much as she was ever going to tell him.

"It lasted for months. I had a cough and couldn't smoke it, so one of the other girls showed me how to inject. The hit was even stronger, so I kept doing it. As long as I did what I was told with the customers, I got as much heroin as I wanted. The only time I was happy was when I was locked back in my room and I could shoot up."

She paused for a minute, her mind sinking into the hell that had been her life for the last six months.

"The door of my room was always locked unless I was working, and then there were always two of them on guard to stop anyone getting away. About two or three weeks ago, poor Jackie got roughed up by one of the punters. We could hear her screaming and some of the girls ran to help and shouted for Ilir to come; that's Aleksander's cousin. He went into the room and hauled the punter out; didn't

191

even do anything to him, just chucked him out. Afterwards he went back up to the room and Marie, the woman at the front desk, went with him. I took a chance and slipped out; I had some money that Josef, one of Aleksander's workers, had given me and I had a vague idea of getting on a train back up to Glasgow, but one of the girls told him I was gone and they caught me."

She paused, her face pale and drawn.

"I thought they were going to kill me. Part of me didn't care, but I couldn't bear the thought of never seeing you again."

Bill's face twisted with grief, but he made himself look at her, a shadow of the daughter that they'd waved off to London with high hopes for her future a few short years ago.

"If you hadn't come for me, I don't think I could have made it. They gave me no food or medicine and I just had the water out of the sink to drink. And the drugs ..."

"Well, I did find you. Now you're safe and we're going to get you well again. That's my promise."

-o-

A little later the nurse popped her head round the door. "Mr Ingram," she said, "a woman called Margaret called and asked if you would contact her. Said she was Carol's aunt."

"Thanks. I'll pop out to use the phone. Can someone keep an eye on Carol while I'm gone?"

"Yes, I think the doctor's coming to examine her shortly, so it's not a bad time for you to have a break. You can speak with him when you get back."

Bill looked at Carol, wondering if he should tell her he was slipping out for a while, but she was sound asleep again.

He picked up his jacket and headed for the lift at the end of the ward, suddenly realising how hungry he was. Stopping at the small shop at the entrance of the hospital on his way out, he purchased a pack of sandwiches, then collected a cup of coffee from the vending machine in the foyer. It wasn't a bad day, but the chill in the air meant he was glad he had his coat with him. He walked briskly away from the busy hospital concourse and headed round the corner to find a quiet spot to phone Anna.

When he rang, she hung up immediately so, after quickly devouring his sandwiches, he walked on, knowing that for some reason it wasn't safe for her to talk and that she'd call him back when she could.

Sipping his coffee as he strolled, he was amazed at the size of the hospital and, quite enjoying the first bit of exercise he'd had in a few days, he decided to keep walking and circumnavigate the building. Before he'd gone far, Anna called back.

"Sorry, I was in the club. I've just managed to get away for five minutes."

"What's up?"

"They're closing the brothel. I overheard Aleksander talking to Ilir. They were talking in a mix of Albanian and English and I picked up enough to know what was going on. They've moved all the girls to a new location and the workmen are in stripping the place already. My guess is that it will be gutted and back in use as a cheap hotel before too long. I thought you should know. Have you called the police yet?"

"No, but Carol's told me everything. It's worse than you could imagine. I was going to phone the police tomorrow, but I may do it today. I'll speak to Carol first."

"OK, but don't take too long, or any evidence from the brothel will be gone."

"Right. Take care, Anna, and don't get caught out. I'll let you know what happens."

He pocketed the phone and continued walking, picking up the pace. Dumping his empty coffee cup in the bin, he reckoned he was more than halfway round the building, so he kept going. He jumped when an ambulance siren wailed close by, startling him. As he turned the corner to walk round to the east side of the building, he could see people running and a crowd gathering. Two policewomen and a male officer were attempting to stop people passing up the street and Bill cursed, as he realised that he'd have to walk all the way back round to get to the front entrance.

He managed to curb his curiosity about the nature of the incident; whatever it was, he didn't have the time to wait and find out. It crossed his mind that being within hailing distance of a hospital wasn't a bad place to find yourself in need of urgent medical attention and he silently hoped that it wasn't as serious as it looked.

He retraced his steps and finally reached the main entrance again. Going up in the lift, he wondered if yet another family was just about to be plunged into their own personal nightmare.

When he got out of the lift, he knew that something was wrong. One of the nurses looked at him, white-faced and fearful, and at the other end of the corridor he could hear somebody crying. The nurse tried to stop him, but he pushed roughly past, hurrying towards the room Carol was in. *Surely she hasn't had some sort of medical emergency now?* Everything had seemed under control; the acute problems she'd been suffering from had been dealt with and all the ongoing issues for her health were long-term ones.

He had a sudden and awful thought. *Did Aleksander Gjebrea or one of his men get to her?* He broke into a run, chased by the young nurse he'd brushed aside. He reached the room, heart thumping, to find it crowded with medical staff. He looked at the bed, but it was empty.

The ward sister saw him, her face ashen. "I'm so sorry," she said. "She jumped. We couldn't stop her."

Bill stood rooted to the floor for a second. He noticed for the first time the open window, one of the curtains fluttering weakly in the light breeze. He walked slowly towards it, not wanting to look but unable to keep himself from advancing towards the opening. The sister was joined by the nurse who'd been trying to catch up with him, and one of the doctors. They all tried to stop him, but he shook his head and, walking the last few paces feeling like a dead man, he approached the window.

Even before he'd entered the room, the feeling had been creeping up on him that what he'd seen earlier on the street below had something to do with Carol, and now, without having looked, he knew he should have gone through the crowd when he was down there, to see her, be with her in her final moments.

Looking down from the spot she'd thrown herself from, he could see the wide circle of people, now being held back by a barrier of blue and white tape and an additional four police officers. The ambulance he'd heard previously was parked within the ring of onlookers, and next to it he could see the backs and legs of two paramedics, who were kneeling over Carol's broken body. He couldn't see her head; a doctor in a white coat was crouching over her, obscuring it. Only the bottom half of her body was exposed, her legs at improbably unnatural angles, a puddle of blood slowly emerging from between them.

It occurred to him that there was no urgency or tension in the movements of the people tending to her; he knew himself that, considering the height she'd fallen from, it was unlikely that there was anything they could do for her.

Even so, he had to be there and he pulled himself away from the window and ran back towards the lift. He angrily stabbed at the buttons, but the lighted indicators above the metal doors stayed stubbornly static. He dived for the stairs to the left of the lift and ran down them with little regard for his own safety or the welfare of anyone who might be coming up towards him.

By the time he'd exited the hospital entrance and ran full pelt around to the other side of the building, his breath was coming in great rasps and sweat was blinding him. As he approached the crowd, a couple of them looked back at him and, somehow sensing that he had a connection with the victim, the mass of people around the periphery started to thin out as they nudged each other, nodding towards him nervously. By the time he reached the ring, it had split, leaving a gap for him to enter through.

Those close to him couldn't meet his gaze, but he saw none of that. As he ducked under the tape, one of the policemen moved sharply towards him and tried to tell him to go back outside the perimeter, but something made him stop.

"Do you know the young woman, sir?"

Bill answered, his voice flat, his face numb with pain. "She's my daughter."

The crowd gasped and drew back. A few of the women started to weep at Bill's stark statement.

"I don't think you should go and see her, Mr ..."

"Ingram. Bill Ingram. My daughter's called Carol. She's been ill ..."

He tried to look over the policeman's shoulder to where Carol lay, still attended by the three medical staff, and he could see one of them shaking his head, sadly.

"Is she still alive?"

"I don't think she can be, Mr Ingram."

While he was talking to him, the young officer tried to guide Bill away from the prying ears of the crowd, to the other side of the ambulance.

"I need to see her, just in case."

"I'll talk to the doctor. Please wait here." He motioned for one of his fellow officers to stay with Bill and approached the doctor, talking quietly to him. The doctor looked over at Bill then walked towards him, accompanied by the policeman.

"Are you sure this is your daughter?" the doctor asked.

"Yes, she jumped out of one of the windows of the ward she was in. I've just come from there."

The doctor looked at the policeman and seemed to make a decision, nodding to him.

"Your daughter is barely alive and it's unlikely she'll survive. We have an airway in place and we're helping her breathe, but her injuries are severe and extensive. I'm afraid I can't hold out much hope for her."

"Can I just be with her, please?"

"I must warn you her injuries are extreme, including those to her head. I'm one hundred per cent sure that she won't know you're there, but you can come over and be with her."

"I don't care. I just need to hold her."

They led him over to Carol. Someone had covered her head with some form of blanket, but he could see a few strands of blonde hair escaping from the side. One of her arms was underneath her, sticking out at a very strange angle, but her left arm was on top of her body and seemed relatively undamaged. The doctor indicated that he could take hold of her hand, and he did so. It was completely limp, but as he gripped it, he thought he felt the faintest of tremors. It might have been just him desperately grasping at the need for a last living connection with her.

Although unsure exactly where on her wrist he'd find it, he attempted to feel for her pulse. He was sure he could detect a faint beat and it comforted him to know that he'd be with her to the last breath, even if she was unaware of it. He knew deep down that no one could survive a fall from that height and, even if she did, she would be left with horrific disabilities.

He felt the paramedic grip his arm at the same moment he became aware that he couldn't feel a pulse any more. He turned to look at him and the sad shake of the head told him everything. The doctor looked at his watch, confirmed the time of death with the paramedic, and signalled to the man on the Ambu bag to stop pumping. Another blanket was collected from the ambulance and they covered her over gently. Bill continued to hold her hand and they allowed him as much time as he needed before gently helping him up, into the quiet of the ambulance.

Both the paramedics and the doctor spoke with him and confirmed that her injuries hadn't been survivable and Bill told them that he'd realised that almost immediately. He thanked them for their efforts and for giving her dignity in dying and, when the crowds had dispersed, he walked back round to the hospital entrance, accompanied by a concerned policewoman.

When he returned to the ward, he was ushered into the sister's office. "We're all really sorry for what happened," she said. "It was such a shock."

Bill could see that she was genuinely upset. "I shouldn't have left her. It's my fault as much as yours."

"Please, sit down. Let me get you a cup of tea." She signalled to one of the nurses. "The doctor who examined your daughter needs to speak to you; I'll just call him and let him know you're here." She picked up the phone as the nurse came in with the tea.

Bill sat down wearily as the nurse put the cup down on the desk in front of him. "I'm so sorry for your loss," she said, and she patted his shoulder before scurrying out.

"The doctor will be with us shortly," said the sister, as she put the phone down.

Bill would have left it at that, but a worry niggled at the back of his mind. He was sure something must have made her decide to kill herself and he needed to check out the possibility that someone from the nightclub had got to her.

"Were there any phone calls, or did anyone come to see Carol?"

"No, the only call was that one for you. There's been nothing since."

"And no one tried to visit?"

"No, I'm sure we would have noticed."

He thanked her and they sat in silence, awaiting the doctor's arrival. The sister waited with him for a few minutes, then excused herself to check on her other patients.

Sitting alone, he saw at least three police officers walk past in the time he'd been there. *Too late*. He knew that any chance of persuading the police to pursue any sort of case against Aleksander Gjebrea had gone with Carol's death. He would simply tell them that she'd got herself hooked on drugs and had ended up in prostitution, leading to her illness and her ultimate choice to take her own life. He would have to deal with Gjebrea in his own time.

"I should have waited until you were present, Mr Ingram, but Carol seemed to have improved enough mentally to cope with the news."

The doctor's voice snapped him out of his trance.

"What?" he asked, unsure of what the man had said.

"I said it would have been better if I'd waited until you were with us."

"What are you talking about? Sorry, I'm lost."

The doctor's face fell. "Has no one told you? Carol's tests came back positive for both HIV and hepatitis C."

Bill controlled his anger. "This is the first I've heard of it. When did you find out?"

"The results just came back today. I told Carol they were here when I checked her over earlier. She didn't want to wait for you to return to hear them."

"Christ, did you not think first? No wonder she didn't want to go on living."

"Mr Ingram, Carol was an adult and we can't withhold information from a patient if they ask for it. Carol insisted that I told her there and then."

Bill could easily imagine Carol demanding her test results, probably knowing what she would do if they were bad; not wanting him to find out first and stop her. But he was still angry.

"I take your point, but you didn't need to mention them at all until I was there, did you?"

The doctor sighed. "I'm sorry. In hindsight, that would have been better, but I can't turn the clock back, much as I'd like to."

Bill relented. It wasn't the man's fault.

"Don't worry. I'm not going to make a fuss. She would probably have found some other way to do it later, even if we'd prevented it today."

The doctor looked gratefully at Bill.

"The police are conducting an investigation just now and they'll want to talk to you. There will be a review of hospital security and it wouldn't surprise me if they put safety locks on all the windows."

"I'll talk to the police before I go. I'd rather get it over and done with."

Bill shook the doctor's hand and waited for the police to come and talk to him. When the door opened again, it wasn't the police, but the ward sister.

"Mr Ingram, we found this when we were clearing out Carol's stuff. The police need to see it once you've read it, they say."

The nurse handed Bill a sheet of paper that had been folded three or four times to seal it, forming its own envelope. Carol had addressed it to "Bill" on the front. That hurt a bit. He would have expected "Dad".

He walked over to the window and unfolded the paper. He read it slowly, with a heavy heart.

Dad,

I addressed this to you as "Bill" to make you understand that I'm an adult, and as an adult I've made terrible mistakes. So I'm making this decision as an adult, too. It was only hard to make in one respect – how much pain it will cause you.

But my staying alive would have caused you as much pain, or more, in the long term; watching me die slowly, with no chance of all the usual things that come with having a daughter, such as grandchildren.

You and Mum have been wonderful parents to me and I'm only sorry I've let you down in such a big way.

I'm also sorry I couldn't face the police. I don't mind if you tell them all about what Aleksander did to me, but it won't do much good. He'll laugh it off; being done for supplying drugs and running prostitutes won't lose him much sleep, even if he gets caught.

I'm glad Mum isn't still alive to see me now and I'm so sad that you've had to go through all of this. Despite all I said about being an adult, I still feel like your little girl and I only hope you can forgive me.

All the love in the world.

Carol

Bill stood looking out of the window, not wanting to let the nurses see the tears running down his cheeks. It crossed his mind that he'd cried more in the last eighteen months of his life than he had in the first forty-seven or so years, and he didn't quite see what the point of the rest of his life was. But other people had recovered from the sort of thing he'd been through, or worse, so he presumed he could do the same.

It was only on the way back to Carol's flat that he realised he was wrong. He had one purpose in life. He was going to make sure that Aleksander Gjebrea would pay in some way for what he had done to Carol, and to Susie.

CHAPTER 13   HOMELESS

Anna was intrigued. Two months after Carol's funeral, she got a cryptic email from Bill telling her to meet him at the north entrance of the Tube station nearest to work. No time or date was given, but the message also told her to wish Carol a happy birthday.

She looked at the map to check. She thought The Elephant and Castle was probably closest to Bloq, but wondered if Kennington might also be a possibility. There wasn't much in it. She tried to picture the layout of both Underground stations and where their entrances were. She usually drove to work; travelling home after a shift in the small hours of the morning would have been next to impossible using public transport and she had a parking spot at both her flat and the nightclub, so it made sense to use her smart car.

She'd never used Kennington, but she'd driven past it once or twice. She knew that both the Bakerloo and Northern lines had station buildings at the Elephant and Castle and they were connected, although you had to walk the length of the Northern line platform to travel between them.

She checked on the travel London website and on Google maps. Kennington only had one entrance and it faced west.

The old brick building that was the Bakerloo line entrance to the station was on the north side of the Elephant and Castle, across the roundabout from the modern glass entrance to the Northern line.

She cursed Bill's paranoia about security, which at times was worse than her own, but she knew that he was right.

Every day she lived on the edge, waiting for the shock and terror of being discovered by the nightclub owner or one of his subordinates.

Anna remembered Bill saying that his daughter would have been twenty-six in August, but the exact date evaded her. At the back of her mind she knew that he'd told her, but she just couldn't recall it.

She emailed him back and asked him what day in August Carol's birthday fell on, but a reply came back almost immediately telling him that "Billie" was out of the office and would not be back until the 4th of September. She risked calling him on his mobile, but that went to voicemail and there was no reply to her terse text.

Suddenly, just as she was thinking she'd have to hang around on a London street outside a Tube station every day until the end of August, it came to her. Carol's birthday fell on the same day as the anniversary of Princess Diana's death. Alison had been a big Diana fan and Bill had told her, when they'd spoken about Carol and Susie at one of their meetings, that it annoyed Carol when her mum made such a fuss about Diana on Carol's birthday every year.

He hadn't given her a time, so it mustn't matter too much, which puzzled her, but he knew her daily schedule, so he'd have a rough idea of when she was likely to turn up. She'd decided to take the Tube that day and leave a couple of hours early to make sure of meeting him before work.

She'd been floored when Bill had contacted her about Carol's death. He'd apologised for ringing again, but wanted her to hear it from him before she read about it in the papers. When she could finally speak, she told Bill that she was on her way; that he shouldn't be on his own to cope with his loss.

But Bill had insisted it was too dangerous; he was pretty sure sometimes that he was being watched.

"They're keeping an eye on me, so I'm trying to act as they would expect me to and not arouse any suspicion."

"You've been to the police, though?"

"Yes, but that would be expected. The police were involved the moment she jumped out of that window."

"So what are you going to do next? What about the funeral?"

"It's all organised, but you've got to stay away. It's not safe."

"Oh, Bill. That's not fair, you were there for me at Susie's funeral."

"I know. And I would feel better with you there, but it just can't be."

"When will it be safe for us to meet up again? I'm not sure I can do this on my own."

"Don't worry. We'll work something out. In the meantime, keep in touch by email. I'll try and not use the phone. I've looked into it. If we open up one of these cloud services on our computers, we can both have access to any information that we store on it. Just make sure you have everything password-protected and hide any stuff on your PC using innocuous sounding folder names."

"I do that already. I've also got somewhere in the flat where I can hide physical stuff. There are a few bundles of papers and stuff behind the hot water tank in the utility cupboard, if anything happens to me."

That had been the last time they'd spoken, but the emails flew back and forth on a daily basis. She knew that Bill had returned to Scotland very soon after the post-mortem, insisting on accompanying Carol's body up to Glasgow with the undertaker while one of the firm's staff drove his car.

She didn't tell Bill, but she'd been in the office at the nightclub when Dhim came in with the paper for his boss. Aleksander always liked to read the *London Evening Standard* before the club opened. Everybody she knew read it; it was free, and was more commonly referred to as simply the *Evening Standard*. Dhim threw the paper on to her desk, and she could see the headline. Suicide at the Royal Free – Probe ordered.

There was a picture of Carol on the front page. She would have to wait for Aleksander to finish with it before she could read the article.

"That silly bitch threw herself out of window." Aleksander laughed. "What a fruitcase."

Anna was appalled at his callous indifference.

"No, wait, that not right word. Fruitloop or nutcase better, not fruitcase."

He and Dhim laughed together. They must have been relieved that she was dead, but all she could see was how amusing they found it. If she hadn't realised before, it was a sobering lesson in how little respect they had for the lives they had wasted.

-o-

Because Carol's mortgage was in joint names and the title was, too, Bill was able to put the flat on the market quickly, which slightly disappointed Anna. She thought he might have kept a London base and it worried her that he might eventually disengage from their pursuit of justice for his daughter, and her sister.

But she kept him up to date with her investigations at the club and she hoped that he was merely lying low at home, using her information to carry out background research on the nightclub, acting out a normal life until Gjebrea and his gang lost interest.

Her efforts to gather information that would incriminate Bloq's management progressed slowly. Fighting her impatience, she carefully dug into the organisation's files, unearthing a slow but steady trickle of material that, together with data she hoped to find on the computer system, would provide at least enough evidence to force the police to investigate Bloq and its owner in depth.

By furtively watching Aleksander's fingers on the keyboard, she'd been able to discover half a dozen of the passwords he used to access various parts of his business and personal records and she reckoned she would have full access within another few months, if she persisted.

She knew she also needed to retrieve his contact list from his phone, which was even riskier. Although they didn't seem suspicious of her in any specific way, they had a natural distrust of anyone they hadn't known for generations and who wasn't Albanian.

She was looking forward to seeing Bill again. Her sense of isolation had heightened when he'd left to go home to Glasgow and the constant threat of exposure left her exhausted and drained every night she collapsed into bed after a long shift at Bloq.

Almost sure of the day he'd arranged to meet with her, she emerged from the station entrance and looked around casually. She'd taken a circuitous route by Tube, changing trains a few more times than necessary to make doubly sure that she hadn't been observed. She wasn't surprised when she didn't immediately see Bill. She assumed he'd be watching her from somewhere to check that she was alone. Sometimes she thought that they were driven too much by their paranoia, but the consequences of making a mistake would be dire – for her in particular, but also for Bill.

Ten minutes passed and she began to get irritated; he's taking things too far, she thought. Doubts began to enter her mind; she was sure it was the correct day, but had she got the meeting place right?

He'd chosen well, though. It was a busy spot and there were a few people hanging about besides her. A young man nervously waited to one side of the station entrance, perhaps for a girl, and a huddle of Millwall fans congregated next to the subway steps prior to taking the Tube to The Den, to board the supporters' buses travelling to the rearranged evening away game at Barnsley. The noisy group gradually grew as newcomers arrived on a regular basis, some from the pub across the road.

Two beggars sat near the entrance. One was a woman of middle-eastern origin, by the look of her, squatting cross-legged on a mat in front of the café; the other was an older bearded man sitting on the opposite side of the station opening, wearing three or four coats, tied with an old belt. As she paced back and forth, she wrinkled her nose in distaste at the strong smell of urine and alcohol that surrounded him every time she came within a few feet of him. He occasionally mumbled something indistinct when she passed him and pointed to an old battered cap that sat between his knees.

As the minutes ticked away, she looked impatiently at her watch. The Millwall fans, their group fully assembled, made their way into the Tube station, chanting loudly, the sound echoing around in the narrow corridor leading to the ticket hall.

There was a lull in footfall in front of the station and she found herself alone, apart from the tramp and the begging lady. *I've got the wrong bloody entrance. He must have meant the Northern line.* It was one hundred yards away on the other side of the Elephant and Castle roundabout.

She went to go down the subway ramp to take her through the underpass to check out the other station when the old man let out something that was between a shout and a groan. She looked over at him and took pity on the poor soul, fishing in her pocket for loose change. Trying not to breathe in, she approached him and dropped a few pound coins into his hat. She glanced at the young woman ten yards away and turning towards her, decided that she couldn't give to one without the other.

"Thanks, Anna."

She froze. Trying to not make a sudden move, she turned slowly round towards the direction the voice had come from, expecting to see Bill poking his head around the corner, but there was no one there.

"Don't move, or look at me. Just listen."

It was Bill's voice but it was coming from the old man who she'd just given the money to.

"Go and give the Iraqi woman a few pounds. You were going to anyway. Then come back and stand next to me."

She did as she was told.

"What the fuck do you think you're doing? Isn't this taking things a bit far?" she hissed at him when she returned.

"I had to show you that I could be completely convincing as a down-and-out. I'll tell you why later. Go and buy me a cup of coffee. When you come back, give it to me and I'll give you a key and an address. When's your next day off?"

She couldn't resist a glance at him. *It's not Bill. It can't be.*

"I'm off on Friday. What time do you want me there?"

"Any time. I'll be there all day. Bring a briefcase with you. Dress like an estate agent, or similar. Now go and get me that coffee; milk and two sugars."

She went into the café next to the station entrance and bought two coffees. She gave one to the beggar woman, who nodded to her, and handed the second cup to Bill. He grabbed her hand to thank her; despite knowing it was him, she still almost pulled her hand away in disgust, so credible was his disguise.

When he did let her go, she felt something hard in her hand, which she coolly slipped into her pocket before walking away, still astonished at his behaviour.

-o-

Two days later, Anna found herself driving up the Walworth Road towards Camberwell, turning her head

211

away nervously as she passed Browning Street, the road Bloq was situated on. She parked just off the Camberwell Road and walked under the railway bridge into the top end of Pelier Street.

She looked at the piece of paper the key had been wrapped in. Bill had written the address inside it and she checked it against the numbers on the houses. *Number fifteen*. She was looking for number two. *Strange*. Pelier Street was short, with houses down only one side, and they were all odd numbers. On the other side, the railway which she'd just walked under ran parallel to the street. Sandwiched between the elevated track and the road were a series of yards, each with one or more railway arch lock-ups at the back. They were occupied by various small traders. The first one, the largest, was a garage offering *MOTs, servicing and competitive tyre and exhaust fitting*. The next yard belonged to a builder, and as she walked down the street she passed a plumber, a carpet remnant saleroom and small removal and storage company. The last one, which had to be the address Bill had written down, looked like a junkyard. Through the steel mesh fence she could see a variety of vehicles and metal objects of all shapes and sizes piled up right to the edge; in some places the fence bulged slightly where part of the metal mountain leaned against it. A small plaque next to the gates, which were also made of mesh but had solid galvanised sheeting covering their bottom halves, told her it belonged to J. Callan, Metalworker. *Even stranger*.

She opened her briefcase and took out a clipboard, which she'd thought might look authentic, and checked the imaginary details on the random printed sheets that were clipped to it.

She unlocked the padlock with the key Bill had given her and removed it from the hasp. Sliding the pin back, she opened the left-hand gate enough for her to step through, closing it behind her.

Inside the gates, she could see that although a large part of the yard was covered by the pile of scrap, there was a clearing that stretched from the gate to the two enormous wooden doors that filled the large arch.

An old camper van, its wheels missing, sat on its axles in front of the left-hand door, the metal pile almost engulfing it on one side. The right side of the arch had small door set into the large one, and the curve of the arch at the top was filled with wood planking, apart from a small fanlight in the centre.

In the only corner of the yard that didn't seem to be covered with scrap, there was a series of metal sculptures of various sizes, of the type popular in some modern houses, gardens and public places. One was obviously a large bird, perhaps an eagle or something similar, but the others looked more abstract.

The small door was locked and the key she'd been given didn't fit. There was a padlock on the large doors, so she tried the key in that, and it fitted. She opened the door that wasn't blocked by the camper van, looking around as it creaked loudly. The interior was dark, but there was a dim light at the back of the arch, which was much deeper than she'd expected. The intense blue flare of a welding torch almost blinded her for a second and even when she looked away, the blue flash lit the high-domed brick ceiling of the arch eerily.

As she approached, Bill laid the wand on the bench and swung the welding mask up from his face.

"What the fuck are you doing, Bill? First you're a stinking tramp and now you're some metalworking artist guy. Have you gone mad?"

"I've got a plan to nail Aleksander Gjebrea. This is where we'll be based and the metalworking is just a cover."

"What about the tramp thing?"

"You didn't know who I was and you had a good look at me. Neither would they."

"I don't understand."

"I can hang around the club and his other properties day and night; check through his bins and see who's coming and going. You on the inside and me on the outside."

"It'll be risky. If they catch you, they'll hurt you, badly. They might just beat you up for being a nuisance."

"You take worse risks every day. Now it's my turn."

She shrugged her shoulders, conceding he was right, and her face softened. "How have you been?"

Caught unawares, he looked at her, a sudden moistness in his eyes. She thought she could hear a slight shakiness when he spoke.

"I'm holding up. It's not been easy, but I don't have to tell you that."

"Bill, I'm so sorry." She took a step towards him and, self-consciously, he let her put her arms around him. He returned her hug, awkward and uncomfortable, unused to physical contact outside his immediate family. They stood for a minute, in the middle of the cavernous brick space, consoling one another.

Over the next month, Bill steadily became familiar around the area as a harmless and amiable Scottish down-and-out, uttering random phrases in a thick Scottish brogue like a man with Tourette's. It was a disappointment that he couldn't further disguise his origins by adopting an Irish or Welsh accent, or one of the English regional dialects, but he wasn't great at mimicking people and he definitely didn't think it would hold up under pressure if he was caught out, so he stuck with an exaggeration of his own native tongue. Every time he spoke, he imagined himself using Robbie Coltrane's voice.

"Breakfast!" he would shout, shuffling along Walworth Main Street past fast food outlets, or growl "Jack Russell!" at some poor passer-by walking their dog in Nursery Row Park. He slept rough a couple of nights, in doorways or on public benches, and sat around on pavements during the day, always with his cap strategically placed to collect loose change.

He tried to annoy folk as little as possible and made an effort to add a little humour to their day. He was always polite and moved on without fuss when asked by shopkeepers or the police.

On the whole, he was mostly ignored or, at worst, verbally abused by the residents of Walworth, but there were isolated acts of kindness, too. These were few and far between and they often came from unexpected quarters; when another homeless man shared a full baguette that was his bounty from a raid on the bins at the back of Subway in Walworth, Bill hadn't had the heart to refuse the gift, but it wasn't a meal that he found easy to stomach.

His preparation for each foray into the area as a vagrant was meticulous. Anna watched it for the first time a few weeks after her initial encounter with Bill's homeless character and was astounded again by his transformation.

The facial hair and durable make-up that aged him twenty years had been purchased at a theatrical supplies shop in Glasgow. The woman in the shop had shown him how to use a special glue to attach the long, matted beard and moustache securely and seamlessly to his face, blending the margins with the professional make-up sourced from the same place. The three layers of cosmetics that he applied were durable and waterproof, designed to stand up to the rigours of the warm, sweat inducing stage lighting of the theatre. It gave his face an unhealthy palior and the theatrical supply lady had shown him a clever trick of applying the final layer of make-up whilst scrunching up his face, which produced the convincing effect of Bill having dirty and leathery wrinkles when he relaxed his facial muscles.

Bill used hair gel to make his hair matted and straggly and Anna was disgusted when she watched him incorporating pieces of dried foodstuffs and other items in it for realism; the type of things that would naturally gather in the hair and beard of a man living rough on the streets.

He'd grown his hair long over the previous few months and had dyed it grey once a week to match his beard. He stained the beard a dirty yellow in places round his mouth as if he'd been a long time smoker and he would occasionally take a drag of a cigarette stub he'd picked up in the street; lit with a battered lighter he kept in one of his greatcoat pockets.

He added a few drops of yellow food colouring to a bottle of eyewash; applying a few drops to his eyes every day gave the whites an unhealthy jaundiced tinge.

Since Carol died he had deliberately lost weight, so he had a haggard, exhausted look; it hadn't been hard to reduce his food intake as he had no great appetite, so overwhelming was the grief that was with him from his first waking moment every morning to the last thing at night, when he would have to force his tired eyes shut to find some sleep; even when he did drift off, his nights were often restless and disturbed and very rarely satisfied his body's need for rest, or allowed a few hours of peace for his troubled mind.

He'd purchased all the clothes he needed in charity shops back home and adapted them by fraying an edge here, breaking the zip of a fly there and applying various disgusting looking substances to mimic the stains that he would have acquired from the harsh and unforgiving lifestyle that he was supposed to be leading. His boots and socks came from a similar source and were treated accordingly, to match the well-worn shabbiness of the rest of his apparel.

"Is it not horrible, smelling like that?" she asked him, wrinkling her nose in distaste as she looked at his completed transformation.

"It's not the worst thing in the world, but I have more sympathy now for the people who live this way permanently," he replied, "They suffer from the heat and the cold; from being miserable, hungry, sweaty and itchy; they get abused and insulted. And they don't get a few days off when they need a shower and a square meal."

"I couldn't do it. And I don't know how I'll cope when you start appearing around Bloq. Just make sure you don't take too many risks."

He showed her the battered old Nokia, with the SIM card removed, that he carried in a pocket of a waistcoat he wore as one of his intermediate layers and the charger he used with it when he stayed in a hostel, which he did from time to time to build up a picture of his life as a street person. It held a few photos, ostensibly of his "lost family", to justify his having it and he could take reasonable photographs with it if he needed it to. He kept the SIM card in the lining of one of his inner coats for use in an emergency.

"Just make sure you do your part," he told her. "It will all be worth it if we can see these evil bastards put away."

-o-

He achieved his authentic smell by applying liberal quantities of stale urine to his outer clothes, using a sponge. He collected it in advance in Tupperware containers, leaving it for a few days to brew. He also carried two flat half-bottles of whisky in his pocket, one containing the cheap brand indicated on the label, the other containing cold lemon tea which he brewed daily to match the colour of the whisky; he would take the odd swig of the real stuff, swill it around and let it dribble unnoticed from the corner of his mouth, but he would only swallow the alcohol free substitute from the other bottle. This gave him the smell and the look of a terminal alcoholic without Bill having to endanger his liver in the pursuit of realism. After a week he was so disgusted with the taste of the supermarket own brand Scotch whisky that he poured the contents away and filled it up with a nice Balvenie malt. Because it was too tempting to swallow the odd swig of the good stuff, he only did this on the hardest of days.

He'd taken a similar approach to his gradual withdrawal from his formal life in Glasgow. Deliberately drinking moderate amounts of alcohol during the day, but acting as if he was much more inebriated than he really was, he made his neighbours, his bank manager and his doctor believe that he was hitting the bottle as a result of his daughter's death. He also went out of his way to convince his cousin Archie, Alison's parents and a few his work colleagues, whom he "accidentally" bumped into one evening, that he was finding solace at the bottom of a whisky glass.

At the same time, Bill set about methodically liquidating all his assets, selling his house and cashing in all the pensions and savings policies he could, borrowing against those that he couldn't. When this was added to the healthy surplus he would receive from the rapid growth in value of Carol's flat, some ISAs and the modest holding of shares that he'd gathered over the years, he ended up with nearly three quarters of a million in cash sitting in four or five accounts, much to his surprise.

Withdrawing some of it as cash as quickly as he could without alerting the National Crime Agency or the Serious Fraud Office, he set about converting the rest of it into non-traceable saleable goods, bought with the credit and debit cards that he held. On a regular basis, he would sell some of these on; this would continue for months after he moved back down to London, eventually turning a large proportion of his accumulated wealth into neat bundles of paper money. These he kept in a safe in the Pelier Road Arch he'd rented for two years at a premium for cash up front, no questions asked, from a disreputable landlord with a swathe of rather downmarket properties on his so-called books. This also stored, in crates of various sizes, all of the high value goods that could be converted into cash at some point in the future. It felt very insecure, but he wanted to be able to disappear at any stage without ties that might make it possible to find him.

Anna came to the railway arch regularly, always parking the car a few streets away, or taking the Tube to

Kennington. Bill showed her the work he'd done to make his London base habitable. He'd fabricated a small timber frame and plasterboard cubicle at the back, large enough to hold a single camp bed, a small wooden wardrobe and a chest of drawers purchased in a charity shop on Peckham High Street.

Next to his sleeping quarters he built a larger booth to house a desk, a couple of filing cabinets, a colour laser printer on a stand, a metal storage cupboard and a large cork-backed noticeboard that incorporated a whiteboard area. The railway arch had a small existing toilet in the back corner, housed in an alcove set into the wall of the arch. It also contained a sink, but only the cold water tap was connected.

Bill added a shower cubicle with an electric shower and a water heater that supplied instant warm water to the sink. The addition of a two-burner camping stove, a small fridge-freezer and a microwave/oven combo to the lock-up meant that he was more or less self-sufficient and could cook simple meals for himself, and Anna, when she visited the archway.

He purchased a number of oil filled radiators to keep each of the living and working spaces warm, and kept a power card filled with cash for the electricity meter next to the doorway.

He'd completed enough metal sculptures for the place to be convincing as his workshop, so he packed away the welder and the angle grinder that he'd been using to make his steel figures, but not before he'd cut a hole in the back wall of the campervan and welded a steel frame into it. He fabricated a small aluminium door, covered it with a plasticised sheet and bolted it on to the frame. From inside the motorhome, it looked like an access hatch for a water tank or an electrical panel, but when it was swung to one side, the opening abutted on to a small wooden access door, identical to the one on the other side, allowing hidden access into the lock-up.

Bill took a crowbar and prised the corner of the mesh fence loose where it met the brick of the railway bridge abutment. This allowed him to sneak in to the yard when the gates were closed, although he had to clear some of the junk from the pile to give him a rough route he could clamber over.

He threw enough plastic bags, empty bottles and assorted detritus into the back of the campervan to make it look like a makeshift dwelling for his homeless alter-ego. After a few days on the streets, he would crawl back in through the gap in the fence, climb over the mound of scrap and into the motorhome. Anyone who spotted him would think that he was simply a homeless person who'd found a clever place to doss down, in a scrapped camper van.

He would lie on the old mattress for a while, in case anyone had seen him come in, then crawl through his hidden hatchway into the lock-up when he thought it was safe. He was quite happy that these precautions would stand up to all but the most severe scrutiny.

Once he was inside, he would luxuriate in the shower for ten minutes, bag up his smelly streetwear, put on his own clothes and stretch out on the camp bed for a couple of hours' kip.

Long before Bill had embedded himself in the community as the local vagrant, Anna had been putting into place her side of the pursuit of justice for Bloq's owner. She'd always been one of the first to arrive at work; as one of three keyholders, she would open up if Aleksander or Dhim weren't going to be in on time, which was fairly frequently. By the time Bill returned to London, they trusted Anna with more and more of the legitimate side of Bloq, which she could have just about run on her own.

Without drawing any attention, she'd gradually started arriving earlier than usual; she could have most of her admin duties done even before the other staff had arrived for their shifts, leaving her more time to work the front of house when the club was open for customers. Aleksander commented favourably about her attitude on more than one occasion, which encouraged her to extend the amount of time she spent in the club on her own.

Aleksander's passwords started to come in useful, although she still had a few to get for various parts of the system. As well as being able to search the network server for files that might help them build a case to give to the police, it also gave Anna access to the network configuration data that Bill had asked her to find. She managed to open up the broadband router settings in an Explorer window and photograph every page of it with her iPhone. She sent Bill the photos and deleted them from her phone when he confirmed that he'd received them.

It was made easier for her by the main computer server always being switched on and Anna having her own terminal in the office, which allowed her to gain entry into the system at any time. Security wasn't helped by the fact that Aleksander made the mistake of keeping many of his passwords in an encrypted file that she had, by a little slice of good fortune, managed to get the password for. He'd opened it one day with her standing right beside him, waiting for the access code for a utility site she was using to pay an account.

Despite giving the impression to the outside world that after Carol's death he had curled up into a corner, moping and drinking himself into numbness, Bill had been secretly busy, on several fronts. Besides sorting out his finances, he had enrolled on an online crash course in computer networking. As a result of his new-found knowledge, it was surprisingly easy for him to set up a virtual private network, or VPN, into Bloq's network. He gave Anna a series of entries to change on the router settings page which allowed him to have a direct gateway into the nightclub's computer system that he could access at any time from his laptop in the lock-up, simply by logging in to the VPN.

During his time at home, in between showing prospective buyers around the house, he'd also purchased a video editing suite for his laptop and made use of the tutorial that came with it to learn the rudiments of how to use it to view and modify video files. Once he'd set up the VPN on his return to London, he was pleased to find that, as he'd hoped, he could trawl through all footage generated by Bloq's CCTV system, which was network based and stored all its files on the server's hard disks.

By the end of September, he felt he was a familiar enough face around Walworth to blend into the background and he started to wander closer to Bloq. He was careful not to target the nightclub too obviously, going through the bins of neighbouring bars and restaurants in Browning Street and elsewhere in Walworth, but he eventually plucked up the courage to have a look through the glass recycling bin in the yard beside the nightclub, harvesting enough alcohol in ten minutes from the dregs in the discarded bottles to fill up a plastic container he'd started carrying specifically for the job.

He returned three days later, repeating his scavenging operation but also making a search of the other bins as well, collecting some tasty filled wraps, discarded as

223

surplus from a function the night before. He stashed them in one of the stock of carrier bags he carried in the pockets of the numerous coats he wore. While these layers allowed him to survive the cooler nights on the pavements and doorways of Walworth, they were stiflingly hot during the day and they added to the unpleasant cloud of odour that he dragged around everywhere he went. The whole outfit was held together incongruously by a black plastic belt around his waist, a counter to the deficit of buttons in his outer layers.

For a while, Anna had been desperate to smuggle out a few original documents, when she felt a photograph or copy wouldn't be enough to persuade the police to prosecute, but Aleksander had a policy of springing the occasional search on the staff when they arrived at the club, or when they left, to discourage petty pilfering and, more importantly, to stop any of them considering making freelance drug sales inside the club to supplement their income.

Now, with Bill around, they planned a dummy run to get a trial package out of the club, using him as the mule. On the day Anna specified, Bill hung around the church next door until he saw her put a blue bag into the larger of the two wheeled bins. He waited a good fifteen minutes then approached the yard where the bins were stored.

To avoid suspicion, on the off-chance that someone in the club was watching the CCTV feed from one of the two yard cameras, he rooted about in the recycling bin, extracting a few bottles and emptying a dribble of spirits from each into his own container. Then, opening the lid of the next bin along, he pretended to search for food and extracted the blue bag that Anna had placed in it. He quickly stuffed it in between two of the layers he had on. He was just about to close the bin when he saw a hat that had been discarded. He quickly slipped it in beside the package and shuffled up the road towards his scrapyard home. He was sure that he had seen Aleksander wearing the hat the week before and when Anna visited Bill's lock-up the next day she confirmed that it was her boss's.

"You see the bird shit on it? That happened on his way into work the other day. I was going to get it cleaned for him, but he told me just to put it in the bin."

"I'm going to wear it, just to piss him off." Bill laughed.

Using the bin proved a successful way for Anna to smuggle important material out. She didn't even have to do it herself. As long as she knew Bill was there, she could put papers into the waste bin and give it to one of the other employees to take out to the wheelie bin and Bill would do the rest.

When he wasn't hanging about Browning Street, Bill explored the nightclub's computer system via the VPN from the safety of the lockup. He had to be careful that nobody was using the computer system when he was logged on, as there was always a chance that another user would notice unusual activity. Even when Anna sent him a text to tell him the club was closing, there was no guarantee that Aleksander or Dhim wouldn't return after she'd left. He would log on and carefully monitor network traffic; if this was quiet, he would remotely access the CCTV control program and check the club's cameras to make sure that it was definitely deserted. Only then would he feel safe to drill deep into the file system for the information they needed.

There were infrequent time-outs with the VPN and while this caused him nothing more than the odd minor inconvenience while surfing Bloq's computer records, he wanted a more secure and steady connection to guarantee access should they ever need to get stuff out in real time, so he sat Anna down the next time she was at Pelier Street.

"We need a better connection to the computer network at the club," he said.

"OK. How do we do that?" She took a look at his face. "Wait a minute; you want me to do something tricky, don't you?"

"Yes, but we can make it fairly safe. Well, as safe as we possibly can. The first part is easy. You need to get me a photograph of the network switch from all angles – it will be somewhere near the server."

"And where's the server?"

"How would I know? I've never been in the back of the club."

"I can't get you in there."

"I know; you don't have to. The server will probably be somewhere in the office, more than likely in a cupboard. It looks like a slightly larger version of a desktop computer, but with no keyboard or monitor."

He showed her a picture of a typical server on Google, and also what a switch might look like.

"I think I know where it is. If not, I'll find it. So I just need to take photos of it?"

"Yes, including a few pictures of where the cables plug into it. Once we have that, we can add an internal wireless access point. I can use a Raspberry Pi with a wireless dongle."

When she looked completely perplexed, he explained that the Raspberry Pi was a small modular computer that geeks liked to experiment with, but with a bit of imagination it could be used for all manner of tasks.

"This is one of the simpler things you can ask it to do. It's already set up for wireless networking; I just need to connect it directly to one of the network connections within the switch and it'll transmit or receive from another wireless connector that we can set up somewhere close by."

She looked puzzled. "Two questions. How do you think I'm going to be able to take this thing apart and add a bloody raspberry, or whatever you call it? And where are we going to put another wireless access point to connect it with?"

"You don't have to take anything apart. I'll buy an identical switch and make all the necessary modifications. It's fairly simple, really, as long as it all fits in the case. All you have to do is take it in, exchange it for the existing one, and then put the old one in the bin. I'll get rid of it for you."

"That sounds too easy; there must be a catch."

"They've never searched you on the way in, so that shouldn't be a problem. The switch has up to forty connections, but it doesn't really matter which order they go in, unless they're labelled, in which case, you'll have to change one cable at a time. It'll only take a few minutes. You can switch them over long before anyone else is there and I'll check it out and see if everything is working OK."

"And the other wireless thingy?"

"We can hide it in your car and connect it to a mobile phone or a 4G dongle via a netbook or perhaps another Raspberry Pi. That will give us a direct data link to here. You'll just have to leave the car in the Bloq yard whenever we need access. You'll more often than not be in the club when we need it, anyway. Remember, we still have the direct network link. This is just a backup; insurance, if you like."

It didn't quite go to plan. They hadn't factored in Aleksander's unpredictable timekeeping. Bill had tested the modified network switch which, although significantly heavier, looked identical to the one Anna had photographed at the club. It worked well with the wireless access gear they'd rigged up in her smart car, hidden in the void under the passenger seat.

On the day Anna summed up the courage to switch the two black boxes, she arrived early as usual and laid out enough work on her desk to convey the appearance of a normal day's routine.

She was halfway through transferring each of the thirty-four individual cables from the old switch to the new one, methodically plugging them in to their sockets in the same order, even though Bill had said it wouldn't have made any difference, when she was interrupted.

She hadn't heard a car pull up, so she jumped at the sound of a key rattling in the lock of the door at the end of the corridor, just outside the office. Bill had explained that the switch was the junction box that allowed all the computers and peripheral devices such as printers, CCTV cameras and point of sale equipment to talk to each other and connect to the Internet, and also to the server, the central store for all of Bloq's data.

Anna knew that with half the cables disconnected parts of the network wouldn't work, but she didn't know which parts. She shut the cupboard door hastily, trying to make as little noise as possible.

When Aleksander entered the office, she was sitting at her desk poring over the following week's staff rota, waiting for her computer to boot up. She watched anxiously as the log on screen appeared and she typed in her password.

"Hi, Anna. How things are today?" Anna had always been convinced that he could probably talk perfectly good English and that he cultivated his Eastern European accent and idioms to give him and the nightclub an exotic veneer, but she was so terrified that he would discover the partly completed substitution that she hardly registered it. When she spoke, she was sure he would notice the shake in her voice.

"Fine. Just finishing the rota for next week. What brings you in so early?"

"Had meeting. Finished sooner than expected. No time for going home."

He walked over to his desk and switched his workstation on. She had a fifty per cent chance that it would connect, but if he tried to access anything else on the network, the odds of her being discovered would rapidly increase. Anna clicked on the icon that should have opened up the club's stock control module, but a pop up window appeared. *No network access. Please contact the network administrator.* She wasn't dismayed. It was one less unplugged connection for Aleksander to find. Nevertheless, she knew that the longer he was in front of the monitor, the more likely it was that she would have to bail out, and quickly.

In desperation, she remembered one of the bartenders telling her the night before that there was an issue with one of the beer taps. She looked over at her boss, who was checking his emails with no apparent problem, so she knew that the router, the gateway to the Internet, was also hooked up.

"Aleksander, we have a problem with the draft Budvar. The boys say they tried to fix it last night, but they asked if you could have a look at it this morning."

"OK. No problem. I just finish emails first. What did they say problem was?"

"They think there's a problem with the python system, or it's a black keg," she said, referring to the refrigeration unit that ensured that the draft lagers and beers reached the taps at the right temperature. A black keg was a barrel that had a leaking internal valve tube. In both cases the beer or lager could come out flat, or like Creamola Foam at the other extreme. She desperately wanted him to leave the office and check it out, so she tried to appeal to his sense of self-importance.

"The boys said you fixed it when it happened the last time."

"OK. I finish reading emails then go look at it."

He sat for another five minutes and, as he left to attend to the Budvar problem, she let out a long sigh. She couldn't risk closing the office door; it would appear more suspicious if he returned and besides, with it shut she would have had less chance of hearing his footsteps along the corridor if he did come back before she was finished.

Almost shaking, she carefully unplugged each of the remaining cables and slotted them into position on the new

230

switch, glancing over her shoulder every few seconds and listening intently for the sound of anyone approaching. When she'd finally swapped all the network cables over, she unplugged the old switch and dropped it into the small bin sitting by her desk, followed by a couple of trade magazines that had been lying on her desk.

She was just about to sit back at her desk when she realised she hadn't connected the power to the new switch. Her stomach lurched at the thought of the consequences of being so careless, but she had time to correct her error before he came back. Returning to her desk, she opened up a window in Internet Explorer and was relieved to see her familiar Google home page load up.

A quick check of the other parts of the Bloq network confirmed that they all seemed to be working normally. She removed the bag from the waste basket and tied it up, just as Aleksander entered the office.

"Here, give to me. I go out to car now, anyway."

Before she could object, he'd taken the bag from her and strode out of the office. She listened, her heart in her mouth, as the door into the yard slammed behind him.

-o-

The first time Bill was beaten up, it came as no surprise. He had been spending more time scouring the bins of Browning Street than anywhere else, concentrating particularly on the yard shared by the nightclub and the church next door, an irony that Bill always found amusing. The bouncers had chased him away a couple of times, but Bill was persistent and eventually they lost patience with him. It happened about a week after he'd retrieved the bag containing the discarded switch that Anna had lost a night's sleep over. The November days, and especially the

231

nights, were getting colder, but he made a point of returning to the club a few hours after having been told emphatically to leave.

He had just climbed into the glass recycling bin when Aleksander and Josef drew up in the Mercedes.

The nightclub boss got out and walked round the back of the car to the bin that Bill occupied.

"What we have here?"

Bill looked down at them vacantly, acting the part but dreading the inevitable outcome.

"We chased fucker already today, boss. Now he get proper warning."

"Wait. Maybe he want say something."

Josef grabbed the lapels of Bill's coat and, with no apparent effort, lifted him from the bin and slammed him to the ground in front of his boss. He placed his right foot on Bill's chest.

"Well? Have you something say to Mr Gjebrea?"

Bill, badly winded despite the thick layers of coats, mumbled something indecipherable.

The man who'd caused his daughter's death stood over Bill. He grinned at his colleague then looked down at Bill, without any sign of recognition.

"Sorry. Did not hear what you say."

Bill muttered again, still gasping with the pain in his back and chest.

"Jusht lookin' furra wee drink," he slurred.

Aleksander Gjebrea leaned closer to Bill's face to say something and recoiled in disgust as the smell reached his nostrils.

"Fuck. Bad fucking smell." He gagged a little and spat on to the tarmac to clear the acid taste from his mouth. Annoyed at showing any sort of weakness, he was quick to turn it into a show of strength.

"Hold him."

He walked towards the rear of the yard. A hose reel was mounted on the wall, attached by a short loop of pipe to a tap; the staff used it to clean the front of the club and the pavement outside with a pressure washer on a weekly basis, although there was also a basic nozzle on the hose itself that could be used for quick clean-up jobs of vomit or discarded food.

Aleksander turned on the water and pulled out enough hose to reach Bill.

"You need bath to stop stink so much."

Laughing, he squeezed the trigger and a freezing jet of water hit Bill in the face, forcing itself into his mouth and up his nose, hurting his eyes with the pressure. He spluttered and coughed, turning his face away in reflex, the bitterly cold water causing intense pain within his nasal cavity. He panicked as it reached his throat, causing him to gasp.

The hose was then turned on the rest of Bill's body, soaking the thick layers that kept him warm. It was tolerable, but very uncomfortable, and he knew that he'd be in danger of hypothermia if he had to spend the night outdoors.

After a good soaking, the jet of water was returned to his face and although he was ready for it this time, it still came as a shock and induced a surprising degree of terror in him. Bill remembered hearing about waterboarding, a method of torture used in the wars in Iraq and Afghanistan, and thinking at the time that it couldn't be as bad as all that. Now he understood.

Bill was worried that his make-up or fake facial hair might start peeling off. Fortunately his torturers became bored with the brutal treatment they were handing out and turned the hose off.

"Next time, if happen again, we use pressure washer. We advise stay away." Josef aimed a kick at Bill's midriff, punishment for causing the bouncer to have wet shoes and trousers, a complaint that he wouldn't have dared mention to his boss.

Bill lay for a while, snot pouring from his nose, gasping and wheezing, before staggering to his feet and stumbling down the road, shivering violently as his body cooled. A few pedestrians looked puzzled at his bedraggled appearance and the trail of dripping water as he made his way back to Pelier Street as quickly as he could manage. No one stopped to offer him help.

-o-

Bill spent the majority of the next week at the lock-up, mostly in bed after developing a painful and debilitating chest infection the day following his soaking. Anna called round twice, arriving the second time with a course of antibiotics that she'd somehow managed to obtain.

"I'm a nurse. I know how to get things in hospitals. You only have to look the part and be confident," she told Bill, when he asked her how she'd acquired them.

He made use of the time she was around to show her how he downloaded the footage of his ordeal at the club from the CCTV storage folders on the server.

"Whoever installed the system must have set it to automatically delete all the CCTV files after four months, except for the three external cameras. They seem to have their footage retained for much longer, maybe even since the system was installed. Good job it's black and white, and fairly low res, or it would have filled up the server."

Anna had a sudden thought.

"Can we look back to find clips of the times when the other tramp got beaten up and when the boy caught dealing drugs was taken away?"

Bill tried to answer, but a fit of coughing prevented him. When he did manage to reply, he wheezed and croaked as he spoke.

"Shit, I should have thought of that. Can you narrow the dates down? Otherwise it'll take forever to find them."

She smiled, despite the serious nature of their conversation. "It was a few days after Stephen Gately died, I remember that."

"Who's Stephen Gately? And which incident are you talking about?"

"I told you; the young drug dealer was bundled into the van at New Year, this year. Stephen Gately was a member of *Boyzone*." She blushed. "They're a guilty pleasure of mine, my favourite group as a teenager, so that's why I know that the tramp was beaten up the October before last. You can Google the exact date."

Bill did as she suggested and looked at the CCTV clips, starting from the 11th of October, 2009, the day the boy band member had died.

Anna's accurate recall paid off. It didn't take Bill long to find footage of both events. Although they had no material from inside the club, and they couldn't see much of the boy's face, the way they'd bundled the youth into the Bloq van was highly suggestive.

The recordings of the tramp being beaten up, from both yard cameras, were very good, although Aleksander Gjebrea wasn't in either of the clips.

The footage of their assault on Bill was also excellent and this time they'd caught the nightclub boss on film. They discussed sending the police all the material they already had.

"They'll not be able to do much with the young guy's case. There's no body and we don't even know who he is. He could be sitting at home watching the TV, for all we know," said Anna.

Bill had to agree with her.

"And even if we did manage to provoke the police into investigating the other case, at worst they'd get a few months," she added.

"Unless the old guy died, but that will be difficult to check out. I think we should carry on as we are; try and track down the young drug dealer and keep up the pressure at the club," Bill said

The second assault on Bill took place just after he'd plucked up the courage to sniff around Bloq again, a few weeks on from his near drowning.

"Boss, that crazy old fuck at bins again." Josef, one of Aleksander's security men, had poked his head round the office door to make the announcement.

Anna cringed. She forced herself not to react.

Aleksander was sitting opposite her, at his desk. He turned to Josef, frowning.

"You make stupid fucker disappear. Me, I not have time spare for dealing with it."

Anna risked watching the yard feed on her monitor, with Aleksander sitting a few yards away, probably looking at the same scene. She watched the screen with horror as Aleksander's two security thugs came out of the building together. Josef got into the van and reversed it back, turning it slightly as he did so, to form a small triangle at the rear of the yard, bounded by two walls and the van body.

Dhim grabbed Bill, who by this time was cowering by the bins, and dragged him behind the van. Anna had to switch feeds at this point. Fortunately, the cameras were positioned so that they could cover almost every part of the yard and Aleksander had swivelled the second yard camera around to get a view of the action in the corner, now concealed from anyone passing by on the street.

She forced herself to watch as they knocked Bill to the ground and commenced giving him a thorough going over.

She flinched with every blow, especially as she could see her boss smiling at the spectacle unfolding in front of him.

She'd initially been worried that they were going to give him a one-way trip in the van, but as it went on she realised that they would have done that right away, had it been their intention. Anna was glad to see that Bill had his arms wrapped round his head to offer a little degree of protection and she hoped that his thick layers of clothing would help pad against major damage, but even so, she was almost at the stage of leaving the office to go and phone the police when the two assailants decided they'd done enough damage.

Bill lay for a considerable time. Anna checked the CCTV feed occasionally, when she could risk it, and eventually she saw him get to his feet using the wall as support and hobble painfully out of the yard and along the street.

After work that night she drove along the most likely route that Bill would have taken on his way back to the railway arch and, although she didn't go in, she was pleased to see a chink of light through the crack in the door; she heaved a sigh of relief that he'd made it back.

She visited him a couple of times over the next few weeks. His injuries were more severe, but strangely they had less impact on his psychological health than his previous attack. Whether he was becoming accustomed to being a victim of violence or he was more terrified of water than pain, he didn't know, but although it took him longer to recover physically, mentally he was over it in five days.

She'd tried to fuss over him, to atone in her own mind for having stood by and let it happen without lifting a finger to stop it, but Bill wouldn't be cossetted, preferring to plough all his efforts into their crusade against Aleksander Gjebrea's organisation.

"Bill, I think I might have something."

It was well after New Year and Bill was back on the streets braving the bitter cold again. Anna had been going to email him to say she would be calling round to Pelier Street but, seeing him shuffling along the street when she arrived at Bloq, she put a message in one of her blue rubbish bags in the bin, knowing that he'd be watching.

The next morning, she drove to Camberwell and walked the half-mile or so to Bill's yard.

She was glad to see he was just Bill again; no dirt or smell. As much as she knew it was necessary and admired his courage and determination, she hated being in contact with him when he changed into his homeless alter ego. They greeted each other warmly, but she wasted no time in telling him about her latest discovery.

"There was a member of staff, a barmaid, who went missing in strange circumstances. The police investigated, but Bloq was only ever involved as part of the routine inquiries."

"When was it? Did you know her?"

"No, it was before I started. About three years ago. I was checking through the staff records, probably in desperation, to see if there was anyone who had left Bloq who we could contact to see if they would be willing to go on record about Susie, Carol or the others."

"That might work, but I'm not sure too many would be willing to stick their necks out."

"You're probably right, but I did a search for every employee that had left in the last five years, making a list of them as I went along. I contacted a few of them, but they either knew nothing or were too scared to talk. Then I got a bit worried that one of them might call the nightclub and say something, so I thought that I'd do a bit of online research for those on the list instead and leave talking to them for later."

She took a big breath.

"When I did a search for this barmaid, Tanvi Gujar, I found this:"

She showed Bill a printout of a newspaper clipping from The Docklands and East London Advertiser, Thursday 11th December, 2008. He scanned it quickly. *Tanvi Gujar, 32, a resident of the Ocean Estate in Stepney, missing since last Wednesday. She lived alone and was reported missing by her parents when she failed to turn up at a family function on Sunday. Staff at Bloq, the nightclub in Walworth where she worked as a barmaid, say that she failed to come in for work on Friday after her normal two days off and they had been unable to contact her. Tanvi's parents phoned the police on Sunday, after she didn't arrive for her normal weekly visit to the family home in nearby Hackney.*

Vishal Gujar, Tanvi's father, said that the family were very worried about their daughter and that it would be very out of character for her not to phone if she wasn't going to be there. He asked her to contact them and appealed for any information that anybody might have that would help to find her.

Bill put the printout on the desk. Like all the other documents connected with the nightclub, it would be scanned and added to the rapidly expanding pile of files

240

stored in the elderly but functional filing cabinet next to him.

"What happened? Did the police ever find anything?"

"I don't think so. There were a couple of paragraphs in the paper the following week and a few lines the week after that, but it just seemed to fizzle out. I can't risk asking around at work and I haven't contacted her parents yet."

"Do you want me to try and talk to the family?"

"Thanks. That would be great. I'd be slightly nervous about someone at the club hearing about it if I went." She looked relieved at his offer. "What do you think?"

"If this is connected and we can get the police interested in investigating her disappearance, it could be a way to get Gjebrea and his gang put away for a significant amount of time. At least we have a name now."

"It's still not enough, Bill. In reality, we're no closer to getting the police to take the whole Bloq thing seriously and if we go to them with little dribs and drabs, they're just going to get fed up and fob us off. We need something more concrete."

Bill turned away from her and stared at the noticeboard they'd started populating with key points from their investigations. Anna sensed something in his manner.

"Bill?" she said.

He turned to look at her. "There is one way to get them."

"What?"

"We film them killing someone."

She looked shocked. "Who?"

"Me."

She stared at him, annoyed and confused. "What are you talking about?"

He sat down on the edge of the desk, facing her.

"We have up to five people that have gone missing or have been damaged in some way by Aleksander Gjebrea or his organisation. There are no witnesses and no forensics linking him to any of them. We probably have enough evidence to cause him and the club a lot of grief, but nothing that will cause him significant harm."

"So?"

"If we can provoke him to assault me again and I disappear, but leave enough forensic evidence at the scene, we can make it look like he's killed me and there's a good chance that he'll be arrested and convicted of murder, even in the absence of a body. He's already assaulted me twice and we have that on film."

She didn't immediately reject the idea.

"It would be a hell of a gamble. You could get badly hurt. Look at what they've done to you already."

Bill knew that it would be impossible to control the level of violence that he would suffer if he provoked them for a third time, and that there was a chance that he really would die in the process, but he was willing to take that risk. If the worst happened and he died, it would make it virtually certain that Aleksander Gjebrea would be found guilty and Bill could reconcile that with the sobering thought that he wouldn't be alive to see it, although he wouldn't risk saying that to Anna.

"There are a few things we can do to stop them if they go too far. I'll carry one of these panic alarms. We'll think of some way that you can call for help without risk to yourself if I'm getting too badly beaten."

"I'm not sure. I would never forgive myself if something happened to you, after Carol." A thought seemed to flash through her mind. "You'd have to disappear permanently afterwards. You could never go home again. And the police would have your DNA. What would you do?"

"It wouldn't necessarily be like that. They would have the DNA of a homeless person. My DNA has never been sampled for any reason and it's unlikely that it ever will be. No one would know about my connection with the victim, apart from you. Anyway, I don't care if I do have to make a new life elsewhere. There's nothing for me at home but memories."

A profound sadness compressed Anna's chest as she realised Bill had just expressed the nub of the situation they were both in.

"I need to sleep on it," she said, as she walked past him and out of the door.

CHAPTER 14   BLOQ

It was a week before Bill spoke again with Anna. He saw her briefly from a distance when she arrived at the club, on one of the days he was back on the streets of Walworth; he wanted to maintain his presence in and around the nightclub without being in their faces.

But it was back within the safety of the arch that she gave him her answer, having asked a question first.

"If I don't agree to this, will you do it anyway?"

Bill could see that she was annoyed and considered his reply carefully.

"Yes, I think so. But I would have to do it differently, and with less chance of me walking away and more chance of them escaping justice."

"Don't try and apply pressure. I've already made my mind up." She looked at Bill for a second then shook her head gently. "I'm doing this against my better judgement. I'm in, but with a few reservations."

"What are they?"

"First. If it looks like you're in any danger of serious harm, I'm calling the police."

"OK. And second?"

"Once we do this, we hand all the stuff we've got to the police and get the hell out of it."

"I can live with that. I don't think there will be much to be gained beyond that, anyhow. And I'd be happier with you well away from that place into the bargain. You've been riding your luck for too long now. I've ordered a couple of panic alarms and I want you to carry one, too. Anything else?"

"No, that's it. How do we do it?"

Over the next few hours, Bill went over his plan in fine detail. Anna picked holes in some of it, but between them they resolved most of the issues that concerned her. After they'd hammered out the last kink in the plan, he asked her what she thought.

He could see she was still angry at him and he waited patiently for her to get it off her chest in her own time.

"You planned this all along, didn't you?"

Bill didn't try and deny it. He had too much respect for her to lie. When he said nothing, she took it as an invitation to carry on.

"The whole tramp thing; it never was just about gathering information, was it?

"No, that's not strictly true. There was an element of that, as well."

"Don't give me that crap. You've been deliberately provoking Aleksander and his thugs, haven't you? And the access to Bloq's computer system, the VPN and me putting that switch thing in; that's to make doubly sure we could get video evidence while they're half killing you. Is that right?"

"I did have it in the back of my mind that it might come to this, but I honestly didn't have any definite plans at the beginning. Everything we were doing was useful; there was always a chance that it would throw something up and we wouldn't have had to do it this way. I'm glad you're on board, though."

"It's fucking dangerous and stupid, but it might just work. I wish there was some other way, but for the life of me, I just can't see how."

-o-

Bill and Anna worked hard for the next few weeks on a number of fronts. Because she continued her shifts at the club her time at Pelier Road was limited, so most of the work fell to Bill. He purchased a van and made a loading ramp that could slide out when the doors were opened.

At Anna's request, Bill set up a plausible financial background for a private nursing agency in her name and she made several visits to a number of medical consumables suppliers, ordering dressings, syringes, needles, bandages, wound irrigating fluid, latex gloves, cotton wool and the like. Bill collected the purchases, suitably attired as a van driver.

Anna also made several forays into local hospitals, wearing her old uniform, and procured a number of items that she couldn't source legitimately, antibiotics and prescription only painkillers, among others. She felt a bit guilty, especially about the Schedule 4 drugs she'd taken; she knew that somebody would get their fingers rapped for that, although there was a possibility that the small amount she'd taken might prove easy to pass off as wastage, hidden in the large volume that was used on a day-to-day basis in each of the departments she visited.

In between spells on the street, Bill used the van to do a number of jobs integral to the success of their plan; he visited a number of second-hand shops until he found a roll of carpet big enough to wrap a human body in, and he purchased a large plastic water tank from a local builders' merchant. He also bought a set of bolt-cutters, a few pairs of gardening gloves, and a couple of greenhouse trickle heaters, which he fitted inside the tank when he got back to the lock-up. He sat it just inside the door leading out into the yard.

Looking up a list of butchers who traded out of Smithfield, the largest meat market in the UK, he phoned round and found one who could supply what he was looking for.

He managed to park the van in East Poultry Lane, a covered access road between two of the Smithfield Market halls, and found the stall of E.H. Rawlston & Sons, Master Butchers, in Buyers Walk. They were happy to accept cash for his purchase of one roasting hog and a roll of commercial grade cling-wrap with dispenser, and they even lent him one of the apprentices with a barrow to transport it back to his van.

On his return to the lock-up, he reversed the van up to the arch doors and unloaded his purchase. He tied the pig's carcase up by the back legs above the tank he'd prepared earlier and used nearly the whole roll of cling-wrap to make an air-tight seal around it. After lowering the carcase into the tank, he switched on the heaters and closed the lid, sealing it with the remaining cling film.

Bill broached the question of the aftermath of the anticipated attack first.

"Anna, on no account can you get medical help for me, even if I'm dying. And if I don't make it, leave me in the lock-up, remove anything that might tie you to this place, and get the hell away. Phone the cops once you're safe. And never do anything that would mean you'd be asked to give a DNA sample, because there will be traces of you here, no matter what you do. Get rid of the van. Make a new life somewhere."

Anna stared at him, stunned.

"Bill, I …" Too upset to talk, she turned away so that he couldn't see her tears.

Bill continued. "I know it sounds hard, but if things get that bad, I at least want it to be worth dying for. It's not that I want to die, but if I do, it can't be for nothing."

Anna recovered her composure. "You're asking a hell of a lot of me, but I'll do as you ask," she said reluctantly. "In return I want you to at least try to take your safety seriously. Don't be a fucking martyr."

Bill could hear real anger in her voice and a determination that he should survive. He was touched that she should care, but having both been hit by the same devastating loss and working together so closely, it was no surprise that they had come to care about each other as much as they did.

-o-

Bill and Anna had started to carry simple panic alarms, which emitted a loud piercing noise when activated; Anna could easily justify carrying it in her handbag if she was challenged; many women carried them, fearful of the threat of being mugged or sexually assaulted.

For Bill, being found to be carrying a personal alarm would be harder to explain, so he secreted it in one of the pockets of a money belt which he wore low down under his two pairs of trousers. Although this made it harder to activate, he doubted whether anyone would want to delve too far into his pile of clothes to search him. Only he knew that, underneath all the grime, he was clean; the smell of his outer clothing would convince anyone frisking him that things could only become more disgusting the closer they got to his skin.

Bill made Anna download a panic app for her phone. He set it up to dial his number when she pressed the virtual button and also send him an email and a text message. He'd started keeping his emergency phone, with its SIM inserted, in the other pocket of his money belt it so that, although it was always in silent mode, he could feel the vibration in his groin if she called. If he was at the lock-up, it would also alert him on his laptop.

Because the Nokia he carried with him on the street was old and outdated, he couldn't install anything as sophisticated as a panic alarm, and because it was essential that he could contact Anna in an emergency, he stored her phone number as the first phone book entry and constantly repeated the series of four or five presses that were required to dial it. While this proved easy in a stress-free environment, it didn't work so well under pressure, with the phone buried deep in his clothing.

As a result, he made a point of dialling her number for a few seconds every time he went out on to the streets and practiced pressing the two keys that redialled the last number.

He kept a more modern smartphone back at the Pelier Street archway, on a similar untraceable pay-as-you-go SIM-only contract, and he used this for all the day-to-day calls that he made when researching and preparing their plans to make Bloq's owner face justice.

It was this phone he used to call Tanvi Gujar's parents. His obvious empathy won him a meeting with them, at their home in Hackney. When he visited them, he recognised the desperation to know what had happened to their daughter that he'd seen in his own eyes when he'd looked in the mirror every day before he found Carol.

He pitched his questions from the angle that his daughter had gone missing in similar circumstances and she'd had a flat in Bethnal Green, not that far from where Tanvi had lived.

He looked around. The family home was one of the few two-storey houses in the area and it was immaculate inside. Photographs of their children dominated one wall of the living room. They had a son and two daughters and he could trace their lives in pictures from childhood, spanning the baby and toddler stage, through primary school, family holidays, grammar school and sixth form college. There were pride-filled university graduation photos of them all, and for Tanvi's sister and brother, there were also wedding pictures and family portraits with the Gujar's grandchildren.

There were fewer photographs of Tanvi as an adult, but in the ones there were, she looked a stunning girl. When he gently probed the older couple, they said that Tanvi was a good daughter, but she'd never married. He'd known there would be a "but"; and he sensed that being single wasn't the only one, and although they did their best to avoid airing their other frustrations with her, the pride with which they spoke about her siblings' accomplishments and social status was in direct contrast to their obvious disappointment with the lifestyle that their older daughter had chosen.

"She's always been very independent." The way her father said this, Bill knew it wasn't meant in a positive light.

"When did you first become worried about her?" Bill asked, trying to steer the conversation around to her disappearance.

"She wasn't the type to phone every day," Mrs Gujar replied. Her displeasure was just as evident as her husband's. Bill was beginning to see why the girl only visited once a week. He felt a little annoyed by their obvious bitterness, but knew that it probably came from equal measures of guilt, and anger at their daughter for putting them in this situation.

"Did the police ever find any trace of her? I only have the newspaper clippings to go by."

"No, they found nothing. Every so often they phone and update us, but I think they are inundated with missing people. Unless there is evidence of any wrongdoing, they are limited in what they can do."

"Did the paper never follow it up?"

"They contacted us a few times in the months after Tanvi went missing, but we didn't appreciate some of the questions the journalists were asking; things about her private life and where she worked."

Bill began to realise that, as genuine as their grief was over their daughter having gone missing, their sense that somehow it had brought shame on the family had limited their efforts to publicise her disappearance. He wondered why they had agreed to speak to him, but when he asked them, he understood immediately.

"We hadn't read anything about your daughter, so we thought that you would look into the matter discreetly, without involving the papers," said Mrs Gujar.

Bill knew that he was unlikely to get anything useful from them, but before he left he asked about her work.

It was a mistake. Instantly, they looked suspicious and when her father replied, it was in a much more guarded manner than previously.

"Why do you want to know about her work? What does that have to do with anything?"

"I just wanted to know the full background. My daughter worked in a bar as well. I wondered if there could be a connection."

Mrs Gujar was now staying silent, letting her husband deal with Bill.

"She never talked about her work and we knew very little about it. It wasn't our choice for her, you know. I mean, she was a university graduate." He stood up, signalling that the conversation had gone far enough.

"Mr and Mrs Gujar, I'm sorry to have intruded on you. I hope you find your daughter. If I get any information that might be useful to you, I'll contact you."

Walking back to his car, he deliberated whether it would be of any benefit to talk to her brother and sister, but the near certain prospect of a unified family reluctance to talk about Tanvi made him decide against it.

However, as he drove off, he realised that he had learned something from his visit. There was a strong possibility that she'd gone missing on the same day she'd left work.

In light of this, on his way southwards, he swung right under The Green Bridge, which lifted the Mile End Park across the road of the same name, then took a left into Ernest Street; Anna had given him the address from the personnel records at Bloq. He found Jubilee Heights and, following one of the residents through the security door, jumped in the lift up to the sixth floor.

Two of the neighbours told him they'd moved in long after she'd gone missing; most of the others were out, or were unwilling to answer their doors, but he managed to speak to an older couple who remembered her fondly. He asked the old man who answered the door when they'd last seen her.

"I'm afraid it was so long ago. Can you remember, Bessie?"

The old lady shook her head, vexed that she couldn't be of any assistance.

"She was a lovely young lady," he continued, "and so nice to us; not like some of the other shower we have in here." He nodded towards the other flats on the landing.

"Thanks, anyway. It would have been useful to know when she'd last been at the flat before she was reported missing. If you think of anything, give me a phone." He wrote his number on a piece of paper the old man gave him.

-o-

Bill was having a rest before getting ready to transform himself into a street person, a process he was beginning to hate and that took him almost an hour from start to finish. He hadn't expected them to call, so he was surprised to

253

hear Tanvi's elderly neighbour's voice when he answered his phone.

"My wife remembered something. She thinks Tanvi's flat might have been empty for a few days before the police came round; she gave the police the spare key to get in; we had one, you see. And when they opened the door there was quite a pile of mail inside. She's been racking her brain, you know."

"Listen, thank your wife for her help and if there's anything else, be sure to let me know."

"Oh, we will. We both miss having her as a neighbour. Thank you for making an effort to find her. I don't think anyone else did."

-o-

"There's nothing to say for definite that any of these people were harmed by Aleksander Gjebrea or his people, but I think they might have been; it would be a bit of a long shot if they were all just coincidence."

Bill spoke quietly to Anna as they sat in the railway arch, sharing a pot of pasta while they discussed their latest discoveries. She thought for a moment before she replied.

"I've a gut feeling that they've all been victims, as much as Susie and Carol. I think we need to put all the information we have into some semblance of order, ready to give to the police when we send them the footage of your crazy assault stunt."

"It's mostly ready to go. We just need to check it all over and pack it into boxes. It's all on disk as well. When they beat me up again, it's imperative that we get hold of the footage and delete anything on the nightclub's server that doesn't match up with our story, or it will all be for nothing. And I think it's crucial that we make it look like they've tried to cover it up. That's where you'll come in. I might not be fit to do it."

"I know. Show me again exactly what I have to do. I don't want to screw up."

-o-

Even in its cocoon of cling film, they could both smell the rotting flesh of the pig when they loaded it into the back of the van. It was wrapped in the old carpet that Bill had bought, and tied up with brown sisal string; they loaded it up early as they knew that it would get worse if it had to remain there for a few days. Everything else was in place.

Bill had been impressed by how quickly Anna had learned how to download CCTV files from Bloq's computer system and do some basic editing on them. She also practiced uploading some of the files she'd edited back on to the server at the nightclub, although they were careful to delete these training files immediately, even if the chances of anyone noticing them were slim.

-o-

Anna found it hard to concentrate on work once she knew that Bill was going to be in the vicinity of the club and she hoped no one would notice how often she visited the office to check the CCTV. She'd deliberately delayed doing the month's VAT return to give her an excuse to be at her workstation so she could keep an eye on the car park area where she knew the assault would occur. Her greatest worry was that Aleksander would tell his men to throw Bill into the van and take him elsewhere to deal with. When she'd voiced her fears to Bill, he had smiled and applied a liberal extra squirt of his stale piss, telling her that they wouldn't want to have something smelling like him in the back of the club's van.

Bill's first evening trying to provoke them was uneventful. He loitered around for a while, rooting around in the bins, but if anyone from the club noticed him, they didn't react. Anna kept an eye on him whenever she could and thought that he was very convincing, even down to the unmatched pair of gardening gloves he wore to keep warm and the impression he gave that he was in pain or distress.

To give himself the best chance of survival and to keep his strength up, he'd decided not to spend the nights on the streets, and he returned to the railway archway by a different route each time.

That first evening, when he returned to his base without being attacked, he found it difficult to relax. The long wait until the next evening seemed to drag on forever, although Anna visited him first thing in the morning. She was disgusted to see him dressed and ready to go despite there being a few hours before he would have to make his way in his seemingly aimless manner to Browning Street. Even though he still had to apply that day's quota of street aftershave, the unwashed clothes were revolting and she asked him why he was ready so early.

"It takes a while to put all this stuff on, you know," he snapped at her.

She thought he was very subdued and she noticed him shivering even though it wasn't particularly cold, especially with all the layers he had on.

"Are you OK?" she asked him.

She thought his smile seemed a little forced and she could see from his eyes that he was hurting. She knew that life on the street must be hard on him, physically and emotionally.

"Yes, I'm fine. It's the waiting I don't like. I just wish it was over."

Bill's voice sounded strained to her; she knew the shadow of what awaited him in the car park of a South London nightclub must be weighing heavy on his mind, but she'd never seen him so deflated; this was the man who had scoured the brothels of the capital for months, desperately searching for his daughter. As she tried to think of something to say to console him, she noticed that he was holding his left arm at a strange angle.

"Let me see that arm. You've hurt it."

He blustered briefly, saying it was nothing, but as a nurse she was going to have her way.

He reluctantly gave her his arm to examine and winced when she manipulated his shoulder. She examined the rest of his arm carefully then questioned him about the computer system in the nightclub to distract him; while he answered, she returned to probe his shoulder with her fingers. He forgot for a moment that the area she was exploring was supposed to hurt.

"The glove, Bill. Take it off."

He stiffened, pulling away from her.

"There's nothing wrong with your arm. Let me see your hand. When did you injure it?"

"Anna, I didn't want you to know about it. I figured you'd think it was part of the damage inflicted by your boss

257

when you found out after they attack me. I knew you'd be angry if you found out before that."

She took hold of his arm again and, very gently, she removed the glove from his hand, trying to ignore Bill flinching while she eased the thick leather from each of fingers in turn. The last one came away too easily and she could feel that the leather fabric of the glove was hard and sticky.

"What the fuck have you done?" she gasped.

"I cut it off." He bowed his head, not able to look her in the eye.

"For Christ's sake, why?"

"Finding a body part will make the police take it much more seriously. Anyway, I have another nine," he joked, weakly.

Anna exploded. "It's not fucking funny. I'll need to take a close look at that. You could end up seriously ill."

He thought it was maybe an overreaction considering he was currently trying to arrange for her boss to beat the crap out of him, but he held his arm out again for her and she took it gently, examining the dressing Bill had inexpertly applied to the stump of his little finger. It was mostly caked in dry scab, but there was a constant seep of fresh blood oozing through the grubby bandage and dripping on to the floor.

"I'll get some fresh dressings for this. How long has this one been on?"

"Since I did it yesterday, after you left."

She opened one of the two small medical cases that she'd purchased and Bill had collected, and picked out a number of items. She poured a little wound flushing solution into a plastic sterile bowl and sat in front of Bill. She carefully cut the soiled dressing away from what was left of his finger; he'd cut it off just above the first joint from the tip and the end was a swollen mess of clotted blood, bruised flesh and splintered bone.

"What the hell did you cut it off with? You've made a fucking mess of it. You're out of your mind."

"A set of bolt-cutters. They're in a plastic bag in the fridge, with the finger."

Bill's face was pale and a stab of guilt briefly ran through her. *He's doing this to make sure Susie's killer is punished. Just be there for him, for fuck's sake.*

She washed the wound in the bowl and injected a little local anaesthetic, before crushing a couple of small, persistently bleeding blood vessels with a pair of haemostats. She applied some Intrasite Gel and a sterile wound dressing, and bandaged what was left of his finger with a skill that Bill had understandably been unable to master.

She helped Bill get his glove on and gave him a strip of antibiotics, telling him to take one morning and night.

"Thanks. I knew you'd be upset."

"You didn't really think it through. It marks you out if Aleksander or the police ever look for you."

"I never thought of that. I just wanted to give the police every reason to assume I was tortured and killed."

"And it *will* do that, but at what cost?"

"It's done now," he said. "We can keep it until we're ready to go to the police, then you can put it where they'll find it."

Anna knew it was pointless to go on at him. He was right; there was nothing she could do about it.

-o-

If it was bad for Bill, the anticipation every evening of the violence that Anna expected to witness against him was just as unbearable for her; maybe even more so, because she knew that she had the ultimate responsibility for ensuring Bill's survival.

The club was packed the following night and no one took any notice of Bill. Strangely, although Sunday was quieter and Bill gave them plenty opportunity to react, they ignored him and he left for the arches in the early hours of Monday morning frustrated and with his nerves frayed to breaking point at the lack of response from Bloq's owner or his hired thugs.

By Monday evening, Anna had strung out the paperwork as long as she could. The club was dead and with only a handful of punters in, Aleksander sent Josef home at eleven, telling him there was no point in having three of them on the door. Dhim's younger and slightly less intimidating colleague left, grinning at the unexpected bonus; he knew that Aleksander would still pay him for the full shift, but he would surprise his girlfriend and maybe get a ride into the bargain. It still left the third member of Bloq's security team to assist Dhim through to closing time.

Aleksander, looking round at the bar staff standing idly talking to each other, suggested to Anna that she should also go home because he was *quite* capable of looking after everything in her absence and she deserved an early night for all her hard work.

Panicking at the thought of leaving Bill unprotected, but unable to think of any reason to refuse her boss's offer, she collected her coat and bag and made for the car park. Driving down Browning Street, she glanced in the mirror and noticed a dark shape crossing behind her towards the nightclub. She slowed down and, as the person passed into the circle of light from the security lamp at the side of the club, she was horrified to see that it was the unmistakable figure of Bill, making his way into the yard for another attempt to provoke Aleksander.

The traffic was heavier than she was used to; normally, she made the journey between two and four in the morning, when she encountered little congestion. She crossed over the Walworth Road, running a red light in her panic and nearly hitting a pedestrian crossing the road on the green man. As she drove down Manor Place, she saw the gesticulating woman framed in her side mirror. *Not that I can blame her.*

She followed the road round to the right when she reached the park, driving the route she took nearly every day on autopilot, and it wasn't until she reached the junction with Kennington Park Road that she realised she was making for her flat, when she should have been heading for Bill's base in Pelier Street, where she had access to the Bloq computer network and its CCTV camera feeds. *I'm a fucking idiot.* While she sat in the queue of cars waiting to turn at the lights, she tried to phone Bill and warn him that she wasn't at the club. It took three changes of the lights for her to get through them, but Bill wasn't answering his phone and, while she knew there could be a good reason for this, it worried her. She pulled over to the side of the road, even though it was a bus lane, and fired off a text to Bill, telling him that she wasn't at work and wouldn't be at Pelier Street for half an hour at least. She'd worded it carefully to avoid the risk of her being identified if they found his phone and she knew the text wouldn't show her own name as the sender. A cyclist shouted at her and an irate bus driver sounded his horn as she pulled back out of the restricted lane and she anxiously scanned the side of the road for a bus lane camera.

Her best hope was that he would get the text and keep away from the club until she was back in front of the CCTV feed, but she had no way of knowing if he'd received it.

The two and a half mile journey to the Pelier Street yard, which she would normally do in ten to fifteen minutes at the end of her shift, took just under half an hour, but it felt like a lifetime. She didn't even bother parking the car discreetly, two streets away, as she normally did. Abandoning it at the kerb outside, she fumbled with the padlock on the gate and nearly broke the key in the lock of the small door, before finally sprinting across to the back of the arch and pressing the power button on Bill's laptop.

Like everything else since she'd left the club, the computer seemed to be in slow mode, taking an age to start up, but once it did, she had almost immediate access to the CCTV cameras at the club. She tabbed through each one, starting with the cameras covering the yard. There was no sign of Bill and the van was still there. She nearly cried with relief, but as she sat watching and the minutes ticked by, she began to wonder if she'd been premature in assuming that meant Bill was safe and healthy.

She checked the screens inside the club. On the camera feed in the foyer she could see Dhim standing at the front door, talking to a couple of women. They looked as if they were remonstrating with him and she would have liked an audio feed, just out of curiosity. On a hunch, she switched to the camera outside the main entrance and discovered the source of the argument: a young man was being sick against the wall of the nightclub, supported by his friend, who was barely able to stand himself. Josef's understudy stood by, making sure they didn't try to enter the club. As she watched, the two women were gently ushered out by the more intimidating of the two doormen and by the look of it, were asked to move their two inebriated male companions along. Despite her worries about Bill, she smiled. *A normal night at Bloq.* It was pretty much a rule not to let hammered punters into the club, especially near to closing time. They spent very little and usually caused more trouble than they were worth.

She worked her way through the remaining camera feeds inside the club and located Aleksander talking to a group of young women. She guessed they were on a birthday celebration, or perhaps a hen night. She wanted to shout at them to keep their distance from him, but even on this low resolution video feed, she could see that most of them were responding, as many had before, to his slick charm.

She returned to the yard scene and watched for a while. Nothing moved. *Fuck, Bill. Where the hell are you?*

She flicked from screen to screen, desperately trying to convince herself that Bill hadn't already been dealt with and wasn't currently lying in a heap in the back of the van, severely injured or even dead.

Just when she'd decided to jump in the car and head back to the club, working out in her head what sort of excuse she could give to Aleksander for her unexpected return, she caught a glimpse of a movement at the corner of the screen, where she could just see the edge of one of the bins.

Bill had told her that she should never interfere with the direction the cameras were pointing, in case there was someone at the club watching, but she wondered if she could risk zooming in on the bin area, using her mouse to work the small control panel at the bottom right corner of the screen; she figured that no one apart from Aleksander or Dhim would bother and they were both occupied. Hovering over the onscreen button to pan the camera round to the right, she nearly jumped out of her skin when the bin lid opened and Bill suddenly filled half the screen, as he attempted to climb out. A bottle flashed as it slipped from his grasp and, although she couldn't see or hear it hit the ground, she could imagine it being loud in the deserted car park.

The picture altered from the ghostly grey that the infrared camera generated in the darkness to much more natural, but still monochrome tones in the sudden brightness of the security light now illuminating the yard. She clicked the small icon that allowed her to watch all twelve screens at once, even though they lacked detail in that mode.

The noise, or the light, started a cascade of events that Anna followed on the grid of camera feeds. The doorman standing outside the club's front door glanced around, probably seeing the light spilling out of the car park, and walked briskly to the corner to see what had triggered it.

He returned to the front door and disappeared from the screen briefly before reappearing in the next frame along, inside the foyer. Anna watched as he spoke to Dhim, who must have told him to stay at his post, because he moved back towards the door and reappeared outside.

She followed Dhim from screen to screen through the club. When he got to the bar, he looked around but couldn't see his boss. Anna enlarged the camera view where she'd seen him talking to the group of women earlier, but he wasn't there. She saw Dhim talking to the bar staff before going through the door at the back of the bar. She switched back to the thumbnail view and could see that Aleksander had gone to the office and was sitting at his desk. She selected full screen mode for that screen and watched as Dhim spoke to his employer, who fiddled with his computer, presumably scanning the same CCTV feeds as she was. She flipped back once more to the multi-screen format, observing that Bill was now slumped in a heap against the bin. By the time she glanced back at the office feed, the two men had gone, but it only took a number of seconds before they appeared together in the car park, striding toward Bill.

She selected the tick box on each of the screens showing the car park and clicked on the multi-view button again. She now had feeds from the two yard cameras filling the screen, but one of them was pointing out into the street. Not quite sure that no one else would be watching, she took a risk and panned the camera around until it settled on Bill and the two men towering over him. A third man, probably the other doorman, parked the van across the car park, then stood at the entrance to stop any curious clubber trying to see what was going on, or from coming to Bill's aid.

She felt sick but she made herself watch, knowing that it might be the only way to save his life. She took her phone from her bag and placed it on the desk, checking the reception and the battery level.

The two men, her boss and his thug underling, stood in front of Bill, who sat slumped against the bin. She couldn't imagine what he was feeling, knowing what was coming; it was unlikely they would repeat last month's moderate beating after he'd failed to get the message. She could see them talking to him, and via the camera at the back of the yard, she was almost able to make out the cold smile on Aleksander Gjebrea's face. As her eyes flicked from one screen to the other, she watched Bill's face suddenly alter, a distinct look of terror instantly replacing the sad, drunk expression that he'd tried to maintain. She wondered what they'd said to him, but as she followed Bill's gaze, a chill seemed to grip her and she closed her eyes as the bile rose in her throat. In his right hand, held loosely by his side, Aleksander Gjebrea was armed with a baseball bat and she knew with a cold certainty that unless she called the police immediately, there was only a slim chance that Bill would survive. She picked up her phone to dial, but stopped halfway through.

An icy calm settled on her and she put the phone down. *He decided. I can't go against his wishes*. But she promised herself that she would stop it if it went too far.

She forced herself to look at the screen while Bill was dragged to his feet by Bloq's resident hard man. She was shocked when Aleksander lifted the bat behind him and swung it in an arc, almost like a golfer, finishing with a sickening sudden halt between Bill's legs. Bill folded in two and, as the second blow caught Bill on his left leg, he collapsed onto his side.

Anna's hands came up to her mouth as the bat rose again and again, targeting a different area of Bill's body each time. Even at the start, when Bill's arms were up trying to protect his head, she counted a couple of blows that came frighteningly close to connecting with his face.

Suddenly the screen froze. She snatched the mouse and tried to cajole the laptop back into life. A message appeared. *Connection error – retrying in 30 seconds.* She clicked on the little network icon in the notification area and selected the VPN option, pressing connect. *Nothing. Fuck.*

Bill had explained to her how to use her mobile to connect the laptop to the wireless access point, or WAP, that they'd planted in the nightclub just for this eventuality, but even as she started to go through the process he'd shown her, it suddenly hit her that it wouldn't work. Her car wasn't parked beside the club, and without the wireless receiver and the mobile network data card, she wouldn't be able to use their backup method of accessing the CCTV feed. *Fuck. Fuck. Fuck.*

She picked up her phone again. She just couldn't take the risk with Bill's life and surely what she'd seen so far would be enough for the police, as long as she could download it at some point.

This time, she'd actually dialled 999, but she quickly hit the button to end the call before anyone answered when the laptop screen went suddenly blank, then opened up with the two yard camera CCTV screens side by side.

Except there was no one there. She could see the front wing of the van and the bins; there seemed to be nothing else, then on the first screen, just past the bins, she noticed a foot sticking out. Glancing across at the second screen, she could just make out a shape lying almost in between two bins. The image was too indistinct to see any movement that might indicate that Bill was still breathing, but when she looked again at the first screen, she thought that the position of the foot was slightly different.

Praying that the connection would be maintained long enough, she searched through the appropriate directory on the Bloq server to find the video files covering the time of the assault. Her shocked mind working in automatic mode, she downloaded them and returned to the live feed, looking for Bill's two attackers.

She found Dhim in the foyer, ushering customers towards the door as closing time came and went. The doorman outside was organising the last few taxis that were necessary for the remaining cluster of clubbers who were making their way home.

Her eyes sliding from screen to screen, she finally located Aleksander at the bar. He'd singled out a rather attractive woman, one of the group that Anna had seen earlier. She thought that she might be in her late twenties or early thirties. As the rest of her friends straggled out towards the exit, she held back and, as Anna watched, her boss guided the woman through the bar and the office, heading for the door to the flat upstairs. On the way, she saw him pick up one of the mobile radios and speak briefly into it. She assumed he was telling his head doorman to close up the club and head home.

She stared at the screen in hate and disgust at his callous behaviour, but switched to the screen showing the main door. A couple of the woman's friends were talking to Dhim. He smiled and shrugged, holding his arms out. She could just imagine him telling them not to worry; that she was old enough to look after herself and that she was quite safe with Aleksander. He made the standard gesture with his hand that indicated that they could phone her if they were worried and that seemed to mollify them.

It's not tonight you need to be worried about.

After the last of them left, followed by the staff whom he checked perfunctorily on the way out, she watched Dhim lock the door and make his way back through the club, switching out the lights as he went. When he appeared in the office feed, she saw him cross over to the door leading to the stairs and open it, but he didn't go through. Instead, he stuck his head around the door for a few seconds before closing it. She presumed he had shouted up to his boss to tell him he was leaving and that the club was empty. There was no sign that he'd received a reply.

She followed him from screen to screen as he left the club by the back exit; he didn't even glance in the direction of the bin. Jumping into the van, he swung it round and exited the car park before driving off in the direction of the main road.

Anna knew Aleksander Gjebrea well and she could confidently predict that he'd be occupied for at least a couple of hours. She grabbed a couple of pairs of rubber gloves from the box, went out and started up the van, then slowly eased it out into the street past her parked car, so as not to alert any of the people in the flats opposite. Her return journey to the club took half the time of the earlier one and as she turned into Browning Street, she switched off the lights and slowed the van to a crawl. She knew that Aleksander wouldn't be able to see if the security light came on, but she didn't want to take any chances. When she reached the club, she got out and gaffer taped a piece of cardboard over the van's rear number plate, before reversing it into the car park as slowly as the vehicle would go, easing it close to the wall where the floodlight was mounted.

She held her breath until the roof of the van scraped under the light, but the infrared sensor beam wasn't wide enough to detect any heat from the exhaust pipe and, because the body of the van now blocked it, she knew she would be able to work in the dark, unnoticed.

She pulled on a balaclava, strapped on the small head torch that Bill had put in the front of the van, and turned on the red light beam that allowed her to see in the darkness, but would be discreet enough not to be noticed by anyone nearby.

Barely able to bring herself to look, she approached the bin area, her breathing fast and sharp, her hands trembling. Bill's foot was in exactly the same position as it had been when she left Pelier Street and her chest tightened as she moved cautiously round the bin to catch her first full view of him. He lay in a shiny pool that she knew was blood, despite it appearing black in the red light of her head torch. His legs and arms didn't look as if they were where they should be and his face was almost unrecognisable; his hair and beard were matted with congealed blood and his jaw seemed to be slack and twisted. The swelling over the bridge of his nose and around his eyes made it impossible to make out where his eyelids were. She braved the horrific smell of his stale urinary cologne, the alcohol and the metallic odour of blood to lean close to his face and listen for breathing. At the same time, she reached into the sleeve of his nearest arm and, trying to put the slimy blood-soaked under layers and the crunch of his broken wrist bones out of her mind, she felt for a pulse.

Nothing. He's dead. She moved her fingers around to make sure – it was difficult to be anatomically correct when the bony landmarks of the wrist weren't in the right places. Just when she was going to give up, her fingers felt the weak thrill of a very faint pulse; at the same time, a long slow rasping exhalation of air came from Bill's mouth. She couldn't see his chest move beneath the thick layers of his disguise, but she had enough evidence that he

270

was alive to make her act quickly to get him to safety, even if she didn't think he had much chance of making it.

From the back of the van, she removed a lightweight stretcher with small wheels at one end and laid it on the ground next to Bill. After opening the back doors of the van fully, she pulled out the two long pieces of wood that Bill had fitted on rollers – when they were fully extended, the guides they were sliding through locked them into place, forming a narrow ramp from the ground into the back of the van.

She desperately tried to roll Bill onto the stretcher, but it took her three attempts and he ended up lying at an awkward angle. Her nursing training told her that this wasn't the way to handle a seriously injured patient with possible spinal damage. When she finally managed to straighten Bill on the stretcher, she used the straps and buckles at each side to secure him on to it. She crouched and grabbed the loop of tape at the top end of the stretcher and, placing it over her head, she straightened up as much as she could, taking the weight of the stretcher across the back of her neck, lifting the end where Bill's head was off the ground.

Pulling backwards towards the ramp, she dragged the weight of Bill and the stretcher on its rollers, until she could slide it on to the bottom of the sloped timbers. Reaching into the van she grabbed a short coil or rope lying on the floor, tied it to the head of the stretcher, and passed the other end through a ring screwed on to the floor at the top of the ramps; she fed the other end back down to the foot of the ramp. By pulling on the rope while pushing and guiding Bill with her legs and body, she inched him up the slope.

Halfway up, she lost control of the stretcher and its bottom half slid off the side of the ramp. She tried to lift it back on, but it threatened to overturn so she decided to lower it back down to the ground and start again. She looked at her watch. She'd already used up twenty minutes.

She got him halfway up the second time when the same thing nearly happened again, but she just managed to keep the stretcher half on, holding it precariously in position until she recovered enough breath to haul it back on to the middle. Forced to rest again after her exertions, she had to steel herself to continue by looking at Bill's badly beaten face and listening to his rasping breath. It took her another thirty-five minutes to get Bill into the back of the van and she collapsed on top of him as the stretcher crested the top of the ramp and slid along the floor. The rope had been useless to her once the top end of the stretcher had reached the ring in the floor, so she'd had to manhandle his full weight as best she could, her feet slipping as she struggled to lift and push a cumbersome weight nearly double her own; it left her exhausted and she still had a couple more tasks she needed to complete before she could leave.

She put on a fresh pair of gloves and gave Bill a shot of morphine, then, from the sticky dark pool of congealed blood next to the bins where Bill's head had been lying, she scooped up a handful and tried to remember all the places Bill had told her to smear it on to; the wheels of the bins, some of the pointing on the nightclub wall, inside the keyhole on the back door of Bloq and in behind the down pipes where they emptied into the drain. This ensured that, no matter how thoroughly they cleaned up the yard, there would always be somewhere the police could find some of Bill's DNA.

She shifted Bill's stretcher to one side and slid the two ramp sections back into the van before shutting the back doors and sliding the side door open. Climbing into the van again, she coaxed her tired muscles to help her drag the now rotting pig, wrapped in its cling-film and carpet, towards the opening. She took the Stanley knife from the small red metal toolbox on the floor of the van and reached inside the end of the roll of carpet, slashing the polythene in two or three places. She repeated this at the other end, nearly gagging as the heavy smell of putrid flesh, released from its shrink wrap, reached her nose.

She climbed through the gap between the seats and manoeuvred the van backward and forward until the open side cargo door was level with the pool of blood Bill had been lying in. She jumped over the seats again and, giving the rolled up pig a final shove with her foot, she managed to push it halfway out, one end on the ground, the other still lodged in the van's doorway.

A sudden blaze of light briefly blinded her; the infrared beam must have been triggered by the heat of her body, or the van's exhaust emissions. She made one final half-hearted attempt to push the pig out of the door, but gave up, squeezing over the seats for a last time and driving off, watching in her wing mirror as the roll of carpet with its rotting contents fell to the tarmac.

Trying not to race the engine too much, she turned right instead of left, knowing that taking a more circuitous route back to the lock-up would confuse Aleksander if he heard the van and checked out the CCTV footage before she could get to it. She stopped after one block and vomited at the side of the road. With no time to dwell on how she was feeling, she quickly checked on Bill, slid the side door closed, ripped the cardboard off the number plate and jumped back into the cab; getting stopped by the police for something stupid wasn't part of the plan.

Reaching the yard without any more setbacks, she reversed the van in the gates and opened the large archway door to allow her to carefully squeeze the van through and park it inside the arch. She closed the door behind her and, instead of crumpling in a heap, as she felt like doing, she opened the rear of the van and pulled out the ramp before sliding Bill down on to the floor.

If she'd known how bad it would get, or how long her attempts to save Bill's life would take her, she would have been too daunted to start. And despite her exhaustion, she knew she had other critical tasks to complete that couldn't be put off if Aleksander or his gang weren't going to expose her part in their plan. In between cleaning his wounds, stitching those that needed it, splinting his many fractures and setting up a couple of intravenous lines to give him saline and plasma, she had to fire up Bill's laptop, download the CCTV files and upload the quickly edited ones to Bloq's server, minus the footage of her collecting Bill's broken body and dumping the pig carcase.

Her mind and body screamed at her to lie down and shut her eyes, but she was determined not to cave in, knowing that she would struggle to get started again if she stopped now, even for a moment.

As it turned out, she wouldn't get the chance to sleep for a further twenty-four hours.

-o-

"Anna, can you come to office. I'd like a word."

She clipped the radio back on to her belt. *What the fuck has he found?* Since she'd arrived at the club, Anna had numbly gone about her work, exhausted and still trying to come to terms with what had happened. She was nearly sure that she'd deleted all the video that could incriminate

274

her in any way and although she'd made a mental list of all the tasks that were necessary to make doubly sure that Bill's sacrifice wasn't in vain, she could barely function and was terrified that she'd forgotten something.

Aleksander motioned her to sit down opposite him. "Anna, we have problem. Already, I think you know about."

The chill of fear spread through her body. Aleksander smiled and she steeled herself to act normally.

"Sorry, boss. I'm not with you. What do you mean?"

"Two parties booked one night. Next Thursday."

Anna's mouth hung open. There was no immediate sense of relief, but as her tired brain slowly registered that her activities of the previous night hadn't been discovered after all, she forced herself to concentrate on what Aleksander was saying and make some sort of intelligent response.

"Y-yes," she stammered. "I knew there were two parties. One can have the private suite."

"Not good. I promise both of them to have small suite when first talked about using Bloq."

"Sorry. I didn't know. Can we ask one of them to change dates?"

"I leave with you. You sort out and tell me when is done. Don't like when customers not happy. OK?"

She nearly smiled, but managed to stop herself. She promised that she'd sort it out and made to leave, putting the task into a compartment in her mind that she'd return to when she could hold two thoughts together.

"Take that bin out when you go. And get someone wash down yard. Must have been fight last night and someone sick. Bad fucking smell. I sometimes wonder what staff do for earning wages."

She grabbed his waste bin from him, hoping that his bad mood had something to do with the confusion he must be feeling over the morning's strange discovery.

Emptying the wastebasket into the wheeled bin in the yard, she could still smell the strong odour of the rotting pig and see the pool of Bill's blood. She swallowed the bile in her throat and went to find one of the doormen, passing on Aleksander's instructions to hose down the car park.

Still, she knew where the bat was now. She'd spotted it in the bin when she'd opened it to empty Aleksander's rubbish. *Still has the fucking bloodstains on it.* She needed to remove it from the bin and hide it somewhere; securing it somewhere safe was one of the key things on her list. She couldn't risk trying to take it away from the club so she busied herself around the place looking for a suitable spot to conceal it while desperately wishing that her shift was over and she could leave.

Her chance came when there was a fracas in the foyer of the club, around midnight. Aleksander and his three bouncers dealt with it in their usual efficient manner, firmly escorting the three men and two women involved out into the street, where their quiet but menacing persuasion sobered the protagonists enough to make them go their separate ways home, grumbling at the wrong they'd been done.

All this took ten to fifteen minutes, which was long enough for Anna to carefully extract the bat from the bin, using a cloth to hold it, and hide it in at the back of the club's store. She dropped it down behind a pile of unused

276

fittings that should have been disposed of years ago. She judged by the dust on them that they had been there a while and were unlikely to be disturbed in the near future. Back in the office, she located the last CCTV video file on the server and deleted it. It was unlikely its absence would ever be noted.

Relieved to have one less thing hanging over her, she contacted the disgruntled customers who had been double-booked and persuaded one of them to move to an alternative night, offering them the minor incentive of some nice Cava as a goodwill gesture. She told Aleksander she'd sorted it just before she finished her shift and left for the Pelier Street railway arch, dreading what she would find.

CHAPTER 15   2, PELIER STREET

When Bill awoke, the pain had subsided to a dull ache but it spared few parts of his body. He vaguely remembered drifting in and out of vivid and frightful dreams and drug-blunted semi-wakefulness. For the first time he felt fully conscious and he tried to assess what damage had been done to him. He couldn't move his arms. He could feel them, but any attempt at movement changed the dull ache into a sharp, focussed agony. He knew that they had some form of dressing on by the prickly, itchy heat he could feel along their length. Despite this, he could move his fingers carefully without precipitating any serious pain in his arms, which gave him a bit of comfort.

Encouraged, he wriggled his toes experimentally, gratified to discover that they all worked. Straightening his right ankle gave him no problem, but when he tried to do the same with his left, it wouldn't move at all and any attempt to push against whatever was immobilising it led to more pain.

His eyes had adjusted to the dimness and he was relieved to realise that he was not in a hospital, as he'd first assumed, but in some kind of tent; a cloth ceiling sloped upwards on both sides, held up by some sort of thin rope or wire, acting as a ridge. Opening and closing alternate eyes, he found that the vision in his left eye was better than in his right, which was fuzzy at best, but both eyes had small strange blobs that seemed to float slowly across his vision on a regular basis. As he rolled his eyes backwards and tilted his head the small degree possible, he could just make out the familiar dark brickwork and he realised he was back in the lock-up under the railway arch. *So she got me here after all*. He was mostly relieved, but a little part of him wondered how his refusal to allow a doctor's involvement would impact on his chances of recovery from what he vividly remembered as by far the most painful and frightening event of his whole life. Then he recalled why he'd chosen to suffer and he braced himself as the familiar dark wave of his sense of loss flooded over him once more. Tears misted his already limited view and he had to fight to control his breathing as the full weight of his daughter's suffering hit him anew.

He understood that he'd had some sort of medical attention; he remembered occasional flashbacks when he'd surfaced momentarily from his heavily sedated state, aware that he was being nursed and, although he couldn't see her, he knew it must have been Anna. He was completely restricted, presumably in splints or casts to immobilise fractured bones in his arms and legs, and he was on some kind of powerful pain relief or sedation that had kept him in a crazy, fitful limbo for a length of time he had no way of judging.

As his jagged breathing settled once more, he tested the movement of his head and found that, with considerable effort he could lift it and rotate it from side to side, although it did cause the dull headache that he'd barely noticed to intensify significantly. Trying to fully open his eyes proved to be difficult, but he had vague memories of one or two brief periods of semi-wakefulness in the days, or possibly weeks, preceding this first period of lucidity, when he had been unable to open his eyes at all.

As he mentally assessed the rest of his body, identifying the more painful parts one by one, he realised that there was nowhere that had escaped damage from the savage beating he'd endured and he hoped fervently that it had all been caught on video. He'd die with despair if it had all been for nothing.

For the first time, he also realised that he could hear sounds, but only in his right ear; he became aware of the rumble of an approaching train on the tracks above him, although it wasn't as loud as he'd remembered it being. He assumed he'd suffered some sort of hearing loss, and hoped it wouldn't be permanent. His jaw hurt badly when he tried to move his mouth to swallow and he could feel something sharp and metallic between his lower front teeth. As the tears dried he lifted his head, despite the pain, to look around.

He was lying in a hospital bed and, because of the tent around it, he could only see the limited section of the lock-up that was visible through the open end of his cloth enclosure and he could only hold his head up for a few seconds before it became too painful. However, if he tilted his head in a certain way, he could see that there was a chair to the side of the bed, nearer to the bottom of it. It was empty but he could hear somebody moving about outside his field of view. He tried to speak but the sharp pain in his jaw stifled the sound before it started. He waited to see if the sound had been noticed, but Anna, or whoever was caring for him, hadn't responded.

After a few minutes, he drifted off to sleep again, but it seemed that only a short while later, he was awoken by the sound of footsteps coming towards him. With an effort, he opened his eyes but his lids were heavy and he could manage no more than mere slits. A sudden sharp pain in his head came from nowhere, almost making him scream and pass out, but it subsided quickly and he could now see Anna standing by the chair, a towel in her hand. Instead of approaching the bed as he'd expected, she laid the towel over the back of the chair and pulled her jumper over her head.

Something stopped Bill from trying to move or speak and he continued to watch as her T-shirt followed. She had a pink bra on and, despite his predicament, something deep inside Bill melted at the sight of her lovely paleness, her narrow shoulders and thin arms framing her upper body. He could just see ribs below the bra, but it was her breasts that held his eyes, constrained and almost overflowing the top of the pink lace cups hiding them from view.

Bill held his breath but a fuzzy blob irritatingly drifted into the centre of his vision, temporarily restricting his view as she reached behind her back and unfastened her bra, which she placed on the arm of the chair with the rest of her clothes.

Part of him felt guilty for looking at all, but he couldn't help himself, and he cursed inwardly as the blob made its way slowly across his field of vision until it rested gently on one side, allowing him an almost unrestricted view as she completed her undressing. He'd missed her skirt being unfastened but her knickers soon joined it on the floor as she pulled them down and stepped out of them. As she stooped down to pick up these discarded items, he noticed small folds of fat forming around her midriff and her breasts elongating comically, nipples downwards, as gravity took over, but when she straightened up he could see that, naked, she was a quite beautiful woman with just a small suggestion of a belly, touchingly attractive, and quite stunning, if slightly small, breasts.

He closed his eyes, part of him disgusted for looking in the first place, the other part remembering his wife's body at a similar age and comparing them in a surprisingly objective way. Anna wasn't as large hipped or big-breasted:

281

Alison's fuller figure had always pleased Bill and usually attracted admiring glances from other men, but Anna's slimmer stature was equally exciting and somehow more vulnerable.

Bill couldn't stop himself opening his eyes again and, as he watched her walk naked away from him towards the shower cubicle, it struck him that as well as being very fond of Anna, an attraction towards her had sneaked up on him which he knew was totally inappropriate. Listening to the sounds of the shower being switched on and the door opening and closing, he realised that the unfortunate and unwanted erection that had suddenly appeared was causing him a not inconsiderable amount of pain between his legs. In a chilling flashback to his horrendous assault, he suddenly remembered the excruciating agony of the first blow to his groin administered by Aleksander Gjebrea and the feeling of not being able to take a breath for what seemed like a couple of minutes afterwards, hands clutching at his already swelling genitals.

Now the pain was a fraction of that, but nonetheless it was intensely uncomfortable and he willed his penis to subside, trying to remove the picture of a naked Anna from his mind. He'd almost succeeded, when he heard her come out of the shower and pad back over to stand beside the chair again, drying herself, unaware of his scrutiny. Still unable to pull his eyes away, he watched as she towelled her hair vigorously, her breasts undulating gently. As she continued to dry herself, Bill forced himself to close his eyes in deference to his troubled conscience and, with some pragmatism, to reduce the pain that watching her was causing in his groin area.

The next time he opened his eyes it was to see her throwing the towel over the bottom rail of the bed, then wasting no time in getting dressed. Bill continued to watch as her skin gradually disappeared under a new layer of clothing; having seen her naked, it only made her body more seductive when fully dressed.

As she pulled her jumper on over her head and moved towards the bed, Bill had a sudden fear that she was going to examine him, or worse still, give him a wash. The stark realisation that since his beating she must have attended to his every physical need, including toilet and cleaning functions, deeply embarrassed him, made worse by the possible impending discovery of his hard-on and the inevitable association she would make with that and her recent state of undress.

To Bill's immense relief, she picked up her watch and necklace, which she'd left on top of the bed, and stooped to put on her shoes. Only then did she come towards the top of the bed to check on her patient. Bill immediately shut his eyes before she could see that he was awake, trying hard but unsuccessfully to concentrate on anything other than his recent memory of her naked body.

She took an aural thermometer, which must have been sitting on top of the bedside table, and placed the tip of it in his ear. It was almost beyond him not to react, but he managed to keep still and avoid flinching. While she waited for it to register Bill's temperature, she gently stroked his face, and used a tissue to dry the vestigial moistness at the corners of his eyes. She lifted one of his eyelids and checked his eye perfunctorily, while he attempted to remain unfocused and immobile. Happy that he had a pupillary light reflex as his iris constricted, she started to check him over, starting with the rest of his head. Satisfied, she folded the covers down to his waist and checked his chest, covered in dark purple weals, cuts and bruises, many having turning yellow and black in places.

Bill cringed inwardly as she lifted the blankets from the lower half of his body, exposing him completely to her scrutiny. He risked a quick glance through half-opened eyelids, but she didn't react when she noticed his penis, pointing accusingly up at his head. *Look, I'm hard. Bill, here, has been letching at your naked body. Dirty bastard!* To make matters worse, he saw her smile, then playfully pat his penis a couple of times before covering him up again.

He realised by her reaction that it probably wasn't the first time she'd seen him erect. With dismay, he wondered if he'd got a hard-on whenever she cleaned him; she certainly didn't seem shocked or surprised at what she'd seen.

She checked the splints and dressings on his legs then pulled the covers back up to his chest. Sitting on the edge of Bill's bed again, she stroked his face and sometimes his hair for a while, talking gently to him, telling him softly that he was getting better; that he had accomplished all he'd said he would and that she was proud of him. He felt a tear drop onto his chest as she stooped to kiss him gently on the forehead, her body lingering gently on top of his for a second as she did.

As she moved away, Bill let out an involuntary sigh. Hearing him, she turned around for a second but, thinking that he was still sound asleep, continued to walk towards the other end of the lock-up. He heard the sound of the microwave and, after a few minutes, the smell of hot chicken soup reached his nostrils. He realised with a start that he was hungry, so when she came back to the bed and pulled the chair over beside him to eat her soup, he pretended to stir a bit, groaning realistically before opening his eyes. She immediately put her soup down on his bedside table at the top of the bed and leant over him again.

"Bill," she said softly, "you feeling OK?"

"Like shit." The words he'd said in his brain didn't come out properly and he almost cried with the pain.

"Don't try to speak. You have a broken jaw, your tongue is still swollen where you bit it and your throat was crushed when they stamped on your neck." She started to cry. "I thought they'd killed you."

She lowered her head towards him until their cheeks were touching and, carefully putting her arms around his head, she cradled him gently, quietly sobbing.

"I've fixed you up as best as I could but I think you really need a doctor. I nearly sent for one, but I knew you'd hate me for it."

Bill could feel his own tears welling up and he wanted to tell her that it was OK, that she'd done really well. He couldn't imagine the effort it must have taken for her to get him back to the lock-up, attend to his injuries as best as she could and still carry on with the rest of the stuff he knew she'd had to do.

In a dull monologue interspersed with racking sobs, she continued to list the damage that had been done to his body. "You have two broken arms, a broken leg and a broken ankle. I've splinted those, along with two of your fingers, which were dislocated. Your jaw is broken at your chin and I've put wire round your front teeth to keep it together. It seems to be holding OK. I was worried they'd fractured your skull; both of your ears were bleeding and I couldn't even see your eyes, they were so swollen. I think you may have a fractured cheekbone, too. I'm sure at least two of your ribs are broken and the bruising all over is terrible. On the plus side, the wound is starting to heal where you chopped your finger off."

She glanced at the bed in the area of his groin and, looking a little uncomfortable, she continued anyway. "Your genitals were really bad. One testicle was about three times the size it should have been; one was much less swollen. I think it must have been hiding behind the other one."

He wanted to crack a joke about how she knew what size his balls were in the first place but it was probably better that he couldn't speak. He'd listened to her catalogue of his injuries with a surprising degree of detachment, knowing that the severity of the damage should be enough to make the CCTV convince the police that he'd been murdered.

"I gave you heavy doses of morphine the first three days and I had to use some ketamine when I cleaned you up, put on the splints and wired your jaw together, to keep you from thrashing about. I ran out of morphine last night, but you slept pretty soundly until now. I managed to get some more this morning."

Bill would have, at that point, confessed his earlier voyeurism to her, such was his sense of guilt, but when he made a further attempt to speak, she couldn't make out what he was trying to say and sweat dripped off him with the pain caused by trying.

"Bill, there'll be plenty of time to talk later on. The less you move your jaw, the more chance there is that it will heal quickly. You've not even needed to drink up until now; you've got a line in and I've got plenty bags of saline, although I'll get you to try some soup now and see if you can swallow it, to keep your strength up."

She got up and returned a few seconds later holding a wide-tipped syringe with a short flexible plastic tube on it. She adjusted the top half of the bed halfway up towards a sitting position and moved the pillows to make him more comfortable. After testing her cup of soup to make sure it wouldn't scald him, she drew some of it up into the syringe.

"I'm going to try you with a little bit at first; see if you can swallow it. Shake your head if you want me to stop. OK?"

Bill nodded. She carefully parted his lips at one side and pushed the tube through between his teeth, until the tip rested on the floor of his mouth next to his tongue and watched him carefully while slowly depressing the plunger. He felt the warm fluid starting to fill up the floor of his mouth so he tried swallowing and, despite some discomfort, he managed it with a bit of an effort. He nodded and tried to smile, but only his eyes showed his gratitude. She gave him some more and, seeing he was coping well with her feeding him, she continued until the syringe was empty."

"I would have liked to place a nasogastric tube, but I wasn't confident enough to make sure it went down the right way and I didn't want to drown you!"

After his "meal", Bill felt sleepy again and hardly even noticed the morphine injection she gave him.

The next time he awoke it was dark, but in the small beam of moonlight coming through the fanlight above the lock-up doors, he could see that Anna had pulled over a camp bed and was sleeping on it, close to him in case he needed anything. He couldn't remember anyone looking after him like this; even when he had broken a leg as a small boy, falling out of a tree that he shouldn't have been climbing in the first place. After the initial couple of days of dedicated concern, his mother had quickly tired of pandering to him and he'd had to fend for himself as the sympathy dried up and convincing him of the stupidity of his actions became her main concern.

-o-

The next day, Anna tilted the top of the bed up more; he wasn't quite sitting but it was more comfortable than constantly lying down and at least it was easier to see what was going on around him. She propped his left arm up on a pillow and wheeled in a bed table, the kind used in hospitals at meal times. She opened up his iPad and, using the stand built into the protective case, she angled it so that he could use it to communicate with her and also to fend off boredom, using the fingers of his good hand.

She explained to him that the first night, she'd managed to get the stretcher on to his bed, which she'd moved close to the van, and had set up a drip to counteract the shock he was suffering from. She had no way of getting blood for him but the artificial plasma seemed to be enough.

The next day she'd gone to the warehouse of a company that specialised in the dispersal of redundant NHS equipment and explained that she needed a hospital bed for a student charity event. They'd sold her one for a hundred quid, promising to take it back for eighty if she returned it in the same condition. Quietly pleased at passing herself off as a twenty-year-old student, she returned to the lock-up via her usual medical supply company with enough sheets and pillowcases to last for a fortnight. After she'd eventually managed to lift Bill's stretcher on to the bed, one end at a time, she rolled him off it and took the opportunity to change his blood-soaked dressings before covering him over.

Another foray in the van, a little further this time, to a firm that manufactured marquees and gazebos, gave her the materials to construct the hospital tent that Bill had woken up in.

A week later, on decreasing doses of morphine, he was gradually coming to grips with what he had been through, with Anna's support. He could read and watch TV or films on his iPad, but he mostly just slept, or listened when Anna was sitting with him, talking.

When she wasn't at work, he enjoyed watching her moving around, looking after him and taking care of everything else that needed to be done in the lock-up, but he was careful to put the memories of her nakedness out of his mind, especially when it came near the time for her to wash him. He developed a technique of feigning sleep and trying to think of a complex engineering problem whenever it came time for his bed bath. Initially this was easy because she always cleaned him once his morphine injection had taken effect, but as she reduced the dose he needed and eventually stopped it altogether, it became more difficult to persuade his brain not to think of her in a sensual way.

As it was, on his fourth day awake, the erection situation sorted itself out because, for the first time since the beating, he was aware that he needed a crap.

Tapping the words out on the iPad as she came to give him his daily wash, he abjectly apologised, but indicated that he needed her to help him to go to the toilet.

Mortified, he listened as she told him he'd been more than once already, when he was all but unconscious in the early days following his beating; that she was used to cleaning up for patients in hospital and thought nothing of it. She brought him a bed pan and managed to slip it under him with surprisingly little effort.

Sensitive to his embarrassment, she left him alone for five minutes while he emptied his bowels, with difficulty, due to his semi-prone position. When she returned, she deftly removed the bed pan and cleaned him in a very matter-of-fact way that reduced his discomfiture a little.

He heard her flushing the toilet and bagging up the cardboard container, before returning to bathe him. He was relieved that his penis behaved itself for once, all thoughts of a sexual nature banished by his recent humiliating experience.

-o-

As he improved, she filled in the blanks in his memory by telling him all the missing details of the horrific assault he'd been subjected to.

"They gave you a real hammering. I was this close to calling the police." She held her forefinger and thumb a few millimetres apart to emphasise her words. "Twice."

She'd told him the bare bones of the aftermath to his horrendous assault in Bloq's car park. He had just one question.

"Did we get them?"

"They've been arrested."

"We got it all on tape?"

"Yes, I'll show you."

He slumped back onto his pillow, a sense of relief sweeping over him.

She fetched his laptop and waited while it started up.

"Are you sure you're ready to watch this?"

She'd waited until she felt he was strong enough physically and emotionally to watch the footage of himself being beaten within an inch of his life, but she knew it would still be hard for him to stomach.

After the clip had finished, he said nothing for a while. Anna sat in silence, knowing that he had to let it sink in; how close he had come to death.

"If I hadn't been wearing all these layers, I wouldn't be here now. They would have killed me."

"I know. I thought they had."

"You saved my life. I don't know how you managed to get me back. And do all the medical stuff as well."

"Apart from when I learned that Susie was dead, it was the hardest twenty-four hours of my life. But it was ten times worse for you. I'm only glad you made it."

She told him of the near disaster when Aleksander had sent her home early, how the VPN connection to the club had failed and of the panic that had resulted from it.

"Did you get my message about me going back to the lock-up?" she asked him.

"No, I don't think so. It will be on my phone if it did arrive."

"Your phone was completely smashed. When the bat got your balls, I think."

Bill took a second to take that in.

"Run through the rest of it. Did you manage to get video of them loading the pig into the van?"

"Yes. I was there when they discovered it. I'd gone in early after I'd got you stabilised. Aleksander went through the roof when the boys told him it was there. You were right about letting the pig rot first. I think they would have opened up the carpet to see what was in it if the smell hadn't been so disgusting."

She smiled, remembering the disgust on their faces. She showed him the footage she'd edited. It did look remarkably like a human body being loaded into the van.

"That's brilliant. Did they not wonder why a pig had been deposited in their car park?"

"I think they assumed that one of the rival drug gangs had dumped it there. They didn't seem to make any connection with you. They must have thought you'd managed to crawl away again. The boys hosed down the whole area with a pressure washer to get rid of the smell. I just hope the police got enough forensic evidence."

"They will have. Did you put some of my blood and hair in the places I suggested?"

"Yes. And I dropped your finger down the drain, as you said. That was difficult. I did it the day I sent the video files to the police, when I was putting the bottles out for recycling. I was scared shitless someone was going to ask why I was wearing Marigolds."

"Did they find it?"

"Yes, they checked the whole club and the car park, from top to bottom. They got a machine in to suck out the drain. You should have seen Aleksander's face when they

292

produced the finger, then the baseball bat from inside the club. He thought it was in some landfill site with the rest of the rubbish that had been collected by the council the day after they beat you up."

"Why?"

She forgot there was a lot he didn't know.

"It was in the bin and I took it out and hid it in the storeroom."

"Bloody hell, Anna. You took some risks."

"It was nothing compared with what you went through."

He looked at her sceptically and shook his head.

"Maybe not physically, but you're under the constant threat of being found out. That's just as hard. Anyway, what about the footage of you picking me up and dumping the pig? Did you make sure you got rid of that?"

"Yes, I deleted it all, including the assault itself, before I went into work. Nobody noticed. I'll show you later; it does look like they've tried to tamper with the CCTV evidence. I think the fact that I wasn't very good with the editing program made it look amateurish and probably more convincing as an attempt to cover up your *murder*."

He logged on to Bloq's server and had a look.

"You've done really well. It looks perfect."

He thought for a moment, in case he'd missed something.

"The pig. Did you find out where they dumped it?"

"You're not the only clever one, Bill Ingram. I don't know if I told you, but Aleksander has a spare iPhone which always sits charging at the club; it's a pay-as-you-go, like ours, I think. They use it as a standby if there's a problem with their usual network, but also to do some of their drug related stuff. Aleksander's own phone is an iPhone, too, and they're both linked, so I was able to use the Find My iPhone app to keep track of where Aleksander and Dhim went when they disposed of the pig. I made a note of where they'd stopped and went first thing in the morning, just before daybreak; it was on a patch of waste ground down by the river where people are always dumping rubbish. Everyone uses it because there's no CCTV, so no one gets done for fly-tipping. The council clears it out every so often."

Bill could imagine an exhausted Anna stumbling about in the semi-dark, searching by smell for the decaying carcase that she would be glad to be rid of.

"It was right by the water's edge and I managed to drag it far enough to tip it over the bank. I cut the string first, so the carpet and the carcase separated. They'll probably be miles apart by now, well down the river."

"How about work? Has no one asked how the police got the video, or why the real footage isn't on the server?"

"I went in every day, trying to act normally. I posted the disk to the police when I knew I didn't have to open up the next day. The police must have been waiting for signs of life at the club before they raided it because, from what I heard later, they only arrived after Aleksander and Dhim got there. I phoned Aleksander from the car and said I was too frightened to come in; that I couldn't afford to be identified by the police in case my old boyfriend found out where I was. I don't know if he believed my story about being abused, or if he thought I was maybe in trouble with the law and using the domestic violence story as a cover, but whatever he thought, he seemed to accept that I genuinely was frightened of the police finding out who I was. The police must have been with him at the time; he was very cautious in what he said and he never called me by name.

"When I turned up at the club the day after the arrests, Ilir, Aleksander's cousin, was there. He told me that once the club could be re-opened, I should run it on a day-to-day basis. We couldn't get in for three days until the police gave us the go-ahead, which was ideal for me, as it gave me plenty of time to look after you."

"So you think they don't suspect that it was you who set the police on them?"

"I don't think so, although Ilir sometimes looks at me strangely and I've caught him checking through my computer after I've been working on it. I'm very careful not to leave anything open that would incriminate me. He told me I'd have to talk to the police, and that I should say nothing about the tramp. He said I hadn't to worry about me getting traced, that the police weren't interested in me. He was there when they questioned me and he told me I'd done well when they left."

Bill seemed reassured by her confidence and she left him to get ready to go to work.

When Anna left, Bill looked at the remaining video mpeg files on the laptop. The only ones he hadn't already seen contained the footage of Anna's efforts to get him into the back of the van. He cursed himself for not putting a pulley at the top of the ramp, which would have made it much easier for her. He watched with awe and respect as she used every last ounce of her reserves to get his broken

295

body into the van, knowing that it was, for her, only the start of an ordeal which he could see had taken a great deal out of her. *You're an incredible woman, Anna.*

-o-

Every day Bill was getting stronger; his broken bones healed under their casts, the swelling subsided and the cuts held together with Steri-Strips knitted together. She had purchased some plaster of Paris bandages and now that the flesh wounds on his legs and arms had healed, she was able to replace the splints and soft dressings with casts. It made it easier for him to sit up; he could now just about use the laptop as well as the iPad and he scoured the Internet for news of Aleksander's organisation.

He could now speak; his tongue and throat were back to normal and his jaw was healing well. The protruding ends of the wire on his bottom teeth now caused him more annoyance than discomfort. She still wouldn't let him eat solids until his jaw had knitted fully, in the same way as she forbade him from getting out of bed, other than to use the commode he'd now graduated to, much to his relief. He still needed her to wash him; a shower was out of the question with his casts and he only had limited use of his arms.

The embarrassment he felt every day for his body's involuntary reaction when she bathed him was lessened by her making light of it, but he still dreaded it, worried that she might be disgusted by him.

He'd caught her smiling on a couple of occasions at his obvious arousal. He was convinced that she lingered longer than necessary and was more thorough, when she washed his genital area, just to watch him squirm. Despite his best efforts to fill his mind with something other than her touch, his body more often than not disobeyed him and

296

he could do nothing more than close his eyes and grit his teeth. Often, she made it worse by leaning over him while she cleaned his back, her breasts sometimes almost touching his face. Even the smell of her hair and her perfume did it for him now.

She would often put her hand on his arm while they talked and while he loved this contact with her, it was stirring feelings in him that he knew made things complicated, even if she was unlikely to ever to respond to them. And she would sometimes sit in a bathrobe after she'd had a shower and, sitting lower than Bill on the chair next to his bed, it gave him a view that a small part of him still felt uncomfortable with, but he couldn't help stealing glances whenever he could.

She continued to work at the club and returned periodically with further information gleaned from combing through the filing cabinets in the office when she got a chance. Bill sifted through it and searched online for corroboration that might strengthen the evidence and add to the list of charges the police could throw at Aleksander Gjebrea.

He was gradually drawing up a plan of the structure of the organisation and all its tentacles. Receipts for containers travelling to and from Albania opened up the possibility that this was one of the ways people were being smuggled in and stolen goods exported.

He continued to trawl through the Bloq's computer files whenever he had time. He'd managed to extract the main email file from Aleksander's own computer, because it was connected to the network and he was lazy about security. Anna supplied him with the passwords for both the logon screen and his email account.

Many of the emails were written in Albanian and despite using an online translation program, he wasn't able to decipher all of them, but if the little he had managed to glean from them was correct, there was a constant flow of money and goods to and from his home town of Vlorë, a port city in the south of Albania. He printed out the relevant emails, in English and Albanian, and added them to the plastic file box that would be delivered to the police to join the other four they already had. With a click of the mouse he also added them to the final USB memory stick that would also find its way into the box.

Bill was deeply concerned that Anna was taking too many risks, but she simply wouldn't stop, determined to persist in her efforts to extract every bit of information that might turn out to be useful, no matter what it took. She also reckoned that the longer she stayed, the less suspicious they would be that she was the one who had provided the police with the evidence.

"Anna, eventually they'll realise it was you and your life will be worth fuck all," Bill said. It wasn't like him to swear, but he was concerned and angry at her stance. Deep down, he knew that he wouldn't change her mind, and that she had a point, but every time she left to go to the club, he worried himself sick until she returned after her shift. "You've got to stop now."

"I can't. Then they'll know it was definitely me. OK, so they don't know who I really am, but they'll find me if they think I'm the whistle-blower. I'm going to go in for a couple of weeks then tell Ilir that I can't risk the police looking in to me further, as I'm on the run; that they've already questioned me once and they might be back."

He still looked unconvinced, so she continued.

"I'll be all right. Firstly, they're not going to risk doing anything to me while Aleksander is awaiting trial for murder. Secondly, I'm a good actress – look how much I've been able to do right under their noses all this time without them suspecting anything." She paused and looked at him, smiling. "You're a big softy," she said, leaning over to give him a hug and kiss him on the cheek.

Bill didn't know why he did it but he lifted his better arm and clumsily put it round the back of her neck to return the embrace. She lost her balance a little and almost fell on top of him. As she put out her hand to avoid pressing on Bill's more painful right arm, their mouths came together and, before either of them knew what was happening, they were kissing, softly at first, but quickly becoming more forceful. Her body was lying across his so she took some of the weight on her elbows, holding his face in her hands as their need for each other took over.

Bill suddenly stopped and half-turned away. "Anna," he said, stammering, "I-I'm so sorry. I shouldn't have done that. I don't know what came over me. I do apologise." His face was ashen and she could see the deep concern in his eyes.

"Don't be silly. I would have stopped it if I wasn't enjoying it. It came as a bit of a surprise, but I can't think of anyone else I would want to kiss me like that, right now."

She kissed him again, this time very tenderly and was touched to see a couple of tears run down his cheek. She kissed them off and stroked his hair.

"You're the nicest man I've ever known, Bill Ingram. And don't forget that I know every inch of your body, so we're hardly strangers. And you can't hide that fact that you find me very attractive." She grinned at his discomfort and Bill's face finally broke into a guilty smile.

"Anna, you're wonderful, but I'm old enough to be your father and I shouldn't have taken advantage of you like that."

"You didn't take advantage. We're both adults and we've become very fond of each other. You're an attractive man; maybe a bit older than I would normally go for." She laughed again and Bill pretended to be offended by her comment about his age.

"I've not been put out to pasture yet. I like to think I've kept myself in reasonable shape."

"You're in good shape, Bill, and quite good-looking in a gruff sort of way, but you're warm and generous, and you care, which is more important than stupid film star looks, although, if George Clooney were available ..."

They kissed again, Bill not quite believing what was happening. He had the sudden urge to confess to his furtive watching of her undressing.

"I've got something to tell you. I've been feeling bad about it and I'd rather you knew."

"Sounds mysterious. I hope you haven't been seeing another woman behind my back while I've been at work. Come clean; who else has been giving you bed baths?"

Bill smiled, but continued. "The first time I woke up here after you'd brought me back here, you fed me a little soup. You remember?"

"Yes. I was so relieved when you came round. I wasn't sure that you were going to make it. Why?"

Bill's face had turned a shade of red. "Well, that wasn't me just waking up. I'd been awake for a short while before that."

"So?" she said. "What about it?"

"I watched you getting undressed, ready for a shower, then I watched you getting dried again and putting your clothes on," he blurted, glad to finally have it off his chest but anxious as to how she might take it.

"Bill Ingram," she exclaimed, "you surprise me. I should be scandalised, but do you know, I feel quite fine about it. No wonder you got so excited every time I gave you a wash!" She burst into laughter at his serious face and kissed him again, this time more slowly and with more intent.

"I could show you again," she said, teasing him. She stood up and pulled her jumper over her head, as she had before. She had on a short top, which exposed more of her cleavage and her midriff. Bill stared speechlessly as she removed this too.

He reached out with his good hand to touch her face, but after a few seconds, she took his wrist and moved it on to her breast. She folded the sheet down and pulled her fingers through the hairs on Bill's chest, watching his face as she did.

Bill let out a sigh and she smiled gently at him. "If you hurt at any point, or you feel uncomfortable, just say so. I'll not be offended. Disappointed, perhaps, but not offended."

She leant over and kissed Bill's upper chest, her dyed blonde hair falling over his sides. He kissed the top of her head and reached with his good hand around her back, holding her gently to him. She moved her hands over the parts of his arms not covered by plaster and across both his shoulders.

She lifted herself fully on to the bed, taking her foot, which had been supporting her weight, from the floor. She now lay almost by Bill's side, resting one leg on top of his, which couldn't have been all that comfortable for her, with the plaster of Paris extending above his knee. The other leg lay along the bed beside him, but Bill's arm, also in its cast, lay under her tummy and he found himself to be in the position where, if she hadn't had a skirt on, his hand would have been resting between her legs. She must have known, because she pressed down on to him, stretching the skirt and making him fully aware that she knew exactly where his hand was. Despite a little discomfort in his arm, he moved his fingers speculatively and was rewarded by her pressing against him even more firmly.

Her mouth had moved on from his upper chest to one of his nipples, which she bit gently. After a minute or two pressing her pubis against his captive hand with increasing vigour, she traversed across his chest with her tongue to his neck and playfully kissed him on either side of his Adam's apple before moving on to his chin. As she found his mouth again with hers, her tongue explored between his teeth and invited his to do the same. She reached down to her side and undid the button of her skirt and pushed the zip down as far as it would go. Arching her back, she pushed her skirt down below her knees and kicked it off. She did the same with her tights but left her panties on, such as they were. Bill had seen similar tiny knickers in Carol's flat when he'd been searching for clues, but it was the first time he'd ever come in close contact with such flimsy underwear being worn by its owner.

Bill felt a dampness between her legs, which he took as an encouraging sign. And, unencumbered by a skirt, she could now press more firmly on his hand, placing it exactly where she wanted. Bill hoped his dislocated fingers would hold up to the pressure, but was thankful the splints had been taken off a few days before. Not quite sure that she wanted him to, but taking the cue from the continued pressure she was applying to his hand, he moved his two fingers, carefully at first, over the mound of her hair and the thin triangle of lacy cloth that constituted her panties. Her soft moan told him that he was in safe territory, so he continued and she adjusted herself by moving slightly up the bed, spreading her legs a little to allow his fingers more room to move.

Bill could feel a warm moist tingling glow at his fingertips and, because the part of cloth he was now in contact with was now what he could have only defined as a thin strap, he could feel her soft wet flesh and damp, curly hair. Even that was only a narrow strip, as she'd obviously trimmed the edges recently. Almost without trying, his fingers slipped under the last remnant of cloth guarding the opening of her lips and were inside her. Shocked at the amount of slippery fluid and amazed that he was responsible for it, he gently explored inside, carefully trying not to hurt her. Her response was to groan louder and press more firmly against his hand, forcing him deeper inside her.

With Alison, Bill had been blessed with a healthy and active love life until she became ill so, not being completely naïve and out of practice, he moved one of his good fingers upwards, taking some wetness with it, until he felt the soft ridge and tiny button that he was searching for. He knew he'd found it when she arched her back and shuddered, breathing quicker now. He moved his finger slowly and gently at first, occasionally dipping back inside her for additional lubrication. She began to murmur his name as she became more excited, increasingly accompanied by some vocal encouragement, along the lines of *yes*, *God* and *mmmmmnnggg*. He moved his finger faster and firmer and she pressed harder against him, removing any worries he had that he might be hurting her.

Bill hoped that she would come quickly, as his injured fingers and the muscles in his arm were starting to tire. She suddenly reached down the bed with her right arm and grabbed Bill in just the right spot, through the bedclothes, making it his turn to gasp with pleasure. She presented her neck to him and Bill obliged by kissing it, moving to her earlobes as she turned her head, all the time trying to concentrate on what his hand was doing to her. Just as Bill thought he might have to stop, she gave a long shudder and cried out a final time, and sank down on to him, gasping for breath.

Bill took the chance to relax his hand, which by now had very little sensation in it. Anna kissed his forehead and his eyes, then moved down to his cheek, finally kissing him gently on his lips, looking at him strangely.

"What?" He said.

"Nothing, that was lovely. How's your hand?"

"Fine," he lied. "I'm glad you enjoyed it."

"Oh, that's just the start, if you're OK."

She pushed herself up into a kneeling position and removed her panties. There didn't seem to be much of them, material wise, in Bill's mind and he wasn't sure what difference it made whether they were on or off.

"Just lie back and relax," she told him.

She carefully brought her knees above Bill's waist and, leaning behind her, pulled the covers from Bill's bottom half and pushed them with her feet to the bottom of the bed. Making him position his arms away from his sides, she straddled Bill, gently lowering herself on to him, guiding him inside with minimal effort. It was Bill's turn to groan as she wiggled her hips downwards, grasping the base of his penis as she did. At first, she barely moved, and seeing him watching her body, she reached behind her and undid the hooks on her bra, knowing that he was incapable of releasing them with his arm in plaster. Her breasts sagged a little, but not by much, when they were released from the confines of their little lacy cups. Bill's eyes drank in the view. She had quite large and dark nipples, slightly oblong and fully erect; almost shining. She took his left hand, the one with the smaller cast on it, bringing it up to her mouth and licking it before placing it on her nipple, holding it there with her hand. Bill watched her face as he gently massaged both the nipple and the surrounding breast, her own saliva making it slippery and silky smooth. Her eyes were almost closed, her mouth slightly open and her chest rose and fell steadily as her breathing quickened again.

Bill couldn't move. His legs were next to useless and his arms weren't much better so he had to leave it all to Anna. He was beginning to hurt a little, but nothing in the world could have made him want it to stop now. She seemed to sense that he wasn't recovered enough for anything too vigorous because, although they both became increasingly passionate, her movements were designed to pleasure without hurting him and, not surprisingly, considering he'd been aroused by Anna for weeks, he came sooner than he'd hoped. She didn't match him this time, but seemed satisfied that he'd finished.

She lay on top of him for a long while, her face resting on his chest. Bill assumed at first that she'd fallen asleep but she'd occasionally rub his shoulder and neck, so he knew she hadn't. As for himself, Bill was amazed that it had happened at all and was grateful that amongst the wreckage that had been his daily life for the last year or so, it was probably the only time he'd felt anything other than pain.

"This doesn't change anything." She still lay on top of him and it had been Bill who'd eventually fallen asleep. When he woke, she'd waited a few minutes before making her statement.

He sighed. "I know. I just don't want anything to happen to you and not only because of this."

"Are you very sore?" she asked, smiling, slightly embarrassed; *for fuck's sake, the poor man is in the early stages of recovery from major trauma!* She cringed.

"A little," Bill replied. "I presume that you don't treat all your patients like this!"

"Christ, don't make me feel worse than I do already. That wasn't meant to happen." She looked at him. He looked hurt, but she wasn't sure if he was winding her up. "I didn't mean that the way it sounded. I'm glad it did happen; it's just that I didn't plan for it, at least not just yet, but I was pretty much certain it was going to take place sooner or later."

"I didn't know. I mean, I knew how I felt about you, but I didn't ever think you'd be interested in me. Apart from the age thing, you're one of the most attractive woman I've ever met and lovely with it. I always assumed there was someone else in your life."

"Thanks for the flattery. I'm just ordinary and I haven't been with anyone since Susie went missing. My partner at the time couldn't handle my so called obsession with her disappearance, so we split and I've been too preoccupied since then to bother."

"But didn't you miss it? I mean, at your age, it's not right to be on your own."

"I could say the same about you. You've never had a relationship with anyone other than your wife, have you?"

"No. Not until now. It never even crossed my mind, and with Carol missing ..."

"I know," she said, nestling closer to him; each a crumb of comfort to the other, for the moment.

-o-

Bill got into the habit of keeping a close eye on Anna when she was at work, not trusting that she was above suspicion, worried that Ilir or one of Aleksander's other associates might try and drag the truth out of her.

He was making good progress physically, but could only move in a limited fashion and he tired easily. He was, however, able to make a start on packing up all the paper files that contained the evidence against Aleksander Gjebrea and his organisation, ready to be shipped over to the police. They already had it all in digital format, as scans; those had been on the disk with the video files of all the assaults that they'd sent to the police, but he knew that the CPS would need the physical copies, too.

He always kept his laptop nearby, with the screen showing the full menu of CCTV feeds from the nightclub and, every so often, he would make a point of waking up his

laptop and checking each of the feeds for Anna.
Sometimes, she was out of the field of view of any of the
cameras, but he would check a short while later and,
ninety-nine per cent of the time, she would appear
somewhere in the club.

He was watching her when the police questioned her for
the second time, marvelling at her coolness; acting the part
of an employee who turned up for work and had no
knowledge of the illegal activities that went on at the club.
He cursed that there was no sound feed with the CCTV; it
would have been much easier to judge how well she was
really doing if he could have heard the conversation. As it
was, he was fairly happy that the police were satisfied with
her story, from their body language. She confirmed when
she returned after her shift that she'd managed to convince
them that she knew little that could help. He worried
slightly that they'd been back to re-interview Ilir and the
staff, concerned that the police were digging because they
didn't feel they had enough evidence.

When Anna came home that night, he had her help him
pack up the final box of files and pop the USB stick in it
before sealing it up. He stuck the shipping labels on all
four boxes; he'd printed them out on an online parcel
delivery website. The sender's name and address was a
small company that actually existed in Peckham, but he'd
ticked the checkbox when he'd paid for the delivery,
stating that they would drop the items for delivery off at
the designated collection point, a local supermarket. Anna
loaded the boxes into the van and the next morning she
handed them over to the girl at the click and collect point,
dressed in a headscarf and wearing sunglasses as a
precaution and taking care not to look at the security
camera. She'd parked the van around the corner, away
from the CCTV cameras in the car park, and used a cheap
sack-barrow to wheel the pile of boxes round to the main

entrance. She was pretty sure that even if the police tried to trace her after the package had been delivered, they would struggle to identify her.

She popped her head in when she picked up her car and told Bill that she'd dropped the boxes off with no problem, then headed for work, thinking of ways to hint to Ilir that she might be moving on.

-o-

At a loose end, Bill made a start on clearing out the lock-up. He began piling things that weren't needed any longer to one side, near the door, putting them in plastic sacks as he went along. His intention was to fill up the van before they left the country and take it to a waste facility well away from South London. He was packing the clothes he'd spent so much time wearing on the streets into black refuse sacks, some of them still caked hard with his own dried blood or sliced lengthways where Anna had been unable to remove them to treat his injuries. As he sealed up the last bag, glad to be rid of them, he tapped the mousepad on the laptop to check for Anna on the nightclub's CCTV system.

As he looked from screen to screen, he couldn't see her and was just about to make himself a coffee while waiting for her to appear on one of the screens, when he noticed a couple of cars in the car park. One was Ilir's 4x4, the other a black saloon, probably a BMW. Wondering if it was the police back at the club again, he returned to scanning the other screens.

FUCK FUCK FUCK FUCK FUCK

Aleksander Gjebrea stood in the centre of his office, a dark-suited man Bill didn't recognise beside him. Ilir sat on the edge of Anna's desk, smoking a cigar.

309

Anna sat at her desk. Behind her stood Aleksander's vicious head of security, Dhim, his hand resting on her shoulder.

Why the fuck are they out?

Bill didn't need sound to know that Anna was in big trouble, but this time it would have helped him decide if she was managing to maintain her composure and convince them that she was on the wrong side of the legal system, like them.

Any hope that she'd be able to resist their interrogation was extinguished abruptly. Dhim grabbed Anna's hair, surprisingly gently, and held her head still. Aleksander approached her, taking hold of her wrists. He leaned forwards, talking at the same time; his face inches from hers. For Bill, his smile when he turned to his cousin and the measured threat of his apparent self-control were somehow more menacing than outright violence.

His first thought was to jump in the van and head over to Browning Street, but he almost immediately realised that a recuperating middle-aged man would be useless against the ruthless criminals who were holding Anna. Forcing himself to control his panic, he realised that while phoning the police would save her life, it would completely blow her cover. The police would take no action without proof that anyone at the club had threatened her and she would never be able to rid herself of the fear that someday one of Aleksander's thugs would catch up with her.

A sudden thought struck him: sending one of the other emergency services to the club would have the same effect as alerting the police. He'd used smoke as a distraction to allow him to get Carol away from the brothel. *It might work again.* He couldn't start a fire, but he could do the next best thing. Using the mobile he'd replaced his

310

smashed one with, he phoned 999 and asked to report a fire. He gave the address of the club and told the call handler that there was a fire in the office, towards the back of the club. The woman on the end of the phone told him to remain on the line, but he'd already hung up. He didn't know if they would be able to trace his phone number despite the bar he had on his phone, but even if they could, it had a pay-as-you-go SIM that wouldn't lead back to him.

Keeping an eye on Anna in a window minimised on the left hand of the screen, he used a small RDP program which allowed him to log on to Bloq's server and find the controls for the club's computerised security system, which controlled the burglar alarm, the fire alarm and the sprinklers. He'd looked at it before now and had briefly familiarised himself with the basic control menu, never expecting that he would need to use it.

Praying that the VPN wouldn't fail him, he found the part of the menu that allowed the operator to override the automatic triggering system, a function that could be used in the event of the sprinkler failing to activate during a fire. Setting off the fire alarm was a one stage process, but setting off the water sprinklers involved three dialogue boxes, one after the other, to avoid setting it off accidentally.

He continued to watch the tableau in the office. Aleksander carried on asking Anna questions and he could see her lips move to answer. It seemed to Bill that she was holding her own and eventually, Aleksander did step away from her and hold his hands out. *He thinks she's legit.*

He barely saw the nod that the nightclub owner gave his cousin. Before Bill could react, Ilir had reached across the desk and pinned Anna's hand to the wooden surface. He took a long drag on his cigar, blew the smoke up towards the ceiling and pressed the tip of the cigar onto the back of Anna's forearm.

She writhed in pain and, with her free hand, tried to wrench Ilir's arm away, but the Albanian's superior strength made her efforts futile. Aleksander moved quickly to grab Anna's arm and, as Ilir removed the cigar from Anna's skin, Bill could see Aleksander saying something to her.

With six clicks of the mouse, Bill set off the sprinklers and, almost immediately, set off the fire alarm, too.

The CCTV feed became grainy as the spray of water misted over the camera lens, but from what Bill could see, the chaotic scene might just allow Anna to escape. He switched to the multi-screen view just in time to see the fire engine arrive at the front and two of the firefighters go to each of the club's doorways.

The main doors were locked and there was no reaction to the thumping on the door by one of the firemen, but the two who had raced around the corner into the car park must have radioed, or perhaps shouted, to the commanding officer because the engine then jumped forward and spun round into the car park, followed by the other two firemen.

Bill clicked on the thumbnail that showed the car park from the back of the property to see the firemen disappear inside the back door of the club, almost immediately coming back out supporting a bedraggled man and, to Bill's immense relief, a similarly soaked woman, who they guided away from the building to the other side of the fire engine. As the fireman rushed back to rear door of the club, naturally concerned to rescue anyone else trapped in what might be a serious fire, he saw Anna slip around the corner and make her escape eastwards along Browning Street.

He kept his eye on the back door of Bloq as two other men were ushered out by the firemen, who headed back inside to check out why there wasn't any smoke anywhere in the building. While this was going on, some of their colleagues were rolling out hoses in preparation for dousing a potentially serious fire.

The three men were trying to shrug off the help of the one fireman remaining with them, as they looked around desperately for Anna. While one of them ran off in the direction that she'd taken, another, who Bill presumed to be Aleksander, was remonstrating with the fireman, gesticulating wildly at the fire engine, which was blocking the way and preventing them from getting either of the cars out. Bill almost laughed as the fireman shook his head, resolutely refusing to move the fire engine while they were fighting a possible blaze.

With no way of knowing which direction Anna would take to give her pursuer the slip, Bill could only wait with dread to find out if she could elude the man who had chased her.

He kept an eye on the scene at the club as the second fire appliance arrived, accompanied by two ambulances and a police car, mobilised when the original firefighting team alerted control about a possible major incident. Bill was sick with relief when the man who'd chased after Anna returned empty-handed, to be rewarded by what looked like a tirade from his boss. At the same time the fire officers were gradually withdrawing from the club, showing obvious surprise and confusion at the lack of any smoke or flames anywhere.

The chief fire officer seemed to be talking with Aleksander Gjebrea and Bill fervently hoped that they were having an

313

awkward conversation about how a cigar had set off the fire alarm and the state of the art sprinkler system. Ten minutes after Bill had triggered them, somebody managed to turn off the sprinklers, but not before they had caused a significant amount of water damage, which would take at least a few weeks and not a little expense to rectify.

Bill was still watching the aftermath of his sabotage when he heard Anna enter the lock-up. Still soaked, pain etched on her face as she held her burned arm with her unscathed hand, she saw Bill and rushed towards him, making no attempt to hold back the tears, which left new streaks down her already mascara-stained cheeks. Bill grabbed her into his arms, careful not to touch her injury, and held her while her sobbing subsided and she drew herself together.

"That was fucking close." The sense of relief in Bill's voice caused her to lift her face to him.

"Thanks. That would have just been the start. I didn't tell them anything, but they would have continued until I gave in. I could see it in their eyes. They found our dummy switch. Aleksander's IT guy was there. That's why they questioned me."

"Strange that they haven't found the VPN."

"It's probably only a matter of time. Can they trace us with it?"

"Not easily, but I'll delete it soon. At least we know now that you can never go back. In a way I'm glad it's over."

"But why are they out, Bill? The evidence was all there."

"Clever, expensive lawyers. That's how. But they'll only be out on bail; just wait. And they'll still be working on

314

the case against Ilir Dragusha as well. It's not over yet."
Even to Bill, it didn't sound completely convincing.

"I thought at first the cigar had set the sprinklers off, that it
was just luck, but when I got outside and saw the fire
brigade there within seconds, I knew that somehow you'd
engineered it. How the fuck did you manage it?"

"I remembered how I got Carol out. Their whole security
system, including the fire protection element, is all
computer controlled. I'd had a look at it a while ago so I
knew it was there. When I saw them questioning you I
nearly panicked and phoned the police, but I realised that
the fire service would be almost as good and wouldn't
compromise your cover at the club."

"Yes. But now I have to try and persuade Aleksander that
I'm not the grass; that I want to avoid the police just as
much as he does."

"No way. You can't contact him again. Now, let me have a
look at that burn."

"Think about it. I was pretty convincing in there. OK, I
would have given in if it had gone on, but they're not to
know that. I think I can convince Aleksander that I'm no
threat to him; that I'm using a false name because I'm on
the run, but that I can't come back after what happened.
I've got nothing to lose; if he already is suspicious, talking
to him can't make it any worse and it might just buy us a
little bit of breathing space. Then we can go."

"You've not to meet him. Phone only."

"Of course. I'm not stupid."

Bill noticed that Anna was shivering.

"Go and get showered and into dry clothes, then we'll eat. And talk. I'll put a dressing on that burn when you've showered."

While she showered, Bill selected a couple of the bags he'd put in the pile by the door and tucked them in behind the filing cabinet in his makeshift office. He cut up some bread and chucked a tea bag in each of the two mugs, ready for her when she'd finished.

He found some antiseptic cream, a little bit of leftover local anaesthetic and some sterile dressings. When Anna came out, wrapped in a towel before getting dressed, he had a look at her wound. It was a nasty round red and blistered burn, but it wasn't large; about the size of a pound coin. He soaked a couple of wound pads in some lignocaine, applied a smear of antiseptic to the wound, and gently placed the dressing over it, using a sticky bandage to hold it in place.

When he'd finished, he made her take one of the antibiotics left over from his own recuperation, and a couple of painkillers. He put on the kettle to brew the tea and fired a ready meal into the microwave, knowing that she'd need something inside her after her ordeal.

Bill marvelled again at her bravery and resilience as she tucked into her food with enthusiasm, but he could see her eyes starting to become heavy as they sat together afterwards, talking quietly to dampen down her residual fear and their realisation that they'd got away with another near-fatal encounter with the evil criminals who had already blighted both their lives.

-o-

While Anna slept, Bill was busy. He deleted all the CCTV files on Bloq's server. He didn't want any footage of Anna remaining for Aleksander and his crew to use to try and find her. The police might have taken a full dump of all the data on the server when they first raided the club, but he doubted it. At most, he thought they might have downloaded the video files for the period around the time of his murder. He'd kept a copy of everything they'd gathered on a couple of memory cards, which he kept safe in his wallet; if they ever needed anything else to send to the police, it was still available.

Bill spent the best part of four hours online, organising travel arrangements and completing the final financial transactions that were essential if they were both to disappear successfully, far away from the scope of Aleksander Gjebrea's influence.

By three o'clock in the morning, he figured the club would be empty. Locating Anna's car keys in her bag, he jumped in the van and headed to the nightclub, driving past it first to check that no one was there. Satisfied that it was unoccupied, he parked the van on the street and walked across the car park to Anna's car. He looked round, suddenly aware that this was where he'd nearly died, and a shiver ran up his spine. It took about fifteen seconds for Bill to open the car, remove the wireless module they'd installed under the seat, and lock the car again. Breathing a little easier once he was in the van, he drove back to the lock-up, making a mental note to erase the night's CCTV files from the server and delete the VPN, completely removing any traces of Anna and himself.

-o-

Two days later, a small padded envelope arrived at the lock-up. Bill checked that the contents were from the airline and put it in the safe. Anna had cut her hair and dyed it back to her natural brown colour. She bought a

317

decent pair of theatrical glasses and dressed herself in the style popular in art and media; Designer coats and dresses from previous decades, sourced in second-hand shops in or near affluent neighbourhoods, worn over leggings or jeans with baggy jumpers and laced up boots. She topped it off with woollen knitted or crocheted hats in various strange shades, and bags made out of recycled materials from an ingenious variety of strange sources.

When Anna had sent the original disk containing the video files and the supporting documents to the police, she'd included a covering notepad document on the disk, telling the police that they shouldn't look too hard for their whistle-blower. She'd been careful to fudge the grammar and spelling a little to cast some doubt on her identity; if they believed that their informant was one of the club's Eastern European staff, then that was a bonus.

She'd phoned Aleksander at the club and the conversation had gone as she expected. She got the impression that he almost believed her, but he had a few doubts. Bill thought he was just being reasonable to try and entice her back to the club. When she didn't fall for it, he was pretty sure that Aleksander and his friends would be scouring London for her.

-o-

"Anna, it's too dangerous for you to stay in London. I'm not convinced that Aleksander really believes you. I think you should get away for a while and I'm not fit enough to travel, so you'll have to go on your own. I've booked tickets in your real name; it will be safe enough because no one knows who you really are." He also knew that her hair colour now matched the photograph in her legitimate passport.

318

"What if I don't want to go? You can't just boss me around."

"Listen, I know you're annoyed, but we're going to have to disappear after this is all over. We need to do some research and work out how to get some money out of the country."

He held her hand gently and he could see the anger leave her face.

"Where do you want me to go?"

Bill handed her a Qatar Airways envelope. She opened it.

"Why Australia?"

"I don't know. I'm no good with languages. We'd stick out like sore thumbs if we didn't go somewhere English speaking."

"OK, I get that. What do you want me to do?"

"I want you to look at a few places that would be suitable for us blend in to, and sort out a few formalities that will make it easier for us to get away from the UK quickly. And you don't have to do it if you don't want to, but it would be good if you could take some money out with you. Rent an apartment in Sydney and leave the money there. We can move on from there later, but the sooner we make a start, the better."

"How dangerous is it, to smuggle cash in?"

"I wouldn't take so much that you'd be in big trouble if you got caught. Hopefully you won't, because it would leave a bit of a paper trail that could be picked up later. I think there's more danger that we'd lose some of the money. I've got a couple of pieces of cheap jewellery and

319

a couple of inexpensive antiques that you can take over as gifts for friends. Leave it in the flat as well; they're not worth that much, but it's a start and it will act as a practice run for when we have to move more valuable stuff later on."

"I'll go, of course, but how will you cope here?"

Bill smiled. "Don't worry about me; I'm well enough now to look after myself."

"I know, but I do worry about you; you're not as young as you used to be." Anna teased him. She looked at the tickets again. "Twentieth of April. That's only a week away. Are you getting fed up sleeping with a woman half your age, or are you just exhausted, needing a break to get your breath back?"

Bill opened his mouth to protest, but he could see her laughing at him. She'd stayed over at the arches nearly every night from the time she saved his life, and they'd shared a bed since, according to Bill, she'd seduced her frail and badly damaged patient who was too ill to fight her off.

Bill had struggled physically at first, but as he got stronger Anna was amused when his appetite for her increased in line with his fitness. She was even more surprised that her own desire almost outstripped his. In her previous relationships, she'd usually been the least sexually active, often blaming work pressures and tiredness whenever her libido waned.

With Bill, they had been through so much together and she'd come so close to losing him that it seemed to instil in her a need for constant intimacy to confirm their existence, even when she should have been too tired to be interested. She could never have foreseen falling for someone nearly twenty years her senior and having the sort of affair that might have been more plausible if they'd both been in their twenties.

"I've not done too badly for an old bastard, have I?" Bill seldom swore, so she knew she was in trouble. He reached out and caught her, pulling her towards him, holding her immobile while he used his free hand to start unbuttoning her top. The harder she wriggled, the tighter he held her until she gave in, laughing, and started kissing him.

-o-

"Yes, you're OK for an old git." They lay naked beneath a sheet, on the narrow bed they shared in the cubicle that served as their bedroom. She smiled at him, half-dozing in the languid after-sex stupor, intensely fond of him, enough to seriously consider spending the rest of her life with him. She frowned. *Am I thinking like that just because I'm a few days late?*

She needed to know for sure, but she hadn't plucked up the courage to use the pregnancy test kit in her bag. She'd been careless; although she'd missed a few days here and there, she'd continued to use oral contraception after she'd broken up with her last partner, in case she found the need to sleep with Aleksander. Even though it had seemed disgusting and inconceivable, she would have done if it had been critical to her goal of putting him behind bars. For the protection of her own health, she would have insisted on using a condom if she'd slept with him, but somehow, when it had all kicked off with Bill, it hadn't seemed right or necessary to use protection; Bill's long-term monogamy made it unlikely that there would be any risk to her on that score and she'd only had one sexual partner in the last five years.

-o-

321

As much to get them out of London and away from the lock-up as to do what was necessary, Bill arranged for them to take a trip in the van to dump everything that was no longer needed. He applied online for a permit to dump the stuff at a recycling centre outside London. It amounted to half a van full, and included the water tank that had held the pig, the cupboards and the filing cabinet.

Bill was getting stronger by the day, and he did most of the work while Anna was still sleeping, but she helped him with the heavier items once she was up and dressed. When the van was fully loaded they set off in an almost holiday spirit, along the A3 towards the South Coast. It was the first really clear day for a while, unseasonably warm for mid-April. The road was busy, but they were in no hurry to cover the forty miles to the community waste recycling centre at Witney, fifteen minutes beyond Guildford. It took no time at all to empty the van. They were helped by one of the staff, who took their permit and eyed up the water tank and some of the office furniture as it was unloaded, undoubtedly planning to keep it to one side and sell it later to augment his wage packet.

When Bill took the road towards Chichester instead of heading back to London, Anna raised her eyebrows and looked at him, bemused.

"I thought we'd make a trip of it. Take in a bit of the countryside. It's not a patch on Scotland, but it makes a change from being stuck in London."

"You old romantic. Is this our first date?"

She looked across at him and laughed. He shook his head at her.

"No, but if you want to think of it like that, don't let me stop you."

"You're actually blushing. It is a date."

The cab of the van was warming up so she squirmed out of her jumper while attempting to keep the seat belt on. She was wearing a thin T-shirt underneath and, as she made a show of pulling the jumper off, Bill glanced over and could make out her shape underneath, held in place by her lacy bra, which just left enough to the imagination to give Bill that familiar glow in his core, not to mention the discomfort in his groin that he attempted to relieve with a judicious piece of repositioning.

Catching him looking at her, she made the most of his discomfiture by stretching and yawning, making the most of the figure which Bill had come to delight in over the short time they'd been together.

"Eyes on the road, Bill," she teased, "it wouldn't do if we crashed now."

"You are one wicked witch!" Bill said, but he was laughing.

They rode on, happy in each other's company, until they reached Chichester. After a couple of hours wandering around the town, they had lunch in a waterfront pub overlooking the estuary in the delightful village of Bosham, followed by a walk along the seafront. In late afternoon, they jumped back in the van and made their way back towards London.

They'd been travelling for an hour when Bill indicated right and turned off the busy main road on to a leafy English lane, lined by woods, fields and the odd very impressive house.

"Another detour! You really are full of surprises today. Where are we going?"

"Just wait and see. You'll like it."

Bill drove on for about a mile until the road opened out on to the top of a low dam, which held back the waters of a large pond. He turned left down small track that led to a car park at the foot of the dam, maybe about fifteen feet below the level of the water on the other side. The old mill stood at one end of the car park, long since converted into a house. After parking the car, they both got out and walked up past the mill house to the dam, following the footpath round the pond.

Rather self-consciously, they took each other's hand as they walked on a well-made path along the water's edge, stopping to look at the wild ducks and the dragonflies hovering amongst the reed beds. Halfway up the pond, the path curved round into the woods and they followed it round until they came out into the open, where the path ran along beside a field. The trees almost petered out, until they came to another pond, surrounded by an isolated copse of thick bushes and taller trees, much smaller than the first one. It had a small jetty that jutted out into the water and they sat on it for a while, their legs dangling over the edge. Bill almost forgot for a brief moment why they had been thrown together, but memories of similar days with Alison crowded into his mind, along with an irrational flash of guilt.

"What is this place?"

"This is called the Black Pond and the big one is Burton Mill Pond. It's a wildlife reserve. I spotted it on the map last night and thought it might be nice to see. Act normal for a day."

Anna gripped his hand, tuned to his moods now. When they returned to the van, this time along the road that circled round past a large stately home and through a farmyard, the evening light was just beginning to fail and, by the time they were back in the van, and on the main road, Bill needed to put the headlights on. Stopping on the way only to buy some fish and chips, they reached the lock-up not long after ten. Tired after their long day and the fresh air, Bill was surprised and, in the circumstances, delighted, when she repeated her earlier tease without Bill having to watch the road.

-o-

Bill dropped Anna off at Heathrow.

They had said their goodbyes before they left the lock-up to avoid the danger of being seen together at the airport. Anna had commented on his lack of shaving.

"Remember, the police might be looking for someone with a beard who may or may not have been murdered. What made you decide to grow it? It tickles when you …you know. Down there." She laughed, blushing slightly.

"I didn't hear you complaining last night. Anyway, I just missed having that nice grey beard. It'll be a foot long by the time you get back."

She kissed him and they held each other tightly for a minute.

"I'm going to miss you," she told him.

"Not if you don't catch that plane. Now, get in that bloody van."

There had been tears when he dropped her at terminal four. He tried not to let her see his, as she walked away from the van through the security bollards, pulling her case behind her and wiping her eyes with a tissue.

She turned and waved once. As soon as she looked away, Bill drove off and returned to the arches. He had two weeks to make all the preparations to put them out of Aleksander Gjebrea's long reach and make sure, as much as he could, that the man he considered to be his daughter's killer would be in prison for a long time.

CHAPTER 16   BLACK POND

When Anna stepped out of the terminal building, she knew that Bill wouldn't be there to meet her. She'd spoken to him the day before she left Sydney and he'd told her to get a taxi back to the lock-up, as he wasn't likely to be back in time to pick her up. He didn't say what he was doing that would prevent him from meeting her, but she was used to his paranoia and wasn't surprised that he wouldn't give any details over the phone.

She had her own key for the lock-up, so she let herself in and turned on the lights. There was no sign of Bill or the van but she could see that he'd cleared away a bit more of the junk that had been lying around, leaving only the basics needed to live, without much comfort.

She threw her case on the bed and went to the fridge to get a cool drink; it had been warm in the taxi in the heatwave that London had been experiencing.

The fridge was virtually empty, but there was a carton of orange juice and, leaning up against it, there was an envelope with her name on it, in Bill's block lettering. She lifted the envelope and placed it on top of the fridge, then poured herself a glass of orange.

She opened the envelope, took a sip of her drink and started reading.

Anna

(it's how I know and love you, so I'll stick with it),

I'm sorry I had to deceive you by sending you away, but I knew that I couldn't do what I had to do with you here.

By the time you are reading this, I will be dead.

The glass slipped from her fingers, shattering on the concrete floor and splashing orange juice everywhere, but Anna barely noticed. Hardly able to breathe, she stumbled to the bed and sat down, reading on.

You'll have a pretty good idea why, and maybe how, but there are some important things I need you to know.

Firstly, I was getting too fond of you and I'm not conceited enough to think that you'd be happy spending the rest of your life with an old fuck like me. What you have given me over the last year or so, since we met, has made the most horrible part of my life a little less unbearable, but I can't put your life at risk, just so that I can indulge myself. And if we stay together, it will *put you in immense danger. Aleksander Gjebrea is not stupid, and he may eventually put us two together, and if he does, he'll spend the rest of his life searching for us, even from prison. The world is too small these days for a couple like us, with such an age gap as ours, to remain unnoticed, and these people have contacts all over the globe. On your own, you have a good chance of being safe, as long as you're careful.*

So here's what you need to do. Much of my savings are in a joint account under your assumed name. There should be no problem getting this money as you have already been writing cheques and making withdrawals from it; it's the dummy company account we set up to purchase supplies, etc. You might get away with using your real name in future, but I wouldn't risk it. Make a completely fresh start and it will be safer for you. You've already used one false identity, so you know how to pull it off. To help with documentation, I've left you a new passport with all the ancillary paperwork. Don't ask yourself how I got it or how much it cost. Use it to get yourself out to Australia (you've already done some of the groundwork), then get yourself another identity when you're there. Find a dead serviceman with few relatives; one who spent a lot of time overseas. Choose a country he was based in around the time you were born, preferably one with chaotic records. Get a birth certificate from there with his name on it. You can work out the rest.

Use my money to get yourself sorted out in London, and for travel costs. Leave some of it here, just in case you ever need access to cash in the UK. You can always find a way to get hold of it later if you want.

As for the rest of the money; some of it is in the safe in the lock-up, in used notes. The key is in the artwork. Open up an account with your new passport and deposit the money into it. Do it gradually, to avoid being investigated by HMRC or the serious crimes squad, looking for money launderers.

Once you are somewhere new, transfer the money by withdrawing small irregular amounts of cash; anything from a few hundred to a couple of thousand. Put it into an account in your new identity. Split up the payments and hold back or add cash here and there so that none of the deposits match up. You have at least a few months to do this without being in any real danger.

As an insurance against things going wrong, you need something you can take with you that can be converted into untraceable cash. You've already taken some over: the cheap looking costume jewellery you took with you was modified with some fairly expensive gemstones in place of the cheap glass they came with. There's more in the safe. Chuck these in your jewellery box along with your own stuff. There's also an art portfolio case that belonged to Alison with some old paintings and drawings that she did during one of her "phases". Among them, there are three moderately expensive art pieces but, to be honest, you'd be hard pushed to spot them; I deliberately chose paintings that, to my mind, looked like shit. I've marked them on the back with my initials in pencil. Hopefully customs officers will think the same. Pass these off as your own; Alison never signed any of hers. You might be surprised to know that the stuff you've already taken out is worth nearly one hundred thousand pounds!

My advice is to invest the remaining third of the money in antique books. Some of them are worth a fortune and are easy to carry; or you could send them with the rest of your stuff. They can easily be hidden amongst a pile of old worthless books you can purchase in any second-hand bookstore and you'd be unlucky if anyone in customs spotted a valuable book amongst the dross. You'll always find a collector wherever you go who is willing to give you cash for rare books, and their value will hold, as well. Just make sure you get provenance details when you buy them.

You can keep some of the money in the bank. Most countries like Australia allow you to take a certain amount of money in legally, but you don't want too much as it will all have to be converted back to cash when you change identity again. The money should mean you will be able to buy a decent property and still have enough left over to buy a small business or live off it while you take your time looking for a job. You could even go back to university!

Don't ever get a job as a nurse. If he ever works out that you are Susie's sister, he will come looking for someone who would naturally gravitate towards nursing.

And never come back to the UK, unless they find you. Then the UK is the last place they'll look. And always avoid places with strong Eastern European connections. It's safer to follow the fate of Aleksander Gjebrea through newspapers; you may leave a trail for them if you use the Internet to search for information about him or his organisation. If you have to, do it anonymously from an Internet cafe far from home, perhaps when you travel abroad.

Lastly, wait a few months before phoning the police and telling them where they can find me. By that time, I'm not sure that they'll be able to tell exactly how long I've been dead, as bacteria and the local aquatic life will have hopefully done their work. You'll know to phone from a public phone, but make sure there are no CCTV cameras about.

Do you remember that trip we had? The little wooden jetty where we sat and watched the ducks? There should be no doubt, when they find me, that I was dumped there by the gang.

I've left the van a distance away, where we parked that day. It should be clean enough, with no traces of us in it, but it would be better if you could get the bus down there and drive it back to London. You can use it to dump anything remaining in the lock-up that would point to us having been there. Give everywhere a thorough clean-up, although the lease is paid up for two years and it will be at least that long before it gets into such a state of disrepair that the owner gets complaints about it. Dump the van with its keys in the ignition in one of the inner city estates, but rub it clean first. It will soon disappear.

I forgot to mention. There are two memory cards in the safe. Everything is on there, should you ever need to give it to the Australian police, if Gjebrea comes for you. It might give you enough time to get away, while they investigate.

My family won't ever connect the death of that homeless man in London to me. While you were away, I made a quick trip to France and sent a letter to my cousin, explaining that I was making a new life there and that he shouldn't try to contact me. I felt bad about it, but if they'd identified my body, it might have muddied the waters.

I'm sorry I had to leave you, but in addition to your own safety, which I had to protect above everything else, I cannot allow that evil bastard to remain unpunished for what he did to Carol. When she was born, it made me a different person and a part of me died when she jumped out of that window.

I'd hoped otherwise, but I've come to realise that, without a body, there's a good chance he'll walk free and I just can't take that risk, so for me there was no other choice. It's all I can do for Carol and also for your future.

Start again and don't look back. You are a wonderful person and I cherished our time together. I hope you remember me fondly, but don't let it ruin your life. You're young and have the ability to do anything you want. Find a young man to make you happy and give you children, but never tell any of this to a soul, no matter how much you trust them. Bury it deep within you and make a new life for yourself.

With deep affection

Bill

The pages fell from her hand on to the floor.

Oh, Bill, what have you done? What have I done? I should have told you.

She sat for an hour, head in hands. Tears coursed down her cheeks on to the floor, forming two dark patches on the dry concrete that slowly coalesced into one.

She re-read the letter, this time taking in the detail, and the sentiment. *Without knowing it, Bill, you've given your child a future. But one without you.*

She straightened up, wiped her eyes and began to follow his instructions.

-o-

By the time Aleksander Gjebrea and Dhimiter Dervishi had been found guilty of four counts of murder, she'd wiped out any trace of her and Bill's enterprise and was on a plane to the other side of the world, six months pregnant. She followed the trial from ten thousand miles away on the BBC; it was notorious all over the world for a number of reasons.

Aleksander's cousin, Ilir, had also been found guilty of being an accomplice in the murder of Anna's sister, Susie.

The police eventually found the bodies of all the gang's victims. After Bill's body had been dragged, wrapped in chain, from the shallow waters of the nature reserve, where it had lain for two months, Josef Gjoni, one of the doormen at Bloq, denied all knowledge of the murder but admitted to the attack on Bill at the nightclub back in February. Sensing a deal, he divulged the details of the murders and the whereabouts of the bodies of Martin Okoye, the young black drug dealer, and Tanvi Gujar, the Indian barmaid. He also told the police the full story of Susie's death and her burial by Dhim and two of Ilir's

333

boys. He pled guilty to four counts of manslaughter and would serve only two to three years, although Anna doubted whether his life in or out of prison would feel entirely comfortable; she was sure that Aleksander's Albanian connections would be utilised to find and punish his former employee for his betrayal. She seemed to remember, from something Bill had been told, that there had been a glint of humanity in Josef's treatment of Carol and she hoped they wouldn't find him.

His testimony had been vital.

The pathologist had got it just about right. Susie had been assaulted by a punter and Aleksander, as the owner, and his cousin, who ran the brothel, failed to provide medical assistance for her in the full knowledge that withholding such aid would nearly certainly cause her death.

The CCTV footage of Bill's assault that had been anonymously sent in, the finger, and all the other evidence corroborating Josef's statement, including him accurately identifying the location of the bodies, persuaded the jury to unanimously convict Aleksander and his accomplices.

A number of witnesses came forward when the case hit the newspapers. They included a girl who had escaped Carol's and Susie's fates when Josef had palmed her a key that allowed her to sneak out and find her way to safety and redemption. As the only survivor of Aleksander's obsession with the corruption of young women who seemed to have the world at their feet, her testimony was one of the compelling reasons for the judge to hand down a long sentence.

The police pathologist's evidence in the case of Bill's murder would also have a profound effect on the length of sentence they received. As the water in the pond heated up in the warm summer months, Bill's body decomposed rapidly and was also partially devoured by the aquatic life in his watery grave. The post-mortem revealed that Bill's injuries from the nightclub assault had healed, but that Bill had had a second finger removed shortly before he was drowned. The prosecution, despite the defence counsel's attempts to pour scorn on the idea that Bill had been held somewhere for a couple of months, successfully alleged that Bill must have been kept captive while his wounds healed, only to be tortured again and drowned once he'd recovered. Three strands of Aleksander Gjebrea's hair were found lodged between the slats of the wooden jetty. The only way Anna could think it had got there was that Bill had managed to harvest them from the hat he'd picked out the bin on one of his scavenging trips.

Martin Okoye's death was a straightforward gangland killing, although the young drug dealer had also been tortured, to try and force him to betray his supplier.

The killing of Tanvi prompted more questions than answers within the ranks of the law enforcement authorities. Josef insisted that he was only involved in the disposal of the body and the clean-up of the room she'd died in and had not seen the murder being committed. Aleksander Gjebrea and Dhimiter Dervishi declined to give a reason for her murder.

She'd been a stunning young lady and Anna wondered at what point in her seduction by Aleksander did she try to get out, ending up dead because she'd seen too much, or just needed to be punished.

Josef Gjoni had speculated, when asked by the prosecution at the trial about Aleksander Gjebrea's motivation for his predation of young, successful middle-class women and instigating their descent to addiction and prostitution, that Aleksander had been involved with an English girl when he first arrived in the UK, who had subsequently dumped him after he'd become completely obsessed by her. He based this on conversations he overheard between Aleksander and his cousin.

It had taken Anna a year to move all the money Bill had left for her, along with the money she got from the sale of her own flat. Finding a key to the safe lightly welded to one of his iron sculptures, she'd broken it off and opened the door to discover that the money, the "cheap" jewellery and the other easily disguised valuable items that he'd collected were there as promised. There were some nervous moments at Australian customs checkpoints on the five trips she made back and forth between London and Sydney, but the so called "dummy run" that Bill had set her up to do, and her time masquerading as a bar manageress at the nightclub, gave her the self-belief that she could do it. Her cover story, that she was researching the possibility of setting up a branch of her private nursing company in Australia, seemed to allay any suspicions about the number of visits she made during that time. She left one bank account open in the UK, with enough start-up money in it to bale her out in case she ever needed to run again.

She'd read all the newspapers and obtained a copy of the trial transcripts, so she knew exactly how her sister had died and, contrary to the accounts of how Bill had been murdered, she was sure she knew exactly how he'd died, too, and why he'd sent her away on the trip to the other side of the world.

When she closed her eyes she could see Bill heading down towards Chichester in the van, turning off the main road onto Burton Park Lane, then onto the track that led up through the farmyard, stopping at the sharp corner where the road bent round to Chingford pond. Carrying a length of heavy industrial chain and the bolt-cutters in a rucksack, it was only a short stumble through the woods to Black Pond, where he hid the bag's contents in the undergrowth. He'd driven the van back round to the car park at Burton Mill dam, where they'd set out on their walk the previous month.

She imagined him waiting until darkness had fallen to avoid being seen, then changing into the smelly and bloodied layers he'd been wearing when he'd been assaulted. She thought he'd discarded them after his assault, but he must have hidden them somewhere.

Stuffing the clothes he'd changed out of into the rucksack, with a rock to weigh it down, he must have thrown it into the mill pond as he walked along the bank. Taking the much shorter trail the pair of them had walked together in the April sunshine, he would have followed the path up through the woods, arriving at the Black Pond again unseen.

It had become obvious why Bill had started growing a beard in the week before Anna had left for Australia. By the time he made his midnight walk to the Black Pond he had enough of a beard to avoid arousing suspicion when the police got round to comparing his rotting corpse with the video footage of the assault in Bloq's car park.

In her mind, she could visualize Bill retrieving the hidden chain and the bolt-cutters, hauling them over to the end of the jetty. Starting at his feet, he would have wound the chain around his legs and his waist, then looped it round the back of his neck to hold it in place while he cut off another of his fingers with the bolt-cutters, wiped their handles thoroughly with a grubby handkerchief, and lobbed them far into the pond.

She could picture him, in agony, replacing the hankie in one of his many pockets and wrapping more and more chain around himself, finishing with three or four loose loops hanging to the front from his neck. With the free end of chain tucked inside the loop, he must have let the loops drop over his arms, sliding down his body, the weight of the chain tightening the loops as they dropped.

She wondered if he'd stood at the end of the jetty for a few seconds, the heavy chain causing him to sway, blood coursing from his finger. Did he think of Carol and Alison, perhaps of Anna herself, before leaning forward and toppling into the cold dark water?

She shuddered and fought against the grief that threatened to overcome her and tried to blank out his final few minutes from her brain.

She'd waited nearly the full two months to phone the police and tip them off about Bill's body. The next day, the headlines had been dramatic:

TORTURED BODY FOUND DROWNED IN CHAINS
AT SUSSEX BEAUTY SPOT

NIGHTCLUB HOMELESS MURDER – CHAINED
BODY FOUND IN POND

When they drained the pond all they found, apart from Bill, was a set of bolt-cutters in the deep mud at the bottom. There were no fingerprints on them, but the DNA of the tissue shreds caught in the blades was a match for Bill and the finger found at the nightclub.

Bloq was closed down a few days after Bill's body was found, the day the members of the organisation were rearrested, and on the only occasion Anna dared to drive past it before her final trip to Australia, she was pleased to see it lying derelict and empty.

Aleksander Gjebrea was sentenced to life with a recommendation that he should serve at least forty years. The other two were given life sentences with only a slightly lesser tariff.

EPILOGUE

The little girl played at the water's edge. Her mother watched her carefully; the large Pacific rollers still packed a punch, even behind the reef. She could hear the sand and shells being sucked back into the sea as the waves retreated.

"Carol, keep back from the waves, love. Make a sandcastle next to me."

"But Mum, I like the water. The waves are fun."

Anna got up and walked down to the surf line. She held her daughter's hand and let the last few inches of the next wave surge over her child's feet. The girl squealed with delight every time a wave overtook them, her mum making a tease of trying to get out of their way.

After a while, Anna lifted her up and walked to the north edge of the cove, where a rocky promontory formed a sheltering arm that made the beach small and personal to her. She'd found the cove, only an hour's drive from her home in the small coastal town of Port Macquarie, on the eastern seaboard of Australia, a week after she'd left London for the last time. It was bit of a scramble to get to, but she didn't mind; it was always deserted.

She absently touched the scar on her forearm where she'd been burned by the cigar; despite it having faded, and being barely noticeable, she always made sure it was covered up with make-up or a long-sleeved top.

She knew she must stop thinking of herself as Anna, but it was the name Bill had known her by and she wanted to

340

hold on to that for as long as possible. Her new friends and neighbours knew her as something other than Anna, or Jill, for that matter, and she never mistakenly used either name outside of her own mind.

It wasn't that she'd shut herself off from ever having a relationship again. She could see the day coming when she could let someone else be part of their lives, but she'd always hold a special place in her heart for Bill, and not just as the father of her child.

She often asked herself if Aleksander Gjebrea would have faced most of his life in prison without Bill giving up his own life. She doubted it. Josef probably wouldn't have turned informant and, without the alleged torture, the judge might have been less severe in sentencing the Albanian. And she was definitely safer on her own than she would have been if Bill had survived.

She'd done almost exactly as Bill had advised and she had no worries now about the legitimacy of her citizenship in this vast country, or the near perfect safety that it had bought her.

"Come on. Let's put some more stones on the pile for Daddy."

The little girl, named Carol Susie after her and her mum's half-sisters, ran ahead, excitedly gathering stones in the small bright green bucket she carried, the matching spade now discarded and carried by her mother.

Anna looked around for a suitable stone; she always took a little time to make sure she got one that she liked, although it didn't really matter. The cairn that she'd erected to remember Bill by when she'd first found this deserted spot grew a little every time she came, although winter storms had twice flattened it and she'd had to rebuild it.

The little girl added her stones to the pile and Anna placed her own stone near the top.

It was a small risk, and he would have been cross with her, but she owed it to him; on the large stone halfway up the cairn, the only one with a flat face, she took a small sharp rock and refreshed the letters already scraped onto it.

BILL

2012

REST IN PEACE

End.

Thank you for reading Bloq. If you enjoyed it, please recommend it to your friends. Four free chapters are available at *www.alanjonesbooks.co.uk* and, if you have a minute, I'd also appreciate it if you could leave a review on Amazon. It is especially important to me, as an independent author with no marketing budget, that potential readers can see what you and other book lovers thought of the book.

If Bloq was to your taste, you also might be interested in my first two books, The Cabinetmaker and Toxic Blue.

The Cabinetmaker wasn't originally written as a crime novel. It is more of a story of the relationship between the two main characters, a Glasgow cabinetmaker whose son is brutally murdered, and a young detective on his first murder inquiry. When the case goes wrong, and the culprits walk free, the two men become lifelong friends, bonded together by a desire to see justice done, a love of playing amateur football and the detective's introduction to an enduring passion for fine furniture by his friend. It averages over 4 out of 5 stars on its ratings on Amazon, and has been very well reviewed by book bloggers since its publication in 2013. You can read four free chapters at *www.alanjonesbooks.co.uk* where there is extra content including an online audio slang dictionary and an interactive location map.

Toxic Blue is an out-and-out crime story with an unusual pair of investigators. A series of tortured corpses of young alcoholics and drug addicts are turning up and only Eddie Henderson seems to know why. When he tries to tell the police, his information is ridiculed and he's told to stop wasting their time. One officer, junior detective Catherine Douglas, believes him, and together they set out to discover why the dregs of Glasgow's underbelly are being found, dead and mutilated. It is seriously dark and gritty, with a fair smattering of violence, strong language and Glasgow slang - it's not for the faint hearted! It also averages over 4 out of 5 stars on its ratings on Amazon, and has been even better reviewed by book bloggers since its publication in 2014. Again, you can read four free chapters at *www.alanjonesbooks.co.uk* where there is another audio slang dictionary.

Glossary

[Broadband router] The box that connects a home or business to the internet.

[CCTV] Close Circuit TeleVision, now a generic term that includes digital security cameras.

[Download] Retrieving files from a remote computer, usually on the internet.

[Encrypted file] A file that you can only access with a password

[Explorer window] Microsoft Explorer is a web browser, used to search the internet.

[Find My iPhone app] A small program that allows you to track all your apple devices.

[Hard disk] The physical unit that stores all the files on a computer, or server

[Logging in] Using a username and one or more passwords to access a computer or website

[Memory card] A very small thin card that stores data; often used by cameras or phones to store photos, videos and data to transfer to computer.

[Mobile network data card] A small card that fits in a computer to access a mobile phone data network.

[Network] A collection of computers and other devices that interact through cables or wireless signal.

[Network configuration data] The software and settings that control the network and the access to and from the internet. Resides in the router.

[Network server] A specialised computer that stores all the data for an organisation. The internet is made up of many millions of servers.

[Network switch] The junction that connects all the network components and computers together with network cables.

[Notification area] The small area on a computer screen that keeps track of all the basic functions, like printers, network, screen, sound and power.

[Raspberry Pi] A very small modular computer is small which is easily programmable and very connectable. It can be used for many digital applications.

[RDP program] A small program that can take over one computer from another, sometimes from thousands of miles away.

[Terminal] Technically a 'dumb' connection to a network without its own storage, but can sometimes be loosely used for any computer attached to the network.

[Thumbnail] A miniature on screen picture or video that expands to a full size window. They allow you to observe a number of videos on screen simultaneously

[Time-out] For some reason, a computer freezes or the screen goes blank. The computer often needs restarted to solve the problem.

[Uploading] Sending files or information from one computer to another by direct transfer.

[USB memory stick] A small memory device that plugs into a socket present on nearly every computer.

[Video mpeg files] One of the commonest format s for video stored on computers.

[Virtual private network, or VPN] A secure connection that connects a computer to an organisation's network via the internet as if it was in the same physical location as the network. This is set up by changing settings in in the network configuration data in the network's router.

[Wireless access point, or WAP] A device attached to the network that transmits and receives radio signals, allowing computers or other devices to connect to the network without cables.

[Wireless dongle] A device that plugs into a USB socket that allows a user to connect to a Wireless Access Point (WAP)

[Workstation] Any computer connected to a network other than the server.

58840135R00208

Made in the USA
Charleston, SC
20 July 2016